BREATHLESS

A Finding Love Novel

Paris Hansen

To Tammy,

Thanks for Reading!

XOXO

Paris Hansen

Breathless Copyright © 2018 Paris Hansen

All rights reserved.

Without limiting rights under copyright reserved above, no part of this publication may be
reproduced, stored in or introduced into a retrieval system, or transmitted, in any form, or by
any means (electronic, mechanical, photocopying, recording or otherwise) without prior
written permission of the publisher, except in the case of brief quotations embodied in reviews and certain other noncommercial uses permitted by copyright law. The scanning, uploading, and/or distribution of this document via the internet or via any other means without the permission of the publisher is illegal and is punishable by law.

This is a work of fiction. The characters and events portrayed in this book are fictitious. Any resemblance to actual events or real persons, living or dead, is coincidental.

Cover Design by James, GoOnWrite.com

Other Books by Paris Hansen

<u>Finding Love Series</u>
Restless
Powerless
Speechless
Breathless

CHAPTER 1

Brooklyn

"Where do you think you're going, Princess?"

Stopping before her hand could touch the door to the exit, Brooklyn St. James fought back the urge to punch the man following her in his handsome face. She wanted to hit him for following her, for using the nickname he knew she hated, for being a sexy, arrogant, asshole...the reasons were varied and plentiful. She'd never go through with it though. Even if it would make her feel a bit better, she knew it wouldn't do her any good. No matter what she did, she knew he wasn't going away. Especially not now that her sister and his best friend were tying the knot. She was stuck with Declan Reese for better or worse, even if she wanted to cause him bodily harm every time she was near him.

Since the day they'd met the infuriatingly gorgeous man standing a few feet away from her had been nothing but a pain in her ass. They fought like cats and dogs over everything and anything. It was a wonder they hadn't killed each other yet. Especially since Savannah and Gabriel had named them best man and maid of honor for their wedding. The job she was honored to have ended up making her spend more time with the man who drove her crazy. Declan, of course, poked at her whenever he got a chance, knowing exactly what would set her off and she always took the bait no matter how hard she tried to ignore him.

Knowing he wouldn't hesitate to drive her crazy over the weekend, Brooklyn had done her best to avoid him. From the minute they landed in Las Vegas for the bachelor/bachelorette weekend, she'd stuck like glue to her friend Meghan. Brooklyn knew it was only a matter of time before Meghan went off with Oliver, the man she was dating, so Brooklyn made plans with her friend from college who lived in town. She didn't want to spend her first night in Vegas alone and she sure in the hell didn't want to spend it with Declan and Braeden doing whatever the hell Braeden had planned.

She honestly didn't think anyone would notice she left the club. When she'd looked back at their VIP booth, it was empty. Brooklyn assumed they'd all went their separate ways and she was free to spend the night however she wanted. Instead, the last person she wanted to deal with was following her through the casino expecting her to answer to him. She refused to give him the satisfaction of her attention, so she did her best to ignore him, putting her hand on the door in front of her so she could push it open.

"I know you can hear me. Quit being a brat and tell me where you're going?"

Pissed, she turned to face the man who made her breath catch every time she looked at him. She glared at him, her body tense with the urge to punch him. "Oh, I'm sorry. I didn't realize my father came on this trip to Vegas with us."

"Cute. I'm not asking for myself. It's almost midnight, and if your sister found out I let you wander around Vegas alone, well let's just say I don't want to leave my daughter without a father."

"Damn it."

Playing the kid card was decidedly unfair, but effective. Brooklyn sighed, her body relaxing.

"Fine. If you must know I'm going out to meet up with one of my college roommates and her boyfriend. I haven't seen her in years, and this seemed like the perfect opportunity."

"Okay, I'm coming with you.

"I'm sorry. Did I accidentally invite you and not remember it? I don't need a chaperone, Declan."

"This is non-negotiable, Princess. Either I go with you, or we can call your sister and Gabriel and see what they have to say."

"Are you fucking serious right now?" Brooklyn asked through clenched teeth. "Where the hell do you get off? I'm not a child, Declan. I'm not your daughter. I'm a big girl, and I'm more than capable of taking care of myself."

"Take it or leave it, Princess," Declan said as he pulled his phone out of his pocket.

She seethed, her fists clenched at her sides. It wasn't that she thought her sister would tell her she couldn't go out, in fact, she knew Savannah wouldn't care. It was the fact the asshole in front of her was willing to bother her sister over something so ridiculous. Like Savannah, was Brooklyn's keeper. She wasn't a child, she was in her thirties; she'd been married for crying out loud. She was an adult, and this man was treating her like she was anything but.

"Fine, it's a free world after all. If you want to follow me around like a creeper, go for it, but I don't have to acknowledge your presence. Don't bother talking to me, don't talk to my friends. You have no say in how this evening is going to go. Don't pretend that you're following me around has anything to do with my sister either. That excuse is fucking bullshit, and we both know it."

Turning back around, Brooklyn pushed through the door, the stifling Vegas heat assaulting her the second she stepped outside. Even though it was nearly midnight, it was still over 80 degrees, which was a shock to the system when leaving the overly air-conditioned casino. With Declan hot on her heels, she followed the signs to the line she needed to wait in to hail a cab.

They stood in awkward silence, while groups of people laughed loudly around them. Pulling her cell phone out of her clutch, she sent a quick text off to her friend Becca to let her know she was on her way. She didn't bother to mention that Declan was coming with her. Brooklyn planned on ignoring his presence as much as possible. Giving her friend a warning would result in a lot of questions that Brooklyn didn't want to answer. Instead, she'd show up at the Neon Museum, buy her ticket for the tour, and forget all about the shadow she'd picked up along the way.

There's no way she'd let Mr. Tall, Dark and Overprotective ruin the first vacation she'd been on since her marriage started to go downhill. Even if the weekend wasn't truly a vacation, the rest of the evening was, and Brooklyn was bound and determined to forget about everything she'd been through over the last few years. She was going to enjoy the hell out of her freedom, and she didn't care what anyone thought about how she did it.

* * *

"Seeing all those old signs was pretty incredible; especially the ones they fixed-up so they'd light up again. Vegas is fun now, but I bet back in the day it was even better. The glitz and glamour, the Rat Pack..."

"The Mob..."

"Nobody was talking to you, Declan," Brooklyn said reacting before she could even think about it.

As soon as the words were out of her mouth, she mentally slapped herself for acknowledging his presence. She'd done such a good job ignoring him throughout the entire tour of the museum she hated ruining her streak. Ignoring him wasn't easy, not when she'd catch a glimpse of him backlit by the neon lights, his dark hair disheveled, the scruff along his jaw dangerously close to needing a trim. She could feel his eyes on her at all times which both thrilled her and made her angry.

The man absolutely drove her crazy. At any given moment, she wanted to punch him or fuck him, neither of which were good options for her. Of course, the first man she felt any kind of attraction to since her divorce was Declan...the brooding, sexy as sin, thorn in her side. He was the last man she should want, but she couldn't seem to help herself.

Nobody with eyes could deny that Declan Reese was gorgeous and despite the way he treated her, Brooklyn knew he was a great guy and a great father. He was everything a woman should want in a man, but he wasn't for her, no matter how badly she might wish otherwise.

Shaking her head, Brooklyn tried to focus on what Becca was saying. They'd left the Neon Museum a half an hour earlier to head to a nearby bar that was equal parts dance club and adult play area. They stood around a tall table, waiting for their turn at giant beer pong, talking about the history of Las Vegas. Brooklyn had to admit there was a lot about the party town she didn't know and it was genuinely fascinating.

Becca's boyfriend Derek and his friend Colin excused themselves to head to the bar to get drinks for the table. Although Declan was nursing water, he offered to join them. Brooklyn guessed it was more to keep an eye on the guys than to help them out. On the cab ride to the museum, Declan had gone on and on about accepting drinks from strangers, touting stats about how many people were drugged every year in Vegas.

Although she'd wanted to tell him she wasn't an idiot, she kept her mouth closed. The number was staggering, and she was sure most of the women that'd been drugged had said the very same thing. While Brooklyn trusted Becca, she didn't know Derek or Colin, and if Declan hadn't have gone with them, she would have offered to get her own drink just to be safe.

"If I'd known you were bringing that delicious piece of meat, I wouldn't have brought Colin along with us. I thought since it'd been a while for you, that having a nice no-strings-attached Vegas fling would be just what the doctor ordered."

"Seriously, Bec? Come on. You know me better than that."

"Doesn't mean you don't need to step outside your comfort zone now that you're single. It's been a long time since your divorce, Brooklyn. You need to move on."

"It's not like I'm not trying to, you know. I'm not sitting around brokenhearted that Frank and I are over and that he's moved on and already married again. Things were over between us long before we made it official."

"I know. Doesn't mean it didn't hit you hard when you found out he'd gotten someone else pregnant after everything you'd been through."

"Can we not talk about this now? I don't want to think about any of that. I want to enjoy the evening and forget about the past. I want to catch up with you, have a few drinks and kick some ass at beer pong. The rest of it can wait."

"Fine. I won't mention any of it again. But how about you tell me more about Declan before the guys get back."

Brooklyn shook her head, then downed the rest of her drink. "There's really nothing to tell. He's best friends with Savannah's fiancé and the bane of my existence. I don't know why he decided to follow me out tonight. Maybe I remind him of his daughter or something, I don't really know."

Becca laughed so hard, her blue eyes filled with tears. "Oh, honey. You definitely don't remind him of his daughter. In fact, I'm pretty sure his daughter is the furthest thing from his mind when he looks at you."

"Well then maybe I remind him of his sister. All we do is argue. He constantly pushes my buttons and treats me like I'm barely worth his time."

"Oh Brook...you are so damn oblivious."

Becca started to laugh again, so Brooklyn glared at her before tipping her cup back again, hoping there was at least one last drop of alcohol at the bottom. She needed the fortification, the bit of courage alcohol gave her.

What she really needed was for her friend to stop talking. For Becca to stop noticing and stop pointing out the little things Brooklyn had been seeing all night. Hell, since she met Declan if she was being honest with herself. Of course, Becca wasn't the first person to point out the way Declan looked at her or the fact that the way he treated her was definitely not like a daughter or sister.

"If we were in elementary school, that man would be chasing you around the playground, pulling on your pigtails then pushing you into the mud. He wants you just as badly as you want him, but neither of you is willing to make the first move."

"That is so not true," Brooklyn scoffed. But she could feel the lie on her tongue as the words poured out. She did want Declan. At least part of her did. The part that knew what kind of man he was. The part that knew he'd be unbelievable between the sheets and against the wall and anywhere else they could find.

The part of her that knew he'd break her heart ...that was the part she listened to the most. That was the part that kept her from ever making a move on the man that made her feel like lava flowed through her veins whenever he touched her. Declan Reese made her feel things she'd never felt with her ex-husband, which meant that when things inevitably ended between them, the heartbreak would be even harder to get through. Finding out her husband had cheated on her and got someone else pregnant nearly destroyed her. Losing her heart to Declan would definitely finish the job.

"Fine. Have it your way. Lie to yourself if you want to, but I'm not blind, and I'm not stupid. I don't think you'll be able to ignore the chemistry between you for much longer, but you can try. Almost makes me want to move back to Washington to watch the fireworks."

Brooklyn opened her mouth to respond but stopped when she saw the guys approaching the table. She took a long look at the three of them, noting that Declan was by far the best looking one of the bunch. Derek was cute in a Leonard from Big Bang Theory kind of way. He was taller than Becca, but shorter than Brooklyn, with dark brown hair. He had glasses he pushed up his nose every so often and wore a button-down shirt over a Justice League t-shirt.

Colin was...well, Brooklyn didn't really know what to think of Colin. How Becca thought Brooklyn would want a one-night stand with the guy, she wasn't sure. There was something about him that seemed a bit skeevy. It could have been his slicked-back hair or the nerdy, yet oddly suggestive t-shirt he was wearing, or the fact his jeans were tighter than any of the jeans she owned. More than likely though, it was the way he looked at her like he wanted to eat her up and she should be happy he was willing to give her his time.

She shuddered at the thought and looked back at Declan. Suddenly, she was actually thankful he'd come, although she'd never admit that to him. Without him there, she would have felt at least obligated to talk to Colin, but now she didn't have to. She could ignore him and his leering eyes and roving hands. How had Becca ever thought she was that desperate? She'd really need to have a talk with her friend about the kind of people she tried to set her friends up with. But she'd save the conversation for after she left Las Vegas. She was still bound and determined to have a great time, even if one man at the table gave her the heebie-jeebies and the other man made her think about all the dirty things they could and should do together.

It was going to be a very long night.

* * *

"How the hell did you two get so good at this?" Derek asked as he and Colin lost their second game of beer pong to Brooklyn and Becca.

The two guys had stupidly wanted to play guys versus girls, no doubt thinking they'd get the women good and drunk. What neither of them had seemed to remember was the girls had met at college where beer pong had been a staple of nearly every party. Someone had to be the reigning champions of those parties, and if it wasn't Brooklyn or Becca, it was Kerrigan or Chelsea. Especially, during their senior year, when they were the ones throwing the majority of the parties in the big house Chelsea's parents had rented for them.

"We tried to warn you, babe, but you didn't think two girls could beat you guys. You should've listened," Becca told her boyfriend as she wrapped her arms around his waist and gave him a kiss on the cheek.

Derek pouted a bit before he started to laugh. Brooklyn looked over at Colin, who did not seem to think losing to girls was the least bit funny. She rolled her eyes and looked behind her at Declan, who was quietly taking everything in. He gave her a wink before taking a drink of his water.

She couldn't believe he was still bothering to hang out with them. He had to be exhausted and annoyed. It was already after 2 am, and none of them had plans to stop anytime soon. She wouldn't blame him if he wanted to leave, but she knew he wouldn't. He was just stubborn enough to stick it out all night if that's what she planned to do.

Although she wouldn't admit it, Brooklyn was torn about heading back to the hotel. She was tired and ready for bed, but she had no idea where Meghan and Oliver were doing their thing, and she didn't want to interrupt them. Plus, it was just depressing to think about everyone else having someone to share their bed with. Savannah had Gabriel. Finley, Savannah's best friend, had her boyfriend, Liam. Meghan had Oliver. Even Braeden, the perpetual playboy, probably had someone with him. She hated the fact being around couples made her feel like she was missing something.

"Alright, who's up for a rousing game of giant connect four?" Brooklyn asked the group, trying to shake off her suddenly somber mood. "Or maybe giant chess?"

For the next hour, they played multiple versions of ridiculously oversized games. Colin had wanted to make them all drinking games, but the rest of them had declined. It was getting late, and they were already well over the line to buzzed. Everyone except Declan of course, who continued to sit on the sidelines and watch the shenanigans. Brooklyn had tried to get him involved in more than one of the games, despite the fact she'd vowed earlier to ignore him. Each time he politely declined, telling her to enjoy her time with her friends.

As four in the morning quickly approached, Brooklyn was finally starting to hit a wall. It had been a really long time since she'd been out that late and she was definitely feeling the effects of lack of sleep mixed with alcohol. While they argued about whether or not a pawn could move diagonally, Brooklyn excused herself from the group so she could use the bathroom.

After waiting in a surprisingly long line, she took care of business, then splashed some cold water on her face to help wake her up. When it didn't do the trick, she realized it was time to head out. She'd text Meghan on the way back to the hotel to let her know she was coming, in case she and Oliver were using the girl's room instead of his. The last thing Brooklyn needed was to walk in on them in the middle of...well, anything.

Using the band on her wrist, she piled her thick, dark hair into a messy bun. Although she'd darkened her hair nearly two months earlier, it was still taking some getting used to. While it had taken her a while, Brooklyn was finally feeling like she could move forward with her life. Changing her hair color, was something she'd always wanted to do, but never could while she was married. Seeing the change in the mirror was a great reminder she was free to do whatever the hell she wanted, whenever the hell she wanted.

Brooklyn took one last look at herself in the bathroom mirror to make sure everything was back in place before she stepped out into the hallway. The black shorts romper she wore was cute and super comfortable but made going to the bathroom a chore. The open back meant she couldn't wear a bra, so each trip to the bathroom, she had to make sure the girls were covered back up before leaving the room. The last thing she wanted was to give anyone a show because she had a wardrobe malfunction.

"There you are. I was beginning to get worried," someone said from her right. Brooklyn didn't recognize the voice, so she continued down the hall to head back outside figuring the person was talking to someone else.

"Hey, I'm talking to you, Brooklyn. I've been waiting out here for you for a while, don't just walk away from me."

Turning to see who was talking to her, she found Colin leaning against the wall next to the women's bathroom, a lascivious grin on his face. He pushed off of the wall and walked toward her, the smile never leaving his face. The way he looked at her made her skin crawl. She backed up a step as he moved closer.

"I've been trying to get you alone all night, but your bodyguard has been making that nearly impossible. Becca said you were single and we could hook up tonight. I had all sorts of plans for you, but you haven't been very cooperative. Hasn't anyone ever told you ignoring people is rude."

"Look, Colin, I'm sorry if Becca promised you something, but I'm not interested, okay. I'm tired, and I don't feel well. I'm going to go back to my hotel and get some rest. I have a busy day planned tomorrow for my sister's bachelorette party, so I'm just gonna go."

Brooklyn turned to walk away from him but was halted in her tracks as he grabbed on to her arm. His gripped tightened as he pulled her to him. She stumbled a little, her heels catching on the floor.

"Come on, Brooklyn. I'm sure you have a couple of minutes to spare for me. I'll make it quick," he told her, his tongue darting out to wet his lower lip.

Brooklyn tried to pull her arm out of his grasp, but he held her tighter, hurting her in the process.

"Let me go, Colin. You're hurting me."

"Stop fighting, and I won't have to hurt you. All I'm asking for is a quick BJ, and then you can be on your way. You owe me at least that much after I wasted my night on you."

"Jeezus. Does Becca know she's trying to set her friends up with sick assholes? I'm not giving you a fucking blow job, Colin. Now let me go before I scream."

"Listen here you little cock tease. You fucking owe me."

Brooklyn tried again to wrench her arm out of his grip as he stared at her angrily although the creepy grin never left his face. The situation was quickly going downhill, and as she realized no one had walked past them since Colin had accosted her in the hallway, she knew she was in trouble. Now that she desperately needed him, Declan was nowhere to be seen.

She shouldn't have been so rude to Declan. She should have taken him up on his offer to escort her to the bathroom, but she'd foolishly thought things would be fine. They'd been at the bar for hours, and nothing terrible had happened. She'd gone to the bathroom multiple times throughout the night without incident. Of course, Becca had been with her each time, but she really hadn't thought Becca's presence would have been that big of a deterrent against creeps. Apparently, she hadn't been worried about the right creep.

She started to struggle again, which only made Colin smile more. He seemed to be getting off on the fact that she wanted nothing to do with him. Bile rose in her throat, a cold sweat breaking out along her skin.

"Let me go," she yelled, hoping someone else might hear her cause she was sure Colin wasn't going to listen.

Ignoring her protests, he started to pull her down the hall toward the emergency exit. She struggled, hoping he'd get tired of fighting against her. She yelled at him over and over again to let her go.

"Stop fighting. I'll let you go once you live up to what I was promised. Five minutes...ten tops."

"I'm not going anywhere with you. Let me go, Colin," she screamed.

She thought about throwing herself into him, wondering if the sudden movement would knock him loose. Then she realized it would put the rest of her within grabbing distance which would only make matters worse. She looked around for things to grab onto, a pipe, a pole, a handle of some sort, but the walls were smooth. There was nothing for her to hold on to, there was nothing she could grab onto to use as a weapon, like a fire extinguisher. She had no idea how she was going to get out of the mess she was in.

"I believe the lady told you to let her go."

Brooklyn's shoulders sagged in relief at the voice coming from behind her. While the words coming from someone else's mouth would have probably meant the same thing, she couldn't have been sure she wouldn't have left the arms of one creep for the arms of another one. Now that he was here, she was safe. She felt it with every fiber of her being. He wouldn't let anything happen to her and not just because his friend was marrying her sister.

"Fuck off," Colin said as he whipped around to face Declan.

The force of the move threw Brooklyn off balance sending her hard into the wall. As she fell, her arm came free of his hold. On the floor, she scrambled away from Colin, crawling on her hands and knees toward Declan, toward safety. He helped her up off of the floor, then pushed her behind him, his eyes never leaving Colin.

"You need to walk out of here now. You need to forget you ever saw her. As much as I don't want to spend the weekend in a jail cell, I will do whatever it takes to make sure she stays safe," Declan said his hands fisted at his sides. "Walk away, man, just walk away. It's not worth it."

Colin growled, taking a step forward, but then seemed to rethink his plan. Shaking his head, he took a step back, his hands held up in the air.

"Fine. You can have her. Fucking cock tease was a waste of my God damn time."

Brooklyn watched as Colin left the hallway. She held onto the back of Declan's shirt, preparing herself in case he came back. Her knees buckled the minute Declan turned to check on her. His eyes filled with concern as he looked her over. He caught her in his arms, pulling her against him as he comforted her.

"You're okay," he whispered over and over as he rubbed her back.

Her hands shook against his chest where she'd grabbed on to his shirt as she started to fall. Brooklyn buried her face in the crook of his neck and tried to absorb his strength. She tried to convince herself she was okay that she never had anything to worry about, but that was easier said than done when her hands were shaking, and her heart felt like it was going to break free from her chest.

"I'm sorry I wasn't here sooner. I'm sorry he had time to get his hands on you."

Brooklyn took a deep breath, inhaling his scent. Like some kind of essential oil, it calmed her nerves and slowed her erratic heartbeat. Or maybe it was his arms wrapped around her that did the trick. She really couldn't be sure, although she knew she liked the way it felt to be held by him, to be comforted by him.

"Let's get out of here," Declan suggested after another minute of assuring her she was safe.

She didn't say a word, just nodded her head against his chest. She knew she was ready to leave, but she wasn't so sure she was prepared for him to stop holding her. It was the nicest Declan had been to her since they met. It was the first time they weren't at each other's throats picking a fight, and she had to admit to herself she was enjoying it. Of course, she hated what led to the moment, but she couldn't hate the outcome.

Letting him lead her down the hallway and back toward the club, Brooklyn realized the adrenaline was starting to wear off. Her arm throbbed where Colin had grabbed her. His grip had been hard and unrelenting, she wouldn't be surprised if she ended up with a hand-shaped bruise around her bicep. Her shoulder also ached from the impact with the wall. Another bruise she was probably going to have to explain. It wasn't like she could walk around in long sleeves for the rest of their time in Vegas. Even inside the air-conditioned casino, it would look weird for her to stay covered up given the ridiculous desert heat.

As they pushed through the crowd, she kept her eyes down. She could only imagine the wreck she looked like with her red-rimmed eyes and tear streaked face. Most of the people in the club would have just assumed she was drunk. No one but her and Declan would know what almost happened, what could have happened if he hadn't shown up.

"Wait, I need to get my purse. I left it at the table."

The last place she wanted to go was back to the table. Would Colin be there? Would she have to explain to Becca and Derek what happened? Her head filled with questions she couldn't answer and wasn't sure she wanted to if she could.

"Don't worry, I've got your purse. Let's just get out of here. Get you back to the hotel."

Declan pulled her clutch out of his back pocket and handed her the small bag that held her phone, ID and some cash. Thankful they wouldn't have to go back to the table, she gave him a small smile, then continued to follow him out of the club. It only took them a few minutes to hail a cab, which Brooklyn was grateful for. The longer they waited, the more opportunities they had to see Colin again. After he left the hallway, she had no idea where he went. Although she'd hoped he'd left the club, he could have easily been sitting around waiting for another shot at her.

Pulling her phone out of her purse, she checked the time. It was nearly five in the morning, but she didn't want to head back to the hotel anymore. She wasn't ready to be alone, and she had no idea whether or not Meghan would be in their room. Brooklyn knew the minute she tried to sleep she'd only be able to think about what could have been. Looking over at Declan as he stared out the window, she hoped he'd be open to staying out a little longer.

"All of this craziness has made me hungry. Would you mind stopping to get some breakfast or something? I'm starved."

Declan turned to her, concern warring with something else in his eyes. For a moment she thought he would deny her. She could tell he wasn't sold on the idea of staying out and not just because he was exhausted. Declan was worried about her which was an interesting change of pace. She'd never had a man worry about her well-being before. Which was just another sad reflection on her failed marriage.

"Look, I'm hungry, and I'm not ready to head back to the hotel. I can go alone, but I'd rather not, okay...just another hour or two...please?"

She hated how desperate she sounded. She hated the look on his face when she said please. Although it was fleeting, it made her second guess whether or not she had read the situation right. Maybe Declan wasn't actually worried about her, he was just worried about what Gabriel and Savannah would say when they found out what happened.

"Fine," he said before telling the driver about the change in destination.

A few minutes later, they pulled into the parking lot of a 24-hour restaurant and lounge, a place she'd heard about many times, but never had a chance to visit. It would be good to spend the next couple of hours stuffing her face with delicious, greasy food while trying to forget the horrible evening she'd had. If only she had a clue as to what her companion was thinking.

* * *

Stuffed full of French toast and a ridiculous hot fudge sundae, Brooklyn sat back against the booth waiting for the waitress to bring back their change. She might have eaten her feelings for breakfast, but she didn't regret one single bite. Gorging herself on sweets was what she needed to put the night behind her. That and the totally normal conversation she and Declan had while they ate.

They mostly talked about sports, especially the Mariners since Declan was a huge baseball fan. It was one of the most mundane yet stimulating conversations she'd had with a man in a long time. The comfortable back and forth, even when it turned to lighthearted arguing, went a long way to help her forget what happened. Although she'd been one hundred percent against Declan following her around for the night, she was glad he didn't listen to her. And not just because he'd saved her from Colin, but because he'd actually made the night tolerable. All of the Colin stuff aside, she'd enjoyed the time she spent with Declan more than she ever thought possible.

Once the waitress returned, they left some money on the table and headed outside to find a cab. It was nearing seven in the morning, and the sun was out in full force already. Brooklyn shielded her eyes while Declan hailed a cab. As soon as she climbed inside, she sat back and closed her eyes. The ride down the strip to their hotel would be quick, but she knew there wouldn't be much if any, time for rest once they got back to the hotel. Bachelorette festivities were supposed to start around nine with a mimosa breakfast before a day at the spa. With any luck she'd be able to get in a cat nap during her massage otherwise she was in for a very long day.

"Hey, we're here."

Brooklyn popped an eye open to see they had indeed arrived at their hotel. Somehow, she'd been so out of it she hadn't even noticed the car had stopped. Climbing out of the cab, she thanked the driver as Declan paid their fare. They slowly walked into the casino, the sounds of the slot machines filled the silence between them. She could tell Declan was nearly as exhausted as she was and for a moment she felt sorry for keeping him out all night.

"Thank you for coming with me last night. I know I was a bit of a bitch at first, but I appreciate you being there," Brooklyn said as they stepped into the elevator.

She leaned back against the wall as the doors closed. Declan stared at her like he wasn't sure what to do with her. He was probably shocked by her apology since she'd never really apologized to him before, at least not without her sister prodding her to do so. He took a step toward her and then another until he was nearly touching her. She stared up at him, wondering what was going through his mind as he crowded her against the elevator wall.

Brooklyn licked her lips, suddenly realizing how dry they were. She took a deep breath, her chest barely brushing against Declan's as she did. Not for the first time she felt the spark between them, the one she desperately ignored every time they were in the same room together. Why was he so close? She wished she could read his mind. The man was an enigma, a mystery she wanted to solve.

He leaned into her, lips slightly parted, his eyes dropping down to focus on her mouth for the briefest moment. Instead of looking back at her, Declan turned away toward the panel, pressing the button for their floor before stepping back.

What the fuck, she thought, her heart nearly racing from his closeness. He'd been about to kiss her. That almost happened. She hadn't imagined the moment or how close he'd been to brushing his lips against hers. Why had he pressed the button again? Was he that eager to get away from her? Anger coursed through her, replacing the lust that had nearly taken over and made her do something monumentally stupid.

"Pushing it again doesn't make it go any faster," she snapped.

"No, but pressing it once does," he told her, a hint of amusement in his voice.

"I pressed it when I came in here."

"No, you didn't."

"Yes, I did," she argued, ignoring the urge to stomp her foot like a child.

"Then why were we still on the first floor, Princess? Can you answer that?"

"Why do you have to be such a pain in the ass? I'm tired, okay. I swear I hit the button."

"Well, we'll have to agree to disagree because you didn't."

Crossing her arms over her chest, she turned away from Declan and watched the floor numbers pass by in a flash. It took very little time for the elevator to reach their floor, but that was all it took for Brooklyn to remember how much Declan annoyed the hell out of her. Kissing him would have been a disaster of epic proportions, yet a part of her couldn't help but wish they'd taken the plunge.

As soon as the doors opened, she was off the elevator and walking away from Declan. She didn't say a word to him before she took off, which she felt a little bad about, but she needed to get away from him and the things he made her feel. Even though he annoyed her to no end, she couldn't ignore the fact he was under her skin. No matter how bad the idea of them was, she wanted it...even if just for a moment, she wanted to see how electric they could be together.

Standing outside her hotel room door, she imagined what could have been had she leaned forward in the elevator. What could have been if she'd taken things into her own hands and took what she wanted from him. She hadn't realized she'd gotten lost in thoughts of Declan until she heard someone approaching her. Turning to her right, she found Meghan walking toward her, disheveled and happier than she'd been when Brooklyn had last seen her.

"Well, well, well...look what the cat dragged in. Doing the walk of shame, I see?" Brooklyn teased as she unlocked the door with the keycard and let them into the room.

She spent a few minutes checking in, loving how happy and carefree Meghan seemed after a night with Oliver. It was apparent there was still something weighing on her friend, but Meghan wasn't letting that get in the way of having a great time in Vegas. Brooklyn wished her night had been as good as Meghan's, but it'd been a roller coaster of confusion. Between the Colin situation and the way she felt when she walked away from Declan, she wasn't sure what the heck to call her night.

All she knew was she wanted a long, scalding hot shower, so she could wash away the night and move on with her life. The day before her could only be better than the one she was leaving behind. She had to believe that, or she'd end up spending too much of her day thinking about Declan and every single way he made her crazy. She just needed to spend the day with the girls and forget the infuriating man who made her feel things she wasn't interested in feeling.

CHAPTER 2

Declan

"Come on. How can you call that a strike? The ball nearly hit him."

"You need your eyes checked, ump. You wouldn't know a good call if it hit you in the face."

"You're a bum. I thought the Mariners were playing the A's today...didn't realize they were playing against you too."

Declan smiled as he listened to Brooklyn yell a continual barrage of disparaging remarks at the umpire behind home plate. Since the game started, she'd spent more time on her feet screaming at the ump then she had sitting in her seat. Unlike most of the people around them, she focused on the game, maybe a little too focused if he really thought about it. He loved baseball more than the average person, but even he wasn't as openly passionate as Brooklyn was.

Although this wasn't the first game they'd been to together, this was the first time Declan was so keenly aware of Brooklyn's every move. Normally Erin was there drawing most of his attention. Even when he could hear Brooklyn over the din of the crowd, he could easily ignore her because he had other people to distract him. Then again, they weren't usually sitting next to each other, their legs brushing against each other, their arms continually touching whenever she was actually sitting in her seat.

Normally he wasn't cursing, yet praising the lack of personal space in the jam-packed rows of the stadium. Normally he didn't notice the way her jersey strained across her chest or how if she moved just so, he'd get a glimpse of her sexy as hell cleavage. Normally he didn't look at her and feel like a sex-starved teenager that was going to die if he didn't get his hands on her soon.

Declan was pretty sure his "normally" wasn't nearly as fascinating as his current predicament, but it was definitely a hell of a lot safer.

"Is your sister always this intense at baseball games?" Braeden asked Savannah as Brooklyn jumped up and yelled at the ump again.

Declan turned away from watching Brooklyn and toward the conversation his friends were having. Not having her in his line of sight didn't make him any less aware of her every move. In fact, he almost felt more aware of when she sat back down or when she shifted to get more comfortable. The entire situation was driving him crazy. He tried to pay attention to what Savannah was saying, while he tried to decide whether or not he needed a break from his ultimate distraction.

"She's that intense when it comes to any sporting event she's watching, no matter where she's at. She'll stand up and yell at the TV if she doesn't agree with what's going on. It's a bit ridiculous, but then again I'm not the sports nut she is. Declan's been to a few games with her this year. I bet he's seen her get really into it."

"To be fair, Andrea's usually with us and Erin too. Those two are just as bad. Get the three of them together, and I'm surprised we've never been kicked out."

"It's probably a good thing your company seats aren't too close to home plate," Savannah pointed out. "That and they don't usually scream obscenities at the top of their lungs. I'm sure someone would complain if they were swearing like a bunch of sailors."

Declan laughed knowing there were times the girls had gotten close to going overboard with their yelling. Separately their passion for the sport was admirable. Together it bordered slightly on insane. He couldn't imagine it any other way.

"Oliver over there isn't much better. He's been known to harass the umps and the players on both teams."

Oliver shrugged, not caring that he was being called out. "Hey, I'm an equal opportunity critic. I don't care who you are if you're making bad plays, I'm going to call you out on it."

"Come on. Get your crap together, ump. This is getting ridiculous."

Turning back to watch Brooklyn, Declan couldn't help but smile as she waved her arms around dramatically. The more she got into the game, the more he couldn't stop wondering if there were other things she was as passionate about as sports. That thought led to another and then another. He wondered what it would have been like to kiss her in the elevator. Where that kiss might have led if he'd let himself lean in just a little bit more. Would it have stayed in Vegas or would he have spent the last week buried between her thighs?

The woman was a pain in the ass and exactly what he didn't need in his life. Yet he couldn't stop thinking about the fact he wanted her. Not just in his bed, which was a terrible idea, but in his life, which was an even worse idea. No doubt, Brooklyn was looking for hearts and flowers, love and romance. She was the kind of woman that wanted a relationship, and a relationship was something Declan couldn't, no wouldn't give her. She deserved better than that...better than him.

He just had to keep reminding himself that the beautiful brunette standing next to him was off limits. Brooklyn St. James was not meant for him, no matter how much he might wish otherwise.

* * *

"You've got less than a week of freedom left, how do you feel?" Declan asked.

Since they'd returned from Las Vegas, his impending wedding had taken over Gabriel's life. While Declan had talked to his friend over the phone or via text, this was the first time they'd seen each other in weeks. So instead of immediately heading back to the Reese Wine Distributions warehouse, Declan had decided to take a break to catch up with his friend. It'd been a surprise to find Gabriel at the restaurant so he figured he might as well take advantage of it.

"I feel like I'm ready to get this thing over with," Gabriel admitted. "I just want to be married to Savannah already. The rest of this stuff is getting in the way. If I had my way, we would have gone to the courthouse or got married in Vegas like Meghan and Oliver."

"Why didn't you? Savannah doesn't strike me as someone who's been planning her dream wedding since she was a little girl."

Gabriel smiled. "No, she's definitely not. But a big wedding was important to her mom and her sister."

"God...her sister. The woman is driving me crazy, Gabriel. Seriously, every damn day she's either calling me or texting me constantly. Did you do this, did you do that? It doesn't matter if I tell her yes, she still checks in with me again to make sure I really did it. If I'd known the best man duties came with the nagging maid of honor, I would have let Braeden have the honor."

"Come on, man. It can't be that bad."

The second the words left Gabriel's mouth, Declan's phone rang. He didn't have to look down at the phone to know who it was. He'd programmed a very special ringtone for the bane of his existence.

"Seriously man, is that the Jaws theme? Please tell me that's not the ringtone for my future sister-in-law."

"Sorry. If I told you that, then I'd be lying."

"Give me the phone," Gabriel said as he reached across his desk.

Declan gladly handed him the phone, then laughed when Brooklyn started talking the second Gabriel answered the call. The man hadn't even had a chance to say hello before she began to pester him with questions. Gabriel put the call on speaker so they both could hear what the most infuriating woman in the world had to say.

"Hello, hello...damn it, Declan. Are you even there? I need to know if you talked to Braeden about his tux. And I need to know if you're going to be able to come over on Thursday to help put together the favors and the centerpieces. Since Finley can't be in town until Friday, I need extra hands. And did you get the wine together for the rehearsal dinner?"

"Hi Brook," Gabriel said as she took a breath.

"Oh hey, Gabriel. How are you? Are you excited for Saturday?"

"You know I can't wait to marry your sister. Is there anything I can help you guys with? It seems like there might be a lot to do so put me to work."

"Oh don't worry, Savannah has a list of things we need you to do. The rest of it is stuff the bridal party can handle. So, Declan can I count on you to be at my house on Thursday? Oliver and Meghan will be there, and I was hoping you could maybe talk Braeden into showing up."

"Yes, I'll be there, Princess, but I wouldn't count on Braeden. He's got a case he's been working long hours on. When I talked to him yesterday, he was picking his tux up from the cleaners and heading back to the office even though it was nearly seven o'clock."

"That's okay. We can make do with the four of us. Thank you for checking with Braeden about the tux. I know how he can get and if he's busy at work, he's even more scatterbrained than usual. Okay, well I'll let you guys go. I'll see you around six thirty on Thursday, Declan. Feel free to bring Erin and your sister if you'd like. The more, the merrier. And don't worry about dinner. I've got it covered."

Declan didn't even have a chance to respond before Brooklyn ended the call. The woman was a whirlwind, and if she hadn't been driving him crazy, he would have been impressed with the way she was handling the details of the wedding. He didn't know anyone else that could have wrangled their group quite the way Brooklyn had...especially given how much of a wild card Braeden could be.

"So that's what I've been dealing with since we got back from Vegas. She's been harping on me non-stop about wedding stuff. I really can't wait until your wedding is over."

Gabriel smiled as he handed Declan back his phone. "I'm sure it's been a real hardship for you to talk to her."

"She's driving me crazy."

"And you secretly like it. I won't tell anyone, I promise."

"Shut up, man. Seriously."

Although he protested, Declan knew his friend was right. He had enjoyed talking to Brooklyn over the last few weeks. Even if she drove him crazy, there was still something about her that drew him in. It could have been the constant arguing they did, the banter that made him laugh just as often as it made him want to shake her. There was something about the woman that had gotten under his skin long before the trip to Vegas. Spending the evening with her had made his awareness of her stronger.

There was no way he could ignore her existence after he nearly kissed her in the hotel elevator after he almost murdered a man for trying to assault her.

He was so screwed.

"You need to cut her some slack about this wedding thing. She just wants the wedding to be perfect. Hers wasn't, and she doesn't want her sister to go through the same thing."

Something in his chest tightened as Gabriel's words registered. If there was anyone who deserved the wedding of their dreams it was Brooklyn. She was precisely the kind of woman who'd been planning the big day since she was a little girl; the type of woman who knew what she wanted long before she ever found a groom. To find out her wedding day had been less than perfect surprised him and made him a bit angry. Any man marrying her should have moved heaven and earth to make sure she got what she wanted. The fact Brooklyn was currently divorced just further proved that her ex-husband was the world's biggest idiot.

"I didn't know that," Declan admitted. "I haven't said anything to her about the nagging and I haven't been mean to her to anything, so don't worry. I know she's just trying to make sure everything runs smoothly. We all know this group needs someone to guide them around or we wouldn't get anywhere."

"I knew it. You've been enjoying all the texts and calls."

Declan scoffed. "I wouldn't say I've been enjoying them, but they aren't as bad as I made them out to be."

"Good. Just promise you'll continue to be gentle with her this week. Just do whatever she asks, no matter how ridiculous it is. Consider it your gift to me."

"Don't worry. I promise to be on my best behavior where your future sister-in-law is concerned."

"I appreciate it, man and so does Savannah."

"You're my best friend, man. You know I'd do anything for you."

Over the decades they'd known each other, they'd been through a lot of ups and downs. They could have easily drifted apart when Gabriel's family moved out of West Seattle or when Erin was born, but they didn't let either of those events get in the way of their friendship. Neither of them liked to admit they almost allowed Gabriel's ex-fiancée get between them, both times she was in the picture because it was embarrassing.

Declan knew no matter what that Gabriel had his back. Even if his priorities were going to change when he married Savannah, he knew Gabriel would be there for him if he asked. And Declan would genuinely do anything for Gabriel, even if it meant dealing with his crazy, gorgeous, captivating sister-in-law.

* * *

Brooklyn

The last week had been stressful. More stressful than preparing for her own wedding had been. Brooklyn wanted, no needed, everything to be perfect for her sister's wedding. She wanted Savannah and Gabriel's wedding to be everything hers wasn't and more. So far everything was looking great. The rehearsal dinner had gone off without a hitch, which was no small feat.

Brooklyn was proud of herself for getting everything together and making sure everyone had a great time. The run through of the ceremony was flawless. Arrow was decorated precisely how she'd pictured it, thanks to Gabriel's staff. The food had been impeccable, although she wasn't surprised about that part. That was the one thing she'd been sure of going into the evening. That and she knew there wouldn't be any issues with the venue, given it was her future brother-in-law's restaurant.

Everything that had to do with the people involved in the wedding was what she'd been worried about. Having both sets of parents at the restaurant at the same time had been nerve-wracking. After years of being estranged following the death of his brother, Gabriel was still rebuilding his relationship with his mom and dad, and her parents admittedly weren't their biggest fans. Brooklyn would never be rude to their faces, but she couldn't understand how anyone could treat their only living son the way they had.

Then there was the bridal party. Braeden was unpredictable at best, and the way he acted around Declan's twin sister was confusing and at times hilarious. With Finley came her boyfriend Liam and the potential for out of town guests to get star struck over the Hollywood actor. Hell, Savannah still occasionally got a little flustered over being in the same room as Liam, and really, Brooklyn couldn't blame her. The man was gorgeous.

Although she'd been told she didn't have to worry about cleaning up, Brooklyn couldn't help herself so she'd taken to rinsing off the dishes they used so they could go through the industrial dishwasher. She wanted to leave as little behind for Gabriel's staff as she could. Plus she wasn't ready to head home yet. She needed some time to wind down, to prepare herself for the whirlwind of the next day. Her big sister was marrying the man of her dreams, and she knew it was going to be magical, but until the reception was over, Brooklyn was going to be on edge waiting for something terrible to happen.

"You did a great job today."

She didn't need to turn around to see who was speaking to her. Brooklyn had been aware of him the moment he entered the kitchen. The fact he was complimenting her was pretty out of the ordinary though. The fact he hadn't run out of the building the moment dinner was over was another shocker. She hesitated for a second, wanting to turn and look at him, but knowing if she did, he was going to be nothing but a distraction like he usually was.

"Thank you. I'm glad everything went well. Savannah and Gabriel deserve to have everything go flawlessly throughout this entire process. Speaking of, are you all set for tomorrow? Can you..."

"Don't worry, Princess. I've got everything handled. The centerpieces and decorations have been taken down and are in my car. I'll bring them to the hotel first thing in the morning so they can decorate the ballroom for the reception."

"I'm sorry. I just don't want anything to ruin Savannah's big day. I'm going to do everything I can to make sure that nothing gets in the way of my goal."

"I promise you. We've got this. Nothing's going to go wrong. Gabriel told me how important this is to you."

"Damn it, Gabriel."

"He didn't give me any details; he only said your wedding day was less than ideal. I didn't pry or ask any questions."

"I just...my wedding was nothing but problems from beginning to end and then so was my marriage. I don't want the same thing for my sister," Brooklyn admitted as she rinsed off the same plate she'd been holding since Declan walked in.

"I'm sorry you didn't get the perfect day you planned. I promise I'll do everything I can to make sure your sister and Gabriel don't have to worry about anything."

"Thank you for understanding why I've been so crazy the last few weeks. I'm sorry I've been such a pain."

"Hey, I get it. Will you look at me for a second?" Declan asked.

Brooklyn hesitated for a moment but then turned to face him. Her breath caught the way it always did when she first looked at him. Though he drove her crazy, Declan checked off every single item on her most wanted list. He was tall, dark, and incredibly handsome. He had a smile that made her weak in the knees, a smirk that nearly incinerated her panties and eyes that seemed to see right into her soul. His forearms were the sexiest damn forearms she'd ever seen, and he had an ass she could bounce a quarter off of...which was a saying she never quite understood, but she was 100% certain it was the case with Declan. He was a great friend and an even better father.

How he was still single was beyond her, and despite knowing it was a bad idea, Brooklyn wanted to be more to him than the sister of his best friend's future wife.

"You know everything that went wrong at your wedding had nothing to do with your marriage not lasting right? Mishaps happen all the time, and people stay married for their entire lives. Your wedding could have been perfect, and you'd still be divorced. Your marriage didn't work because your ex-husband is an idiot. Simple as that."

"You don't know anything about my marriage," Brooklyn protested, although she didn't know why. Frank didn't deserve her defending him, though she was probably defending her poor decisions more than the man she'd married.

Her ex-husband was an idiot and a philanderer and an asshole. She knew he was the reason their marriage ended. Not the fact his sister spilled red wine on her pristine white dress before the wedding, or because his mom was an extremely loud drunk, or because the best man speech was embarrassing and completely inappropriate. It was because Frank had a tough time keeping it in his pants...even on their wedding day. Of course, Brooklyn didn't learn of that particular infidelity until after their divorce, but she should have figured it was what he was doing when he was missing for nearly thirty minutes during the reception.

"No I don't, but I know you. And anyone who would let you get away is an idiot. Plain and simple."

Brooklyn's jaw dropped as she watched Declan leave the kitchen. The man was usually an antagonistic thorn in her side, arguing with her about every little thing and pushing every single one of her buttons. He rarely ever said anything nice about her, especially not to her. Yet he just had and then walked away from her like what he said wasn't a big deal. He had no idea how much his words genuinely meant to her, but someday he would.

Turning back toward the sink to finish up her task, Brooklyn continued to run Declan's words through her head. To hear someone unrelated to her and who wasn't a friend tell her she wasn't responsible for her marriage ending, meant the world to her. The fact that it was Declan who said it, only helped to solidify the crush she was developing on the hard-to-read, difficult to avoid man. He was the last thing she needed, but all she could think about. She needed to figure out how to get him out of her system. Too bad she was fairly certain it wouldn't be that easy.

CHAPTER 3

Declan

Looking around the ballroom, Declan had the sudden urge to pat himself on the back. Sure, he wasn't responsible for the set-up or the dinner. He wasn't the reason people were having a great time, some mingling near the bar while others danced to the greatest hits from the 80's and 90's. It didn't matter that his contribution to the evening was minuscule when compared to how massive an undertaking it all was. When Declan watched his best friend slow dance with his new wife to an upbeat song he hadn't heard in twenty years, he felt like he'd been a part of a miracle.

The ceremony was beautiful, filled with laughter and love and a bunch of tears. Declan wasn't too proud to admit some of those tears had come from his eyes as he watched Gabriel vow to love Savannah for the rest of their lives. It didn't help that he'd already shed a few tears when he watched his daughter walk down the aisle as the flower girl. Although at 17 she was far older than most traditional flower girls, Erin had been so excited when they asked her; she didn't care if the honor usually went to little girls.

Declan smiled remembering the look on her face as she threw rose petals along the aisle. It was adorable, but it also reminded him that she was growing up. In no time she was going to be eighteen and too soon after that she was going to go off to college. Even if she went to a school nearby, she'd still have to stay in housing on campus, meaning for the first time since she was born, Declan would go home to a house that didn't have her in it. The thought made him rethink the wine he'd had with dinner.

The song changed to a slower one, drawing his attention back to the dance floor. People paired up or left the floor altogether, but Gabriel and

Savannah didn't even seem to notice. They were lost in each other, which was just how things should have been. On the other side of the dance floor, he saw Brooklyn watching her sister. She looked happy for the couple, yet there was a hint of something else in her eyes. If he had to guess he'd say it was longing. If anyone was the poster woman for love, it was Brooklyn. It didn't matter that her first marriage didn't work out, he knew she still believed in happily ever after. She wanted to find it, and he had no doubt she would.

She looked up then, her eyes meeting his, a huge smile blossoming on her face. For once, she seemed happy to see him. Surprisingly, they'd made it through the day without a single argument. They'd worked well together making sure everything within their control went perfectly. For one day they proved they made a good team. Without overthinking it, Declan crossed the dance floor, his eyes never leaving hers.

"Would you care to dance?" he asked as soon as he was close enough she could hear him.

He reached his hand out to her as he asked; holding his breath until she gave him an answer. She didn't hesitate to place her hand in his and let him lead her into the crowd. Part of him wondered if he was making the right decision, but the other part didn't care. He just wanted to hold her in his arms, even if for only a song or two. Stolen moments were all he could ever let himself have.

The second they found a place on the floor, her eyes lit up with a smile. With their hands still clasped, he pulled her against him, her free hand moving to his shoulder. Placing his other hand against the small of her back, he began to move them slowly. As her eyes locked with his, it felt like everything around them seemed to fade away. They were the only people on the dance floor moving to a song he could no longer hear.

Having Brooklyn in his arms felt better than he'd ever expected. It felt right to be with her at that moment reveling in the love that filled the ballroom like air. When he looked at her, he could see forever in her eyes, and it no longer seemed like a scary concept. For eighteen years, he'd convinced himself that forever wasn't something he wanted, though as he pulled her closer, forever didn't seem like such a bad idea.

"I told you everything would work out," Declan said, needing to do something to take his mind off of his struggles.

"You just couldn't wait to say that could you?" she asked, a knowing smile gracing her lips.

"Hey, I'll have you know, I've been waiting hours to say those words," he joked. "But seriously, you did a great job organizing everything for your sister. You should be proud."

She looked up at him, her eyebrows furrowing in confusion at his compliment. He couldn't blame Brooklyn. He didn't spend a lot of time saying nice things to her. It wasn't that she didn't deserve them, it was that he couldn't be nice to her without wanting more. If he angered her, if he pissed her off, then the chances things would go further diminished. She'd get mad and stomp off, and he wouldn't have to worry about kissing her when he knew it was a bad idea.

"Thank you. I'm just happy that Savannah and Gabriel are happy. Things could have fallen apart, and I think they'd still be over the moon. Those two are more in love than anyone I know."

Declan watched something unmistakable pass over her face. A blink and you miss it moment where he saw a hint of sadness in her eyes. She wanted what her sister had, everyone knew that. She thought she had it once upon a time, but apparently, her ex-husband was the biggest dumbass in the world. He wanted to assure Brooklyn that someday she'd find a man who would love her the way she deserved to be loved, but he bit his tongue.

He didn't want to dwell on the anger that boiled in the pit of his stomach as he thought of Brooklyn with another man. He had no right to claim her, yet that's what he yearned to do. It didn't matter that his brain was working overtime telling him how bad that idea was. Having her in his arms for something other than a comforting hug had the rest of his body working overtime to prove his brain wrong. Even his heart seemed to be overlooking the memo his brain was sending out.

With her body pressed against his, it was hard to ignore how perfectly they fit together. How easy it would be to lean in, press his lips against hers and instigate the kiss they'd both been wanting for a long time. The kiss he almost started in the elevator in Vegas. If it weren't for that asshole Colin the night might have ended differently, but there was no way Declan was going to make a move after what happened. It was probably for the best though. Making a move was the last thing he should do. He just had to keep reminding himself of that.

One slow song melted into another. Declan knew he should let her go, but he couldn't. Thankfully Brooklyn didn't seem eager to walk away, so he tightened his arm around her and brought their clasped hands in to rest against his chest. The moment felt so right. He wasn't surprised when Brooklyn laid her head against his shoulder.

Neither of them said a word. Declan couldn't be sure about her, but he didn't want to ruin what was happening between them. He was the king of saying the wrong thing, especially with Brooklyn. For once, he didn't want to piss her off. He just wanted to savor her. Savor the intoxicating berries and vanilla scent of her and the way she absently played with the hair behind his ear.

As the second song came to an end, Declan slowly released his hold on her. He didn't want to let Brooklyn go, but he knew there was no way the DJ would play three slow songs in a row. Plus, he needed to back off, so he didn't get caught up in how natural it felt to have her in his arms. They needed to go back to arguing and driving each other crazy. She lifted her head off his shoulder, her eyes meeting his. He could tell she was just as affected by their dance as he was. It wasn't just a dance. It was a moment they'd been avoiding for months.

"Hey Brooklyn, sorry to interrupt, but we're going to start putting some things away, and no one seems to know where the boxes for your centerpieces ended up."

Saved by the bell, Declan thought as Brooklyn turned from his arms to face the hotel's event coordinator.

"Hey Sarah, I think Eric said he put them in the supply closet with the rest of our stuff. Let me go get them and then I can help with clean up."

"I'll go with you. You're going to need help getting the boxes down," Declan said as he followed Brooklyn off the dance floor.

"I'll be fine. I can handle it on my own."

"No, you can't," Declan insisted, which was met with a groan and Brooklyn nearly sprinting toward the exit.

Pissing her off wasn't really what he wanted, but it was what they needed to shake off the intimacy of their dance. He continued to follow her out of the ballroom and down the hall. He could tell by the tension in her shoulders she was irritated with him. Good. It would make things easier.

"Just go back to the ballroom, I'll get the boxes," he said as he tried to reach for the handle to the door.

"I don't need help, Declan."

"I'm not offering to help. I'm saying I've got this and you don't need to be here."

That was definitely the wrong thing to say. Brooklyn glared at him before batting his hand away from the door handle. She pulled the handle down and pushed the door open with much more force than necessary. Oh yeah, she wasn't happy with him, which he hoped meant they could get back to their usual routine.

She didn't hold the door open for him, and since he wasn't paying attention, it nearly hit him in the face as he walked into the tiny closet. The door closed behind him, engulfing them in darkness.

"Damn it, why didn't you just hold the door open?" Brooklyn asked irritation evident in her voice. "Did you see where the light was?"

"I think there's a chain for the light near where you're standing," Declan told her.

Of course, he could have pulled his cell phone out of his pocket and used it to make her life a little easier, but what fun would that be? If she was going to be annoyed with him, he might as well enjoy it. She swore a few times, cursing him at least once before she found the chain. There was an audible click before the room was lit up by a single light bulb above their heads.

"Alright, let's get this over with," she said as she looked around for the boxes they'd brought in that morning.

Declan knew just where the boxes were since he'd helped put them up which explained why he knew she was going to need help getting them down. He wasn't just trying to annoy her, although he was enjoying himself. Even if she'd still been wearing her heels, she wouldn't have been able to reach the shelf the boxes were on. It'd been a stretch for him, and he was at least four inches taller than her.

Brooklyn spotted the boxes before he had a chance to point them out. Moving over to the wire shelving unit she reached up, her fingers barely brushing the bottom of them. Standing on her tiptoes, Brooklyn tried to push the boxes closer to the edge and then over, but they hardly moved. He watched in utter fascination as she continued to work out a way to get the boxes down. She tried jumping up to reach for the boxes, nearly falling on her ass as she came down on unsteady legs.

"You're going to hurt yourself. Let me help."

"It's okay, I've got this," Brooklyn said with a grunt as she tried again to push the boxes off the shelf. She was now using the bottom shelf to make herself just a little bit taller, but it still wasn't doing the trick.

Declan knew she was two seconds away from climbing the wire shelving in her dress. If he didn't stop her and she got hurt, he'd never forgive himself and neither would her sister. The woman was one of the most stubborn people he'd ever met, too bad for her; he was just as stubborn. She needed to realize he was trying to be helpful, not trying to keep her from being independent or whatever the hell her deal was currently.

The room was tiny with very little room to maneuver for one person, let alone two. There wasn't enough room to stand next to Brooklyn and reach the boxes, and he couldn't pick her up to get her out of the way. The second he stepped forward, he knew he was going to regret the move in one way or another, but it was too late to change his mind.

As soon as his chest met her back, she stilled, her arms above her head still reaching for the boxes. He waited for her to move or say something, but nothing happened. She didn't even continue to try for the boxes. Like a frightened animal, she froze, waiting to see what he would do next. Before he even made it, Declan knew his next move was epically stupid. He should have backed up and left the room, let her figure things out on her own. Instead, he reached over her to grab the boxes, his hands moving along her outstretched arms. His eyes fluttered closed, as his entire body became in tune with hers.

The hitch in her breath, the shiver that ran down her body. He felt it all. The last thing he should've done was touch her, but he couldn't help himself. Touching her was all he'd wanted to do for months, and the desire had gotten harder to ignore since the weekend in Vegas. He knew her skin would be silky soft. He knew she'd feel good pressed up against him. He knew she was having just as difficult a time fighting their attraction as he was.

Yet at the moment he waited for her to react. Waited for her to elbow him in the stomach or yell at him about being in her way. Instead, she relaxed into him, a sigh escaping her lips.

"I knew you'd need me," he whispered into her ear.

He half expected that to be the moment she decided to punch him. He wouldn't deny the fact he deserved it, but whatever was about to happen, he wasn't going to stop it.

"I don't need you," she said half-heartedly as she pushed back against him.

He groaned as her ass made contact with his rapidly hardening cock. Things were starting to get real.

"You're playing with fire, Princess."

"I'm not afraid to get burned," she taunted, her ass brushing against him again.

He knew it was a bad idea, but he couldn't stop himself. Not even if the walls started coming down around them. The moment was over a year in the making. Hours of her prancing around in sexy outfits whenever they went out. Hours of watching her shake her ass and flirt with men that weren't him. Hours of watching her cheer for the Mariners, getting mad when the umps made the wrong call. Hours of her fretting over her sister's wedding because she wanted the big day to be perfect.

Hours of arguing with her over the dumbest things because he didn't want to admit she'd gotten under his skin.

From the moment he met her, Brooklyn St. James had begun making herself comfortable in his brain. He thought about her more often then he'd ever admit. Her smile, the way she smelled like heaven, her passion for baseball that rivaled his own, her laugh. There wasn't a damn thing he didn't like about her, and that realization pissed him off.

Declan knew they were destined to arrive at this moment. Since the day they met, he knew they'd end up where they were. Maybe not in a storage closet at a hotel in Downtown Seattle, but in each other's arms. Maybe they just needed to get it out of their system to move past their antagonistic relationship into something that would cause fewer waves amongst their group. And maybe he was going to grow wings and never have to sit in traffic again.

It didn't matter that once he had her, he wouldn't want to go back. It didn't matter that whatever was between them couldn't go anywhere. He needed this, needed her.

He didn't wait for an invitation or for her to make another move. Instead, he moved his hands back down her arms, pushing gently so she'd lower them to her sides. His hands grazed along the sides of her breasts, then down her sides to the skirt of her dress. Pulling it up until he could get his hands underneath it, he nearly groaned when his fingers made contact with the bare skin of her thighs.

"Touch me, Declan."

He did groan then, her words adding fuel to the fire burning within him. Grateful that her hair was up in a messy bun, he brushed his lips behind her ear, then down along the curve of her neck and over her shoulder. Peppering kisses along her bare skin, he moved his hands along her thighs, heading for the place he was dying to touch. He could feel the heat from her core before he even touched her.

Rubbing the heel of his palm against her clit only proved to aggravate them both. He needed to feel her slickness against his fingers, needed to feel her body clench around him as he brought her to orgasm. She writhed against his hand, then whimpered when he moved back up her body so that he could slide it underneath her silky panties.

"Don't worry Princess, I'm going to take care of you," he whispered as he nipped at her earlobe.

"Less talk, more action," she demanded through clenched teeth. "Just fuck me Declan. I don't need foreplay. I just need your cock filling me up."

"Jeezus..." he groaned dropping his head against her shoulder.

Those words falling from the lips of the woman he'd been dreaming about for months nearly undid him. Not wanting to disappoint her, he removed his hand then turned her around to face him. Her skin was flushed, her lips parted, eyes glossy with desire. He met her gaze for just a moment before he removed his wallet from his jacket pocket, then took his jacket off and threw it on the wire rack behind her. He pulled a condom out then threw his wallet on top of his jacket, while Brooklyn went to work undoing his pants.

With precision he was surprised they could muster his cock was free from its confines and covered in the condom in mere seconds. His knees nearly buckled when she took him in her hot little hand, stroking him from root to tip. She needed to stop, but he wasn't about to tell her to. Instead, he pulled at her skirt until it bunched around her waist. With the dress out of the way, he reached around her until he cupped her fantastic ass in his hands, a groan escaping his lips when his hands slipped against silky skin instead of silky fabric.

Hauling her against him, he lifted her until she could wrap her long, sexy legs around his waist. He used the shelves behind her to hold her still as he pulled her panties to the side and notched the head of his cock at her entrance. His eyes met hers looking for a sign that she'd changed her mind.

"Come on," she urged her nails digging into his shoulders.

He was thankful for the layers of his tux otherwise he was sure she'd draw blood. She chewed on her lower lip waiting for him to make a move. She wiggled her hips trying to force him into action. If he weren't so close to losing his mind, he would have continued to tease her. Watching her grow frustrated with his lack of effort made his dick harder if that was even possible. Knowing she wanted him just as much as he wanted her made his balls ache with the need for release. His heart hammered against his chest, and for a moment he felt like he might pass out.

Without warning or a second thought, he thrust into her, surprising them both. He stilled, allowing them both a moment to catch their breaths. It was finally happening. The moment they both knew they'd never be able to outrun. Never in his wildest dreams could he have imagined the way he'd feel having her wrapped around him. He knew she'd feel good, but the way her pussy gripped his cock like a vice was unbelievable.

He slowly started to move, his body rocking into hers. With each thrust and retreat, Brooklyn's legs tightened around him, like she was trying to keep him buried inside of her. He fucked her slowly at first, but it did nothing to slake his need.

She tightened her grip on his shoulders as he picked up speed.

"Harder...please Declan, I'm so close."

Her head fell back, eyes closed as he pounded into her. If he wasn't careful, she was going to end up with a bruise across her back from the shelf he fucked her against. She didn't seem to care as she tried to pull him closer, her moans and her body urging him to take her harder.

His thrusts became erratic, his balls tightening. Declan reached between their bodies to rub his thumb against her clit. There was no way he was going to come until he made sure she'd gotten off. She shuddered at the contact, so he continued to tease the swollen nub until she writhed against him.

"Oh fuck...fuck..." she muttered as her orgasm came crashing down. If he thought she was tight before, it was nothing compared to how she gripped him as she succumbed to her pleasure. Declan nearly shot off the second her walls started to convulse around him but managed to hold it together so he could prolong Brooklyn's orgasm.

Once she started to come down, he drove into her, pressing her hard against the shelf. It only took a couple of thrusts before he began to shake. He came a second later, his body tensing as he held himself against her, hot spurts of cum filling the thin barrier between them.

Declan relaxed his hold on her but didn't put her down. He couldn't trust his body or her legs. The last thing he wanted to do was explain how either of them got injured looking for boxes in a storage closet. Gabriel would kick his ass if she knew what they'd been doing.

The second he thought about his best friend, the post-orgasmic euphoria fled from his body. He felt like he'd been doused in freezing cold water. If he hadn't been holding her up, he probably would have jumped back to put some space between them.

Fuck. What have I done? he thought as he tried to figure out how to extricate himself from the situation without making matters worse.

Slowly he set her down, making sure her legs could support her before he backed away. Her brows furrowed as she watched him, the look of satisfaction that had been on her face moments earlier was long gone. His palms started to sweat as he removed the condom, making sure to tie the end in a knot. He looked around the room, looking for somewhere to dispose of the evidence, but found nothing, so he shoved it into his pants pocket.

Without looking at her, he started to do up his pants, not bothering to tuck his shirt back in. He didn't have to worry about Erin since she was with his sister, so once they finished, he wouldn't be heading back to the reception. He needed to get the hell out of there. Needed to deal with how being with Brooklyn made him feel. Fuck, he shouldn't even be thinking about how she made him feel. They couldn't do it again. It was a mistake. It was too damn good.

He was in so much trouble.

"Declan…"

His name falling from her lips always made him feel good until that moment. She sounded hesitant, worried and he'd done that to her, and he was about to make it worse. He couldn't let her know how much being with her had affected him. She couldn't know that she was going to be his undoing. He rubbed a hand over his face, then looked over at her. Unshed tears shimmered in her eyes. She knew without him even saying anything that their moment was over.

"Brooklyn, this was a mistake. It didn't mean anything. I shouldn't have let you push me into it. I'm sorry, but we shouldn't have done this."

"What…how can you say that?" she asked, her voice shaky as she tried not to cry.

"We can barely stand each other most of the time. I just…this…it shouldn't have happened."

She winced at his harsh words, her shoulders starting to tremble. His chest burned with each lie he spoke. It killed him to hurt her, but he couldn't run the risk of her wanting more. There couldn't be more. He wasn't good enough for her. She deserved someone who could be the love of her life, and that definitely wasn't him.

The sound of her sobs filled the tiny closet. Without thinking he took a step toward her wanting to comfort her even though he was the asshole who'd hurt her. She jerked away from him, then pushed him out of the way so she could get to the door.

"Fuck you Declan. Don't fucking touch me," she yelled before yanking the door open.

His eyes met those of Oliver's over Brooklyn's shoulder. Meghan was standing next to him, but she only had eyes for her friend. Brooklyn barreled out of the room, nearly taking her friend out as she did. When Meghan followed her down the hall, Declan was left alone with Oliver, his friend's questions written all over his face.

"What the fuck just happened, man?"

Declan had no idea how to answer the question. He was angry at himself for being a dickhead. Pissed that he'd let things go that far then turned around and hurt one of the most amazing women he'd ever met after the best sex he'd ever had. He was a monumental dumbass, and there was nothing he could do to fix it. The realization made him angrier, and instead of holding it in, he took it out on his friend.

"None of your fucking business," he growled before grabbing his wallet and jacket off of the shelf. He shoved his way through the door, bumping against Oliver, who was blocking his way. He didn't apologize as he did, just shot his friend a warning look, then stalked off down the hallway until he found the entrance.

Declan wasn't sure how one of the best nights of his life could so quickly become a shit show, but he knew he was the only one to blame. He just hoped he hadn't done irreparable damage to his friendships because he couldn't keep his dick in his pants. The minute he realized Brooklyn was worth whatever hell came down upon him, was the minute he realized he was utterly and totally screwed and not in a good way.

CHAPTER 4

Brooklyn

This was a mistake. It didn't mean anything. I shouldn't have let you push me into it.

For the better part of two weeks, Brooklyn had done her best to forget about what happened at her sister's wedding. Every once in a while, she'd have a flashback to how it felt to be touched by him, to be filled by him. Then his words would smack her in the face again like they had that night and anger would course through her.

Thankfully, she hadn't seen Declan since the night in question. It would have been hard for her to fight off the urge to punch him in the nuts. He deserved it. Hell, he deserved more than that considering the way he'd made her feel like some fucking siren that'd led him to his doom. They both knew they'd been dancing around the inevitable since the moment they met. It was only a matter of time before they broke. Given their close proximity leading up to the wedding, it wasn't a surprise it happened there.

What had been a surprise was Declan's reaction and more importantly her reaction to what he said. She had no idea why she cared so much about him thinking the moment was a mistake. Or why her chest ached when she thought about how he said it didn't mean anything.

It didn't mean anything…at least that's what she kept telling herself. For some reason, the words that came out of his mouth the night she stupidly gave in to the attraction between them had cut straight to her heart, and she was trying her damnedest to figure out why. All while trying not to think about that night at all.

She was a mess. And there was really no one she could talk to about it. Only a handful of people know about what happened, and Oliver and Meghan were a bit too busy to even think about Brooklyn's problems. Her best friend Kerrigan was on vacation with her fiancé Ben and thus not available to listen to her whine. So instead of talking out her issues with her friends, she was keeping everything bottled up inside, which made her both depressed and angry.

Her sister said she was a delight to be around, which was Savannah's subtle way of saying she was being a bitch. Instead of working out front, Savannah made her wash dishes in the back where no one could be offended by her. Of course, she couldn't tell Savannah why she was in such a bad mood. Brooklyn didn't want her sister to know she'd finally broken down and hooked up with Declan. She especially didn't want her to know she'd then broken down in tears when he rudely pushed her away.

Brooklyn was embarrassed by the entire situation, even more so by the fact, her body went weak every time she had one of the hot yet inconvenient flashbacks. She hated knowing she'd have a hard time turning Declan down if he wanted to go again. Despite the hurt his words caused, his body had done more damage. A quick fuck in a storage closet had made her feel more than she'd felt in a long time. Had meant more than she cared to admit.

"Hey Brooklyn, do you have a second?"

The uncertainty tainting the words made Brooklyn cringe. The last person she wanted to be hesitant to talk to her was Erin. Even though Erin was Declan's daughter, Brooklyn liked her and felt a connection with her that went beyond employer/employee. Since she'd started working at Delectable Delights back in June, Brooklyn had gotten used to having her around. Now that school was back in session, Erin didn't work as often as she had over the summer and Brooklyn found herself missing the time they got to spend together.

"Of course. You know I've always got time for you," Brooklyn said as she turned around to face her. "What's up?"

After grabbing a towel to dry her hands on, Brooklyn leaned back against the sink and watched Erin pull out one of the stools they kept tucked under the counter. The teenager still seemed hesitant to talk to her, but Brooklyn could tell it wasn't because of her lousy attitude. Erin was usually bubbly and confident, talking a mile a minute about whatever was going on in her life. The fact that she was sitting on the stool, not making eye contact and wringing her hands together in her lap meant she was nervous about something.

"Whatever it is, you can tell me," she said, hoping to ease Erin's anxiety.

"Sorry. It's nothing big really, but I was kinda hoping you might be able to help me. I need to write a few essays for college applications and scholarship applications and well...words are not really my thing. I'm much better with science and math, but these essays are critical, so I was hoping given you're a writer and stuff that you'd be willing to help me out," Erin said before stopping to take a breath. "I could pay you, or we could work out a trade or I mean, I don't know, I just need help and dad said you'd be the best person to ask and I agree. So, will you...please? It would mean a lot."

Brooklyn wasn't sure what to think about Declan recommending that Erin ask her for help. After what happened, she wouldn't have been surprised if he'd asked her not to work at Delectable Delights anymore. It was already pretty obvious he'd gotten someone else to make the deliveries to DD, or he was coming in when he knew she wouldn't be there. Usually, she would have seen him at least twice during any given week when he delivered their wine.

"Of course, I'll help you. I'd love to. I'm sure this won't surprise you, but I enjoy writing essays and proofreading other people's work. My sister says I'm weird, but I can't help it."

"Oh my gosh, that's great. I really appreciate it. Just tell me what you want in return, money or I can clean your house or whatever."

Erin's glasses fell down the bridge of her nose as she excitedly listed off the things she'd do in exchange for Brooklyn's help. Every once in a while, she'd do things that reminded Brooklyn of her dad, and it made her heart clench. She had his bright green eyes, but her hair was a few shades lighter. Erin was the total package, brilliant, funny, and gorgeous. It was a wonder she didn't have boys knocking down her door.

"It's fine, Erin. I've got the time, and I'm happy to do it. I don't need anything in return. Just kick ass in college, and that'll be enough for me."

"Thank you, thank you, thank you!" Erin said as she rushed over to hug Brooklyn. "This means so much to me. These essays are everything."

"Hey, it's no problem. I'm glad I can help. I remember writing essays for college applications. They're difficult, and it would have been awesome to have someone else read them before I sent them in."

"Ummm..." Erin said as she took a step back. "So now that you've said yes, I've got something to admit and I'm hoping you'll be able to keep this between us."

Brooklyn knew she should have said no. She should have told the girl she couldn't keep things from her father that would have been the right thing to do. But she wanted Erin to trust her. For some reason, Brooklyn felt it was important the girl had an adult in her corner that wouldn't judge her, who would help her with whatever she needed. She knew Declan loved his daughter, but he was blinded by wanting to keep her safe. And her aunt, Declan's sister Andrea, was nearly as bad.

"I swear, it's not a big deal or anything, I just don't want my dad to know I'm applying for out of state colleges. I kinda told him I needed an English tutor because I was struggling in class. He thinks I'm only applying to the University of Washington, but I have to get out of here. I'm not applying for any colleges in the state, which is why the scholarship applications are so important. Out of state tuition is much higher."

That was not what Brooklyn was expecting to hear, although she couldn't say she was surprised. Given how protective Declan was, it wasn't shocking Erin wanted to go to school out of state. Brooklyn knew Erin loved her dad more than anything, but it was hard for anyone to figure out who they were when they were under the constant watch of a parental figure.

Although she understood what Erin wanted, Brooklyn couldn't ignore the fact she felt like she should try to talk some sense into the girl. Declan would be pissed when he found out, pissed and hurt his little girl didn't want to be around him anymore. Not to mention how angry he'd be with Brooklyn when he found out she knew and didn't tell him.

"Look, I get it. I do, but don't you think keeping this from your dad is only going to make things worse? He's going to find out eventually and then what? He's going to be mad and probably pretty hurt."

Erin turned around and started to pace. It was apparent Brooklyn wasn't telling her anything she didn't already know. Erin was a smart girl. She'd probably thought the situation through backward and forward and sideways. Looked at every single variable, pros and cons, worst case scenarios and whatever else she could think up.

"I know. But what if I apply for these schools and I don't get in? Then I've hurt his feelings for nothing. I don't want to say anything until I have actual news. I'm going to apply for early decision for my number one school and regular timeline for my backups in case I don't get in. Early decision letters usually come out the middle of December, so I should know more in a couple of months. Then I'll tell my dad."

Brooklyn couldn't argue with her point. Why say anything until there was something concrete to say? Of course, she also had a bad feeling about Erin not saying anything. The decision to go along with Erin's plan was probably going to bite her in the ass eventually, but it didn't matter. She wasn't Declan's favorite person, and he certainly wasn't hers. If he got mad at her for helping his daughter, then so be it.

"Fine. I won't say anything to your dad, but only on one condition."

"Name it," Erin said as she stopped pacing. She looked at Brooklyn like she had the answer to all of her problems. "I'll do whatever you want as long as we can keep this from my dad until I know more."

"Send an application to the University of Washington. I know you don't want to go there, but at least do that for him while you're planning on leaving him behind. He's gonna be crushed, so at least give him this one thing."

Erin sighed, but Brooklyn could tell she was relieved that applying for a school she didn't want to go to was all Brooklyn was asking for in return.

"Okay, if that's what it'll take for you not to tell my dad, then I'll apply. Heck, I'll send an application to every school in the state that has a veterinarian program so that you'll keep this secret for a couple of months."

Brooklyn smiled at the girl. "I don't think that's necessary...although if you wanted to apply to Washington State, I could put in a good word for you. It would definitely make a good back-up school, far enough away to get some freedom, but not so far away your dad would lose his mind."

"I'll think about it. I mean they are ranked fourteenth in the country and I know it's a good school, but I really want to go to North Carolina State. The program is ranked third in the country, and North Carolina is beautiful. It doesn't hurt that it's the furthest away from here. I promise though it's not the only reason I want to go there."

"I know. I promise I won't say anything to your dad. We're not talking at the moment anyway, so that won't be a problem, but I don't recommend keeping the secret for long if you can help it. I get why you want to go away for school, but he loves you and no matter how overbearing he gets he deserves to be kept in the loop about this."

Erin sighed again, the kind of overdramatic, exacerbated sigh that teenage girls were known for. Brooklyn wouldn't have been surprised if there was an eye roll to go along with the sigh. The last thing she wanted to do was lecture the girl, but Brooklyn knew Declan wasn't going to be happy about his daughter's plans.

"I know he loves me. He'd do anything for me...which is what he's been doing since I was born. He gave up his future for me. Going away for college isn't just about me figuring out who I am, but it's also for him and Aunt DeeDee. Both of them need to get lives that don't revolve around me or that stupid company. I want my dad to have all the things he gave up to have me. He's a little too old for the professional baseball career, but he could fall in love, get married, maybe have more kids. I don't know, but I feel like he wasted a lot of time putting his life on hold for me and I want him to stop doing that. I want him to stop using me as an excuse to keep from actually living."

Brooklyn's mouth opened, then closed, then opened again. She didn't know what to say, but she knew she had to say something. Most teenagers would have been so self-absorbed they wouldn't have noticed or cared about what their parents were going through. They wouldn't have noticed the sacrifices they made for them. Brooklyn was ashamed to admit that was precisely the kind of teenager she'd been. The fact Erin not only noticed but also wanted something better for her dad proved she was more mature than most kids her age.

"You have to know he doesn't regret the way his life turned out. He doesn't regret giving things up for you. Not baseball, not being in a relationship. He would give it all up all over again for you without even thinking about it."

"How do you know that? Has he said something to you?"

"Not in so many words, but you only have to look at the man when he talks about you to know he'd do anything for you. He loves you so much and is so proud of the woman you're becoming. I guarantee he'd do it all over again if he had to because you're the most important part of his life."

"But he could have had so much more. He didn't have to spend the last eighteen years alone."

"Technically he wasn't alone, although I know what you mean. Eventually he'll get out there and figure out what he wants to do with his life, but for now, he wants to make sure you have everything you need. Your dad and I might not always get along, but I have to say you lucked out in the dad department. I know he can be tough to get through to, but I think he'll understand where you're coming from."

"I'll think about telling him sooner, I really will, but for now I think its best this way. What he doesn't know can't hurt him and all that," she reiterated. "Thanks for the talk Brooklyn and for being open to helping me out. I really appreciate it. I should get back to work though before Jeanine comes back here to scold me."

With an awkward wave, Erin backed her way through the swinging door that led to the front of the bakery. Shaking her head, Brooklyn turned back to the sink to focus on the dishes she still needed to wash. She had no idea what to do about Erin's secret. She didn't want to betray the girl, but she also didn't want to piss Declan off any more than she needed to.

Despite their differences and everything that'd happened between them, they were going to have to get along for the sake of their friends. It wouldn't be fair for their friends to have to deal with the constant fighting whenever they were near each other. Now that the awkwardness of their closet rendezvous hung between them, Brooklyn had a feeling the tension was only going to be worse, and it wasn't like she could explain to everyone why she had so much animosity for the man.

As much as she wanted to punch Declan in the face, she knew she was going to have to be the bigger person and suck it up. She could be hurt all she wanted in the privacy of her own home, but around everyone else, Brooklyn was going to have to act as if Declan hadn't ripped a piece of her soul out when he let those words fall from his lips while she was still fixing her dress. It wasn't going to be easy, but Brooklyn had dealt with far more difficult and heart-wrenching secrets, what was one little interlude in the grand scheme of things.

* * *

Declan

He'd been avoiding her for weeks. Not for his sake, but for hers. He'd been an ass the night of the wedding, and she didn't deserve to have it rubbed in her face. Although she could be a giant pain in his ass, Brooklyn was a fantastic woman. She shouldn't have to deal with him and his issues.

So instead of fessing up about what was going through his head that night or acting like an even bigger asshole, he altered his delivery route so she wouldn't have to deal with him while she was at work. He steered clear of the group get-togethers so he could give her the space she deserved. He fought the urge to call her when Meghan's news made the rounds. He knew he was the last person she'd want to comfort her, even though he wanted to.

Since the moment he opened his mouth and crushed her, he'd regretted it. He'd acted rashly, out of fear, out of necessity, maybe both. He wasn't too proud to admit to himself that he'd freaked out. It wasn't just about how amazing the sex was. It was how it made him feel. There wasn't a single person he could talk to about his feelings and he sure as hell couldn't admit them to Brooklyn. She was the kind of woman that deserved to marry the love of her life and have children and Declan knew without a shadow of a doubt he was not that man. He couldn't be that man.

He just wished he could take back what he'd said or at the very least take back how it had made her feel. He'd never meant to hurt her. If he could go back, he'd handle it differently, although the result would be the same. He couldn't be with her, no matter how badly he wanted to be. He'd thought about steering clear of her forever, but that wasn't possible or plausible. They had too many friends in common, and now that she was helping Erin with her college stuff, Declan knew it was time to call a truce.

With any luck, they could both forget about what happened that night and go back to being normal.

Everything would be fine again.

Except he couldn't stop remembering how she felt pressed up against him. What it felt like to finally be buried inside of her. He couldn't forget the way her moans filled the small space or the way she cried out his name when she came. But he also couldn't forget the pain in her eyes when he accused her of talking him into having sex with her like he didn't have a mind of his own.

When he saw tears fill her eyes, Declan knew he'd gone too far, but there was no way he could step back at least not in that moment. For the first time in eighteen years, sex had felt like more than just scratching an itch, and it had scared the shit out of him. Instead of focusing on why, he lashed out and blamed Brooklyn, despite the fact it wasn't completely a surprise. Since the moment he'd met her, Declan knew Brooklyn was different. He knew she could break through every wall he'd built around himself.

Knowing that was precisely why he'd tried to stay away. It was why he'd picked on Brooklyn and pushed her away whenever he had the chance. He would have kept doing it if Gabriel hadn't forced him into close proximity with her. Why couldn't he have chosen Oliver or Braeden as his best man? It would have made his life a hell of a lot easier and a hell of a lot more boring. Just the way he liked it...usually. Since the night of the wedding, he'd started having doubts, but there was nothing he could do about them. He had Erin to focus on, and she would always be more important than anything else.

Looking at the clock on the dashboard of his truck, Declan realized he'd been sitting outside of the backdoor to Delectable Delights for twenty minutes thinking about Brooklyn. Worrying about Brooklyn was more like it. He wasn't sure what he was about to do was a good idea, but it needed to be done. He could have waited until the next group get together, but he figured she was less likely to kick him in the nuts at the bakery, even if they were in the kitchen where no one else could see them.

Quickly grabbing the clipboard from the passenger seat, he jumped out of the truck and walked toward the back. With every step, his heart rate ramped up, and his hands started to sweat. He was fucking nervous which was a new feeling when it came to someone other than his daughter. Declan tried to shake it off as he pushed the door up and pulled out the ramp. He went to task loading up the dolly with the wine Savannah or Brooklyn ordered, slower than he usually went about it.

Usually, he was in and out of a business in minutes, but he was too damn nervous to get his shit together or to care about messing up the schedule for the rest of his route. He'd skip lunch if he had to in order to make up the time. Having a woman screw with his work schedule was yet another first. Declan had never let someone get to him the way Brooklyn had, and it was scary and horrible and amazing all at the same time. If only he could let things happen between them.

He shook off the thoughts he shouldn't be having and pushed the dolly up to the back door of DD. He knocked on the door like he usually did then pulled it up, the mouthwatering scent of chocolate and sugar assaulting him as he walked inside. Brooklyn stood at the metal table in the center of the kitchen, a cupcake in one hand, a frosting bag in the other. She looked up as the sound of the dolly reached her. The surprise on her face when she saw he was there was immediately covered up by a mask of indifference as she went back to frosting the cupcake.

For a moment, Declan watched her ignore him. To most, it would look like she was going about her business, but he could see she was fighting against her nature. Her jaw was clenched, her shoulders tense, if she wasn't careful she was going to squeeze the life out of the new cupcake she'd picked up. She wanted to say something to him, to lay into him or insult him like she used to. Part of him wished she would. He wanted her to be the one to break their silence, but he knew it had to be him since he was the asshole that started the whole damn thing.

He unloaded his delivery onto one of the wire racks then turned to look back at Brooklyn. She'd stopped working and was watching him. When she realized he'd caught her staring, she scowled but didn't drop her gaze or go back to the cupcakes. She met his stare, daring him to finally say something. Without a word, he slid the clipboard across the table toward her.

He knew he was being a fucking coward. Despite his grand plan to come inside and thank her for helping Erin, he just stared at her instead. She deserved more than that. She deserved an apology, a moment to yell at him for making her feel the way he did. But he was struggling to nut up and do what he'd come in there to do. The delivery was just an excuse he had access to, Declan could have continued to avoid her, but he didn't want to, and he knew he shouldn't. Now that he was in front of her he wasn't sure why he'd talked himself out of staying away.

With a sigh, she picked up the clipboard and the pen attached and signed her name on the dotted line. The sound of her putting the dot in her last name echoed through the quiet room. She was angry, and he couldn't blame her. Silently, she slid the clipboard back over to him, the way she looked at him made him squirm a little. He picked up the clipboard and turned to walk away. He needed to get out of there, needed to get away from her disapproving glare and the hurt he could still see there.

He had to walk away. Leave Brooklyn still hating him. That would make things a hell of a lot easier, but it wasn't the right thing to do. He wasn't an asshole. Not usually. And he didn't want to be one now. Especially not to the woman helping his daughter. He just needed to make sure they were both on the same page. Nothing else could ever happen between them. He would never let Brooklyn know the real reason he had to stay away from her. He could never let her know that she had the power to destroy him. He couldn't let anyone know Brooklyn could hurt him far more than Kara ever did.

Turning back to face her, he realized she was still watching him, although the look on her face was no longer one of anger, but sadness. Of course, as soon as he realized it, the look was gone, replaced with rage once again.

"Look, I just wanted to say thank you for helping Erin. I appreciate it."

"I'm not doing it for you," she said, her eyes dropping back to the cupcakes in front of her.

"I know. You're doing it in spite of me, and I appreciate it. She's the best thing in my life. I don't want her to suffer because I'm an ass."

Declan hadn't planned on letting that particular fear be known. When he'd suggested Erin ask Brooklyn for help, a part of him worried she'd turn

Erin away because she was his daughter. He knew Brooklyn wasn't that type of person. Declan also knew how much Brooklyn liked Erin, so it wasn't a realistic fear to have, but he couldn't help it. He knew he'd deserve Brooklyn's anger and whatever else came from that. He just never wanted his daughter to be affected by the stupid decisions he made in his life, which was one of the many reasons he'd spent the last eighteen years alone.

"I adore Erin. She's a smart kid, and she deserves every opportunity she can get. I would never hold your actions against her. It's not her fault you're a dumbass. Also, it's not like I could say no and then explain to her it's because you fucked me in a closet and then made me feel like I'd somehow taken advantage of you."

"Look..."

"Save it. I think it's better for everyone if we just forget all about that night. No one needs to know about it. We never have to talk about it. Let's just move on."

Sighing, he ran a hand through his hair, then gripped the back of his neck. He was going to hate himself for what he was about to say, but he couldn't help it. For once he wanted to be honest with Brooklyn even if it ended up being cruel and unusual punishment for them both.

"Forgetting about it seems to be easier said than done. I've tried for weeks to forget about what happened, but I can't. I can still hear you, still feel you. I know it's probably for the best, but I'm not sure I want to forget."

"Declan..."

"It can't happen again, we both know that. But it doesn't mean I have to forget about how great it felt to finally have you in my arms. To finally get what I wanted no matter how bad of an idea it was. I'm sorry about the shit I said. I didn't mean any of it. You didn't talk me into anything, and it wasn't a mistake. I said what I did because I was scared. Because no matter how much I enjoyed it, no matter how much I want you, I can't have you and it was easier to push you away than admit any of that to either of us."

He waited for her to respond, to tell him to fuck off, to forgive him, he almost didn't care which, he just wanted her to say something. The silence stretched between them. It was both uncomfortable and comforting. If she wasn't saying anything, she wasn't telling him to go to hell, but she also wasn't telling him what he wanted to hear. He wanted to know they were going to be okay; that they could be in the same room together without her wanting to kill him.

"I don't know what to say," she said finally, her words catching ever so slightly. She cleared her throat as she rubbed at her eyes with the back of her hand. The last thing Declan wanted was to make her cry again. He should have just kept his damn mouth shut.

"You don't have to say anything," he told her, fighting every urge he had to walk around the table and wrap her in his arms.

"Yes, I do. You hurt me Declan. The words you said, the way you pushed me away while my fucking skirt was still bunched up around my waist. I was still coming down from a pretty good orgasm, and you threw it all in my face. Made me sound like some lecherous seductress that'd planned everything. Now you tell me you didn't mean any of it and I'm supposed to what, just forgive you? Is that what you want?"

"I don't expect you to forgive me completely. I know what I said was cruel. I'm hoping we can go back to normal or as close to normal as possible. We have too many friends in common to let our situation cause problems. And with everything Meghan and Oliver are going through right now, our issues seem ridiculous in comparison."

Brooklyn sighed. "You're right about that. This is nothing compared to what they're dealing with. Fine, I forgive you for being an idiot. And I forgive you for what you said today too. I know you thought you were being helpful by being truthful, but I didn't need to know any of it. It doesn't change anything. We can't be more than this, two people who have friends in common. We can't do anything else about the attraction between us. It's not fair to either of us to even think about it. So again, can we just let it go and move on?"

It felt wrong. Declan didn't want to agree to what she was asking, but he knew he had to for her. No matter how badly he wished things could be different, he owed her at least that much.

"If that's what you want, then yes, I can let it go and move on."

"Thank you," Brooklyn said softly. "Now don't you have other deliveries to make or whatever?"

Smiling, he nodded. "Yeah, I should probably get out of here. I'm a bit behind already as it is. So, I'll um see you at Gabriel and Savannah's on Sunday?"

"Yeah, I'll be there."

"Right then...okay, well have a good day, Brooklyn."

With an awkward wave of the clipboard, Declan backed away from the table, only barely avoiding running into his dolly. He quickly turned around, pulling the dolly behind him. He needed to get out of there before she realized she made a mistake forgiving him before she was smart and took it all back. Pushing open the back door, he stopped so he could pull the dolly through the door. Just as he was about to let the door go, he heard the doors leading to the dining area push open and the unmistakable voice of his best friend's wife.

"What the fuck, Brooklyn? Declan? At my wedding? Seriously?"

"Shit," he muttered before letting the door go so he could get the hell out of there. He knew Brooklyn didn't want anyone else to know about what happened and he'd been stupid enough to start a conversation with her in a place where her sister was bound to hear them. Declan had a feeling his hard-earned pardon was quickly going down the drain as Savannah started pestering Brooklyn with questions.

Loading the dolly back into the truck, he climbed in and threw the clipboard back on the passenger seat. Now Brooklyn was going to want to kill him for an entirely different reason. Their truce was probably completely out the window.

"Well, it was good while it lasted," he muttered, then started the truck so he could get on with his day. He had deliveries to finish before he dealt with the inevitable phone call from his best friend and the reaming that would come along with it. Even with that looming over his head, he couldn't be sorry about what happened between them. Someday maybe things would be different, and he could give her what she deserved. Until then, he'd have the memories of that night to keep him going.

CHAPTER 5

Brooklyn

Something was wrong. After a month of being friendly and actually acting like they liked each other, Declan was back to giving her the cold shoulder. When he did deign to give her attention, it was with the same scowl he used to give her back before her sister's wedding. Back before they'd talked things through, before they called their truce. She had no idea what was going on, but it was beginning to piss her off.

It wasn't the fact he was being an asshole. It was because he'd chosen Friendsgiving to display his newly returned tendencies. Of all nights, with everything going on, why he couldn't have waited was beyond her. The more she thought about it, the angrier she got. It was probably a good thing she was relegated to the kitchen, so she could finish putting the final touches on dinner.

She was also glad the group was in the den watching football instead of the living room. Given the open concept of her sister's house, she had a feeling she'd be getting the stare down the entire time she worked on dinner. Then she'd have a difficult time controlling her need to punch him. Thankfully, the den was far enough away from the kitchen that they didn't have to yell over the noise she was making, but close enough she could still hear her friends. Occasionally, one of them would come to the kitchen to get a new drink or to check on her since she'd volunteered to take care of everything on her own.

Brooklyn quickly checked on the rolls in the oven and made sure nothing was burning, then turned to the potatoes that were ready to be mashed. The thought of picturing those potatoes as Declan's head made her laugh as she measured out the milk and butter to add to the pot. Before

Brooklyn could turn on the mixer, her phone dinged with a text. She hesitated to check it but figured she should do it before she forgot.

I'm sorry. He found out...

The preview of the text on her homepage had her heart rate ramping up. When she realized the text was from Erin, it barely calmed her down. She entered in her password, then pulled up the full message which also contained a picture of a bank statement with a handwritten note on it. We need to talk, love Dad.

I'm sorry. He found out when he checked my bank account. I have a feeling he's pissed, but I wasn't home before he left for dinner at Uncle Gabriel's. He doesn't know you know or how much you helped me, but I bet he's made assumptions. I'm sorry, Brooklyn. I didn't mean for this to happen. I should have listened to you. Please let me know everything's okay.

"Well shit," Brooklyn muttered as she sent a quick text back to Erin saying everything was fine. Even though she had a feeling everything wasn't going to be okay, she didn't want Erin to take on the burden of the fallout. It wasn't her fault Brooklyn didn't tell Declan what she knew. That was all on her. She decided to keep the secret even though she knew it was going to end badly if Declan found out she knew.

Now his lousy attitude made sense. He knew Brooklyn was involved even if he didn't know how.

Putting her phone back in her pocket, she went to work on the potatoes. Her earlier desire to use the mixer against Declan gone now that she knew what his problem was. She really couldn't blame him for being mad at her, although she was still a bit irritated that he'd brought his anger to Friendsgiving. If anyone needed a night of fun and relaxation, it was their group of friends. With everything Meghan and Oliver were going through, they didn't deserve to have to deal with Declan's lousy mood.

When the potatoes were a perfect consistency, she transferred them into a serving dish, then pulled the golden-brown rolls out of the oven. As she put them onto their serving dish, she heard someone enter the kitchen behind her. She quickly glanced over her shoulder, not surprised to find Declan standing behind her. He stopped to lean against the island. Before he could even open his mouth to say anything she beat him to the punch.

"I know you have something to say to me, but it has to wait. Our drama can't ruin Friendsgiving, so you'll just have to wait until after everyone leaves to yell at me."

"How did you know?"

"Besides the scowl on your face every time you looked at me? Erin just sent me a text. She found your note at home and wanted me to know."

"So, you were..."

Turning to face him fully, Brooklyn pointed the tongs at him, to emphasize her point. "I said it has to wait Declan and I wasn't kidding. Our friends deserve a fun, drama-free night. So, whatever you have to say to me, save it and in the meantime, can you at least try to pretend you don't hate me, so our friends can have a good time?"

Declan stared at her, and for a moment she thought he might argue with her and force the issue. She should have known better though. She might not always be his favorite person, but he loved the rest of the group like they were family. He wouldn't ruin their holiday just because he was pissed off at her.

"Fine."

"Good," Brooklyn said as she grabbed the dish of rolls and held it out to him. "Now that we've got that out of the way, can you put this on the table and then let everyone know dinner is ready. I don't want dinner to get cold while we stand here and stare at each other."

With a huff of irritation his teenage daughter would've been proud of, Declan grabbed the rolls from her and walked out of the kitchen. Brooklyn suppressed a giggle, knowing that if he heard her, it might screw up what little peace she was able to muster between them for the rest of the night. She went back to putting everything else in serving dishes and placing them all on the dining room table as the rest of the group filtered out of the den.

"Perfect timing Brook, they just blew the whistle for halftime," Braeden said as he walked into the kitchen to grab a new beer. "Anyone else need a fresh drink?"

As Braeden delivered drinks and everyone took a seat, Brooklyn looked around at her friends, noticing just how happy everyone was, even Declan. Although her life had taken some unexpected and tragic turns over the last decade, Brooklyn knew she was where she was supposed to be. Surrounded by people who loved her no matter what. She'd surprisingly found joy working with Savannah at Delectable Delights, a job she'd initially taken on just so Savannah could have more time to date.

Now over a year later, she was having fun getting up early, learning the recipes, meeting the customers. It was surprising and exhilarating, and Brooklyn was so thankful she'd taken the step even though she had no idea what she was doing. When she graduated from college, Brooklyn thought she had her entire life planned out. She'd marry Frank and become a freelance writer while they traveled around. Then when they were ready, they'd start a family, and she'd become the mother she always dreamed of being.

Shaking her head, Brooklyn tried to free herself from the thoughts of her past. It was not the time to dwell on what was and what would never be. Instead, she needed to stay in the moment and relish in what she had. It was Thanksgiving, after all, so she'd spend the week being thankful for where she was and the love in her life. She'd have plenty of time to revisit the past when she celebrated her birthday in a couple of weeks.

"Okay, who wants to carve the turkey?" she asked, knowing that if anyone was going to be able to distract her it was her friends and she was right.

* * *

Declan

The minute he'd seen the transaction on Erin's bank account, Declan knew he should have stayed home. Seeing the evidence proving his daughter was keeping secrets from him had made him less than desirable company, Friendsgiving or not. Knowing Brooklyn had a hand in helping Erin keep the secret, was the only reason he decided to go, even though he knew it was a bad idea. He needed to confront her for overstepping. It didn't matter that Declan didn't have any actual proof she'd done anything wrong. He knew she was involved somehow, and he planned on letting her have it.

Having to sit through the football game and dinner and the endless string of stupid games had just made his mood worse. More than once he'd gotten close to blowing up. All he wanted to do was take out his anger on Brooklyn then go home so he could sternly tell Erin he was disappointed and hurt. He'd never yell at her, had never yelled at her in her nearly eighteen years of life. When he was angry with her, he usually took time to calm down before sitting her down to talk. He never wanted to raise his voice at her in anger, but he didn't have a problem shouting at Brooklyn. Especially since she was getting in the middle of his family business and keeping secrets with his daughter.

He'd had it all planned out until the end of their game of Never Have I Ever. He wasn't a big fan of the game, especially not the way it was intended to be played. Declan always learned far more about his friends than he wanted to know, although he had to be honest he hadn't been grossed out like he usually was whenever the game was played. It probably had a lot to do with the fact he was learning new things about Brooklyn with every question asked.

Declan had been into the game until Oliver said what ended up being the last never have I ever. Never have I ever had sex on my wedding night. Declan had known the two married couples, and the only other person in the room who'd been married would drink, but when Brooklyn never raised her glass, he wanted to go over to her and wrap his arms around her. He'd known her ex-husband was an idiot, but this news blew his mind.

He had no idea how the man could have kept his hands to himself when his new wife was as hot as Brooklyn. Declan wouldn't have been able to keep it in his pants on his wedding night if she was his bride. Consummating their marriage wouldn't be a problem. He had no idea how not doing it was even a possibility. If he'd been the one to marry her, they would have left the reception early and wouldn't have gotten a wink of sleep the entire night. There's no way Declan would have been able to help himself. It shocked him that her ex hadn't felt the same.

It also made him feel a bit sorry for her, which he knew she'd never want, and he wasn't stupid enough to tell her. Instead, he'd decided to take it easier on her when he finally got to confront her about Erin. After having something so personal revealed in front of her friends, she didn't need him to be an ass to her on top of it.

From his spot on the couch, he could see Brooklyn and Savannah working to clean up the kitchen. Braeden and Gabriel were in the den watching ESPN. He should have joined them when they went in there after Oliver and Meghan left, but he wanted to have some time alone to think. Everything was changing. He could feel it, and he wasn't sure what to make of it.

Finally deciding to take the plunge, he got up and walked into the kitchen. Savannah turned to him and smiled, while Brooklyn ignored his presence for the most part. He could tell she was aware of him by the way her body tensed up just a little. The change was barely perceptible, but he was strangely in tune with her ever since the night of the wedding.

"Hey Sav, why don't you go hang out and I'll help Brooklyn with the dishes," he suggested.

"Are you sure? I mean really, Brooklyn should be the one to go rest since she's the one who did all the work earlier."

"I'm fine, Sav. You look like you're about to fall over. Why don't you head upstairs? Declan and I will finish up in here and then head home," Brooklyn told her sister. "Not together or anything. We will head to our separate homes...damn it."

"Thanks for the clarification," Savannah said with a laugh as her sister started to blush.

Declan tried to stifle his laugh while Savannah handed her sister the dish towel and then hugged her. He loved how flustered Brooklyn seemed to be. It was far from the commanding figure she'd been before dinner. He wasn't sure if it was the revelation from the game or the fact that her sister knew what'd happened between them that had her off-kilter. Declan hoped it was the latter so he wouldn't have to feel bad about enjoying the moment.

Savannah gave him a quick hug before hurrying out of the kitchen. Brooklyn turned back to the sink, setting the towel down next to it. She didn't say a word as she went back to washing dishes. Part of him wondered if he shouldn't leave her alone. He had a feeling she wouldn't even be willing to talk to him if she hadn't put him off earlier. The fact she wouldn't even look at him proved she was embarrassed about what came out during the game. It took all he had in him not to pull her into a hug, but he knew the last thing either of them needed was for him to touch her.

"If we're gonna talk, you're gonna help out. Grab that towel and start drying," Brooklyn said.

Declan grabbed the towel and did as he was told, still not sure exactly what to say. He'd been so angry earlier; he'd figured his anger would carry him through their conversation. Now that he was calmer, and she was more vulnerable, he didn't have his anger to fall back on. Instead of saying anything, he absently dried the dishes she handed to him. There was something so comfortable about standing next to her doing such a mundane task. He didn't want to ruin the mood.

Declan had no idea how long they stood there washing and drying the dishes in silence. It could have been an hour for all he knew, but it definitely wasn't long enough. As Brooklyn handed him the final dish, he fought the urge to lick all the plates so they'd have to rewash them. He had no idea what the heck was happening to him, and he wasn't sure if he liked it or not.

"Look can we get this over with, please? I'm tired, and I just want to go home," Brooklyn said as she turned to face him. "I'm sorry I didn't tell you about Erin's plan. She asked me not to, and while I did tell her she should tell you immediately, I didn't want to betray her trust."

"She's a kid Brook. My kid. She shouldn't have any secrets from me."

"Really? Was being a teenager that long ago for you that you don't remember what it was like? I thought she'd appreciate having at least one adult in her corner that wasn't related to her."

"I remember exactly what being a teenager was like. Look where it got me and what it cost me."

"It's not like she told me she was doing drugs or having sex or taking part in human trafficking. She applied for a college outside of the state. It's not the end of the world. She doesn't even know for sure she'll get in which is why she wanted to wait to tell you anything. Erin figured there was no point in telling you something that would hurt your feelings if nothing was happening. You need to talk to her about this. She has some good points."

"She was working at the animal shelter after work today, so she wasn't home before I left. I also knew I was too angry to stick around and wait for her. I've never yelled at Erin before, and I didn't want tonight to be the first time but seeing that charge on her bank statement pissed me off."

"Why is it a big deal? I guess I don't understand why it matters where she goes to school as long as she's getting a good education."

Declan scowled, irritated that she had the nerve to ask him what the big deal was. Who did she think she was? Everything to do with Erin was a big deal, from the moment Kara told him she was pregnant to the moment of his death, Declan lived for that girl and that girl alone. She was his world.

"You don't need to understand why it matters. All you need to understand is Erin means everything to me," Declan said harshly.

Brooklyn sighed and ran a hand over her ponytail. She barely looked at him, but it didn't stop her from continuing to argue with him about the situation. A situation she had no right being in the middle of since she had no idea what it felt like to be a parent.

"So, are you planning on following her around from class to class every single day? I'm almost surprised you don't do that now."

"You don't have to be such a smartass about this. I'm not going to follow Erin around, but if god forbid something were to happen at least she'd be close by and not all the way across the fucking country. I don't expect you to understand since you're not a parent."

Brooklyn flinched as he spoke, but he ignored it. His anger was back full steam, and he wasn't going to watch his tone just because she was sensitive. It was clear she didn't comprehend what he was saying or why. But it didn't matter because it wasn't her place. Erin was his daughter, his responsibility and no one else's. He didn't want to have to worry about her on the other side of the country where she knew no one and had no support system. College was scary enough without adding all of that to the mix.

Declan wasn't used to anyone questioning the decisions he made for Erin, at least not someone outside of his family. Even his sister Andrea, who'd helped him raise Erin, didn't question him very often. She would agree with him about this. No way would she be okay letting Erin go to college somewhere so far away.

Neither of them spoke. Declan wasn't sure what was left to say, and it was apparent they were going to have to agree to disagree. He could tell the embarrassment he'd assumed she was feeling before was long gone, replaced by an irritation only he seemed to be able to aflict on her. She reached past him to grab the towel he'd discarded earlier.

Her arm brushed against his as she moved, the familiar zing of electricity zipped through him at the contact. Even when she was pissing him off, he couldn't ignore how badly he wanted her. Hell, he probably wanted her even more than usual because she didn't hesitate to stand up to him, to question him.

"I'm gonna go. Have a good night, Declan. Happy Thanksgiving," Brooklyn said quickly before hurrying out of the kitchen. He heard her yell goodnight to the guys and then to her sister before rushing out the door. She was gone before he even had a chance to react.

Running his hand through his hair, Declan looked around the room. The kitchen was clean, and he wasn't in the mood to be around other people. He said a quick goodbye to Gabriel and Braeden and then headed out to his car. Not for the first time after one of their get togethers, he wished he still lived in West Seattle instead of twenty minutes east in Issaquah.

By the time he pulled out of the driveway, his head pounded, a headache taking over the area behind his eyes. He should have listened to his gut and stayed home. He'd had a little bit of fun at Friendsgiving, but Declan wasn't sure it was worth the annoyance or the confusion. And now because he'd spent the evening with his friends, he had to wait another night to talk to Erin about what she did. He had to stew in his anger for longer than he'd like, and he had to do it knowing Brooklyn was pissed at him as well.

Happy Thanksgiving indeed.

* * *

"She's right you know."

Declan turned to look at his twin sister, shocked by her statement. Andrea was nearly as overprotective as he was of Erin having been there for his little girl since the day she was born. Erin's mother didn't want her, and Declan's father was less than pleased that he'd gotten some "whore" knocked up and ruined his chances at a professional baseball career. If it hadn't been for Declan's mom and Andrea, his father would have disowned him and thrown him and Erin out on the streets the minute she was born.

Thankfully, they were able to live with his parents until he graduated from high school. Then he and Andrea had used the inheritance they'd gotten from their grandparents to buy a house in Issaquah, where the schools were better, and they were far away from their disapproving father. Declan knew he would have never made it if he hadn't had Andrea by his side. He owed her so much and would likely never be able to repay her.

"Wait. What? You agree with Brooklyn? I thought you'd be just as eager as I am to keep Erin close to home."

"Dec, she's not a little girl anymore. Don't you think she deserves the chance to spread her wings and see what life's all about?"

"What if someone attacks her or she ends up with some life-threatening illness?"

"Declan, those things could happen to her here. Just because you're close by doesn't mean it won't happen or that it would make things easier for her," Andrea pointed out. "Hell, either of those things could happen if she never even went to college. They could happen to you or me or anyone. We can't all live in a bubble."

"What if she ends up getting pregnant?"

"Again, that could happen to her here, Declan, there are no guarantees. You can't project your mistakes onto her. Erin's a smart girl, with a good head on her shoulders. She knows what she has to do to make her dream of becoming a vet a reality. She won't let anything get in the way of that. Thousands of kids leave home and go far away for college every year, and most of them come home completely unscathed. You have to have faith that Erin will be one of those kids. You can't hold her back because you're afraid of what might happen. You couldn't do that when she was a kid, and she was learning to ride a bike or when she got older and started driving a car. You have to let her live the life she wants and trust she'll be smart about things. But you also have to let her make her own mistakes."

Declan sighed. "I just don't want her to get hurt. I don't want anything bad to happen to her.

"Nobody ever wants anything bad to happen to their children, but you can't hold her here. She's not going to be forty years old living with her dad while she works some menial job. Erin is destined for great things, but she can't achieve those things with you hovering over her or holding her back."

"I don't want to hold her back."

"Then don't. Send me off to North Carolina with your blessing. That's all I want."

Declan turned to find Erin leaning against the kitchen island. He hadn't even heard her come in. He had no idea how much of the argument he and Andrea were having she'd heard, but it didn't matter. For the past four days, they'd all talked ad nauseam about Erin leaving, about the dangers and about why he wanted her to stay.

"Look, Dad, I need to see what I can be on my own and so do you. I'm so lucky I ended up with you as my dad, but you basically stopped living when I came along. I'm super grateful for everything you've given up for me, but its gotta stop. You're still young, and I have it on good authority that you're a hottie, so you've gotta stop using me as an excuse not to live your life. If I'm across the country, you'll have no choice but to do that."

"Erin, you aren't going to college on the other side of the country so that I can live my life."

"No, I'm going to college on the other side of the country so that I can live mine. You and Aunt DeeDee will get to finally see what you've been missing out on all these years. That's just a bonus. Maybe you can finally let yourself find out what kind of relationship you could have with Brooklyn."

"Nothing is going on with Brooklyn..."

"Sure there isn't. Go ahead and keep telling yourself that, Dad. You might believe it, but nobody else does."

"You're too young to know what you're talking about."

"She's not wrong, Declan," Andrea said before ducking to avoid the towel he threw at her head.

"I'm not a kid anymore. I'll be eighteen in a few months, and then I'll be off to college, and I do mean off. Even if I don't get into NC State, I'm not staying in Washington."

"I know...I just don't know what I'll do without my little girl."

"Dad...I'll be just a phone call away. We can do a video call whenever you want unless I'm in class or studying or working...well, we'll make it work. I need to do this and honestly, so do you."

Declan let out another sigh. "I know. I...you're right, but it's going to be weird, and I can't promise I won't bug you too much. It'll take me a while to adjust to not having you around all the time. I won't be able to stop by your room to check on you or ask you how your day went."

"Well I guess it's a good thing modern technology is so awesome then," Erin said. "We'll make the most out of every school break and holiday. Everything will be okay. We'll be okay. I promise."

Erin's eyes filled with tears as she stepped toward him. Declan pulled her in for a hug, his arms wrapping around her so tight he was afraid he was going to squish her, but he couldn't help it. When he was seventeen, he never thought he could love anyone as much as he loved her. His life revolved around baseball and his family, two things he loved to the extreme, but none of them rivaled the way he felt about his daughter from the moment she was placed in his arms. She was a piece of his soul, the best part of it, if he was honest. Declan would do whatever it took to make her happy even if it meant sending her away and breaking his heart in the process.

"We'll make it work, I promise. I love you, Bug."

"I love you too, Dad."

Letting her leave was going to be tough, but he wouldn't stand in her way. Erin needed to find her path, and she was right, he needed to find his. He'd spent the last eighteen years living his life for her, using her as an excuse to stay safe. He couldn't go after the baseball career he'd always dreamed about, but he could finally give in and find out what a real adult relationship was like. The thought scared the shit out of him, but it was about time he gave it a shot.

Now he just had to hope he hadn't pissed Brooklyn off so much she no longer wanted anything to do with him. It was going to take baby steps for him to be ready, so he had time to get her back on his side, and he knew just the first step to make.

CHAPTER 6

Brooklyn

The excitement filling the arena was palpable, and the game hadn't even started yet. It'd been so long since she'd gone to a hockey game Brooklyn had forgotten how exhilarating it was just to watch the teams warm-up on the ice. Growing up, she'd been such a sports fanatic that her dad had taken her to every kind of sporting event he could in Seattle, including junior league hockey. Sometimes they'd even venture up to Canada to watch the NHL team in Vancouver, but all of that ended when she went off to college. When she'd started dating Frank, she felt she had to suppress her love for sports because he hated them. She rarely went to events with her dad during those wasted years, but now that she was free she was doing her best to make up for lost time.

She'd been going to as many Mariners and Seahawks games as she could since her divorce, both with her father and with her friends. Brooklyn had even taken road trips to Portland for basketball, yet this was her first time back in a hockey rink. When Declan invited her to go to Vancouver, she couldn't pass up the opportunity.

It was supposed to be a guy's trip, but Gabriel had to cover a shift at the restaurant and Oliver had opted to stay home given everything he was dealing with. Which was where Brooklyn and Andrea came in. Brooklyn had almost stayed home for the same reason Oliver had, but the pleading look on Declan's face after she told him she didn't think she should go had changed her mind. She hadn't been sure at the time why he was so eager for her to come, but the tension between Andrea and Braeden in the car ride to Vancouver answered her question.

They were worse than Braeden and Declan ever were, and Brooklyn had no idea why. The two didn't necessarily fight like the guys did, but they definitely didn't give off warm fuzzy vibes. Brooklyn knew they'd been close as kids; she'd seen pictures of them together ranging from elementary school to high school. At some point after high school, things had changed. Braeden stopped being as close to the twins and had gotten closer to Oliver.

Brooklyn wasn't clear on their friendship dynamics, but from what she'd gotten from Gabriel, no one knew what happened between the three of them to change things. Gabriel and Oliver just assumed it had something to do with Erin coming into the picture and didn't ask too many questions. Erin's arrival had changed every relationship Declan had, so Brooklyn wouldn't have been surprised if Erin was the reason things changed with Braeden. She just didn't know how Andrea factored into the situation.

"Hey Brooklyn, are you coming?"

Looking around, she realized the three of them were nearly halfway down the stairs to their seats. She'd been spacing out, thinking about the past and her new group of friends, courtesy of her big sister, and hadn't even realized she'd stopped walking while they kept going. She smiled down at Declan who was waiting for her while Andrea and Braeden continued down the stairs.

She quickly made her way to where he was, then followed him the rest of the way until they were a few rows up from the ice. They were a few sections over from the bench and near one of the faceoff circles. She'd figured their seats were going to be awesome based on the number of their row but had no idea just how awesome they were until that moment. Brooklyn had never gotten the chance to sit so close to the ice even though she'd always wanted to. She couldn't wait to be right next to the action. Just watching players skate by during warm-ups was getting her excited for the game.

"These seats are amazing, brother. Thanks for letting me tag along," Andrea said in appreciation as she watched the home team skate past them.

Brooklyn stopped gawking at the ice so she could thank Declan for bringing her. When she turned to look over at him, she expected to find him watching the players skating by like his sister. Instead, he seemed to be watching her, their eyes meeting as soon as she turned his way. Her cheeks grew warm as she suddenly became aware of the undercurrent of tension between them. For her own sanity, she'd been trying to ignore it since he picked her up, but in that space, crammed into tight seats in tight rows, she knew it would end up being impossible.

"Thanks for letting me tag along too. I've never been this close. It's been so long since I've been to a game I forgot what all of this felt like."

Declan didn't say a word, he just smiled at her then took a drink of his beer. Brooklyn turned back to watch the players for another few minutes until they were signaled it was time to leave the ice. She could feel Declan's eyes on her the entire time, but she didn't look over at him again. Since Friendsgiving, things had been easier between them, but there was still something lingering underneath the surface.

After the holiday, Declan had come by Delectable Delights to apologize to her and let her know she'd been right. Hearing him say those words had been a shock, one she still hadn't quite recovered from, but it had helped to heal the wound he'd unknowingly inflicted that day. Declan had thought her silence and irritation was from him arguing with her about his daughter's future, but it wasn't. Brooklyn knew he wanted what was best for Erin and that he was just worried about her. Even if she didn't agree with him, she wouldn't have held any of that against him.

He'd struck a nerve that day when he'd pointed out she didn't understand anything because she wasn't a parent. He didn't know about her past or that she'd give anything to be a mother, so she couldn't hold his words against him, even if she wanted to. She'd rushed out of her sister's house that night because she didn't want to scream at him, she didn't want to break down in front of him. She let his words sink in and then she ran for the hills so she could scream and cry in the privacy of her own home.

Once she'd finished, she realized how it had looked and knew he thought she was mad at him. Brooklyn had planned on giving him until after Thanksgiving to see what he'd do. If he hadn't come to apologize to her, she would have gone to him because she owed him an apology as well. She shouldn't have been in the middle of his family business, and she shouldn't have acted like she knew what was best for his daughter.

Since that day things had been better than they'd ever been between them. They talked on a regular basis. Usually during his deliveries to DD, but sometimes on the phone at night or over text. They'd managed to strike up a friendship filled with so much sexual tension Brooklyn wasn't sure they were going to be able to hold out much longer. And she was pretty sure neither of them would end up regretting it.

They took their seats, waiting for the game to start. Declan sat between her and Braeden, while Andrea sat on her other side. Having the two-person buffer between them seemed to be a necessity, even if it meant Declan had to sit next to him. While the Zamboni moved along the ice, Brooklyn made small talk with Andrea. She looked a lot like her brother, but where he was all hard angles and sharp edges, Andrea seemed a bit softer. She had a tomboyish air about her but took the time to curl her hair and put on make-up. When they first met, Brooklyn had immediately felt a kinship with her.

While she talked to Andrea, Declan and Braeden checked their phones, completely ignoring each other. Someday she'd figure out what the hell the problem was between them, but at the moment she was enjoying herself too much to care.

"So, are your parents coming up for Christmas?" Brooklyn asked.

She felt Declan stiffen next to her and noticed anger pass over Andrea's face for a split second before she answered the question with a shake of her head. Neither of the Reese siblings spoke for a moment, and the silence was more uncomfortable than the atmosphere between Braeden and Andrea. Brooklyn had struck a nerve with her question, but she wasn't sure what the deal was.

She knew very little about Declan's family, aside from what Gabriel had told her. They retired to somewhere in Florida after the twins took over the company. Outside of the members of the family that she knew, that tidbit was the extent of her knowledge about the Reese family. Although she had no idea there was drama there she felt terrible for opening her big mouth.

"Their dad's a pretty big asshole, so they don't really get along with him," Braeden piped up his eyes still focused on his phone. "In case you didn't catch that by the super awkward silence we're all sitting in right now."

It was obvious neither of them wanted to elaborate on what Braeden said, and Brooklyn knew better than anyone what it was like to want to keep the past in the past. She wasn't willing to air her dirty laundry, so she wasn't about to make Declan air his no matter how curious she was about his relationship with his parents.

"Thanks, Braeden. Okay then, change of subject have you guys finished your Christmas shopping yet?"

The tension quickly dissipated as they talked about happier things. Declan had gone all out buying gifts for Erin, a new laptop and a new phone, which he admitted were both selfish presents since she was going to be leaving him soon. He'd also bought her a bunch of other things like concert tickets to see her favorite band. For some reason, he'd felt the need to spoil her, so he went with it.

Brooklyn loved the way Declan lit up when he talked about his daughter. It was one of the things that drew her to him. He was wickedly attractive with his overly long dark hair, piercing green eyes, and strong jaw. He was tall and had a body to die for. She knew his job kept him in shape but had been surprised to find out he also went to the gym daily. He played softball during the summer and joined pickup games of basketball and touch football whenever he got a chance. Once an athlete always an athlete, she guessed.

Surprisingly though, the fact he was gorgeous wasn't what made Brooklyn stop and take notice of Declan. She'd been around enough attractive guys to know outer beauty meant nothing. Hell, her ex-husband was the perfect example of a good-looking guy turning out to be nothing more than a raging asshole. Declan might push her buttons and drive her crazy, but he was a great friend and brother and a fantastic father. No matter how good looking a guy was, there was nothing more attractive than a guy who was wonderful to the people around him.

Once the game started, there wasn't much room for conversation as Brooklyn got into the action. The game was intense, the teams trading rough hits into the glass while chasing the puck around the ice. They were evenly matched throughout all three periods which made for an exciting game. Brooklyn was on her feet more often than not, cheering for Vancouver since they were the closest she had to a home team. Between periods she ran up to the concourse to use the restroom and grab provisions, leaving the guys and Andrea to do their own thing.

"Man, I forgot how much fun hockey games were," Brooklyn said as soon as the game was over and they were done cheering Vancouver's victory.

"I'm glad you could come. I love watching you get so into it. Brings a whole new level of enjoyment for me," Declan said as they started up the stairs. She looked around for Braeden but when she didn't see him, she figured he must have gone up the stairs on the other side of the aisle. Andi was making her way up the stairs in front of them, a few people separating her from where they stood.

"I can't tell if you're being sarcastic or not," she said as she glanced back at him to see if she could read his expression. Even then she still couldn't tell what he was thinking so she decided she didn't care. Instead she shrugged and gave him a smile before turning back around to head up the stairs.

"I'm very passionate about sports. I can't help it. My sister doesn't like to go to games alone with me because she says I'm embarrassing. I would say I hope I didn't embarrass you tonight, but I honestly don't care."

Declan's throaty laugh gave her chills in a good way. She could feel him behind her, closer than necessary as they waited for the long line of fans to walk up the stairs in front of them.

"Embarrassing is not the word I'd used to describe your passion about sports, Princess. Sexy as hell, is more like it."

The low rumble of Declan's voice and the sensation of his breath against her ear had Brooklyn heating up in no time. The chilly air of the arena was nothing compared to her heated skin. She was getting close to having to pull off some of her layers of clothing to cool off. Part of her wanted to pull him into the nearest utility closet and put them both out of their misery. If they'd been alone, it would've been far closer to happening than either of them were probably comfortable with.

"I guess it's a good thing it doesn't embarrass you, Declan, because I don't plan on changing any time soon and I have a feeling we'll be going to a lot of games together."

"Who am I to get in the way of someone's passion? Damn it," he said, his hands landing on her hips as he fell against her. "Hold on."

Before she could respond, he pulled her off the stairs into one of the rows of seats. The big man behind him glared at them and pushed past, zeroing in on the people that'd been in front of Brooklyn. The man was obviously in a hurry and didn't care if he ran over people in the process.

"Let's hang out here for a second. Even if we get outside quickly we'll have to sit in traffic trying to get out of the parking lot," Declan said as he took a seat.

Brooklyn followed suit and then looked behind them to see if she could find Braeden and Andrea. Hopefully, they'd made it to the top and could wait a bit before trying to kill each other. Looking over to the other end of the row, she saw that stairway was just as congested as the one next to them. They were smart to wait, especially given that the guy behind Declan had been seconds away from trampling them.

"If we were smart, we would have gotten a hotel room, so we didn't have to make the drive back down tonight, but Gabriel was in such a hurry to get home to your sister. When things changed and he and Oliver decided they weren't coming, we didn't think to change the plan. I'm sorry."

"It's okay. It's not like I've got to work tomorrow or anything and you're driving so I can always tell Braeden he has to stay awake so Andrea and I can pass out in the back. At this time of night, the border crossing shouldn't be too bad, and there shouldn't be any traffic, I bet it'll only take a couple of hours to get home instead of the nearly four it took to get here. Plus, this has been a super awesome start to my birthday weekend, so that's all that matters to me."

"Wait, it's your birthday?"

Brooklyn nodded, surprised Declan didn't already know since her sister didn't seem capable of not talking about it. Savannah had been going on and on about the plans she had for the last two weeks. If it had been up to Brooklyn, she'd have opted to do nothing. Even though she loved making a big deal of celebrating other people's birthdays, she hated her own. At least she had for the last few years. While she'd like to thank Frank for that particular dysfunction, she knew it was ultimately her fault that she let it get that far.

"That makes way more sense. Your sister kept asking me if I was free tomorrow night and I had to keep telling her no. Every time she looked both disappointed and angry, and I didn't get it. I thought she and Gabriel were having some sort of Friendsmas thing or something."

"Friendsmas?"

"Fuck, I don't know. They had Friendsgiving. Why not Friendsmas?"

Brooklyn thought about it for a moment, trying to come up with a reason Friendsmas didn't work, but she couldn't.

"Okay, you can have Friendsmas. But no, that's not why she was inviting you over tomorrow. We're getting together for my birthday, although I told her many times we didn't have to do anything. I was happy to just have dinner with her and the parents and of course Gabriel."

"Hold on. Are you saying you don't like to celebrate your birthday? That doesn't seem right."

Brooklyn shrugged. She didn't really want to explain anything to Declan. Not because she didn't want him to know, but because she didn't want to bring down the fun they'd had. Her past was a bit of a downer, and she didn't want their night to end on that note.

"I'll tell you about it another time, but yes, tomorrow is my birthday, my sister is having people over at her house to celebrate. It'll be fun and glorious, and I'll be the center of attention so everyone can worship me on the 33rd anniversary of my birth."

"Since I'm not going to be able to come, I'll leave my comments about worshipping you unsaid. Just know I really do wish I could be there, but I've got a standing date with Erin tomorrow night, and I have a feeling this might be the last time we do this since next year she'll be in college."

"Has she heard back yet?"

"No, but last year the college sent their acceptance letters out before Christmas, so the tension is pretty high in our house. Since the mail doesn't get delivered on Sunday, those tend to be the worst, but the rest of the week is still pretty bad. Erin can't come straight home after school because she either has to work with you guys or she has her volunteer hours at the shelter. I'm pretty sure she spends her entire shift texting me to see if I've checked the damn mail yet. I'm not sure how she's getting any work done with all the texting."

Brooklyn smiled knowing exactly how excited Erin was. Whenever they worked together, Brooklyn encouraged her to text her dad. She wanted to know just as much as Erin did if she'd been accepted into her top school. As much as she would hate to see Erin leave, she knew how much it meant to the girl to get into one of the top five veterinary programs in the country.

From the conversations they'd had it was evident that all Erin had ever wanted to be was a veterinarian. She loved animals and enjoyed the time she spent volunteering at one of the local animal shelters. Erin was continually trying to talk people she knew into adopting dogs and cats or at the very least fostering them so they'd get to enjoy human contact instead of being locked in a cage. The girl was so convincing Brooklyn was thinking about adopting a cat.

"Looks like we can finally make our escape. I hope Andi hasn't killed Braeden yet. I don't know much about Canadian laws, but I'm pretty sure murder's illegal up here too, especially when it's pre-meditated. Let's go," Declan said as he stood then offered her a hand.

Brooklyn took it, allowing him to help her up. "What is the deal there and why did you guys invite her if they don't get along?"

Declan shrugged. "When Gabriel dropped out, she seemed like the logical choice. We've all done stuff together for years without too much issue. I mean sure they snipe at each other, but hell, we all do. The last few months though something's been going on with her, but I'm too afraid to ask what it is."

"I don't blame you. Your sister's kinda scary, but in a good way."

"You don't have to sugar coat it, Andi's scary as fuck. She's always been a bit of a ball buster. Hell, when we were kids, she was the first one into a fight while the four of us guys just stood back and watched her. Andi sent more guys running back to their mommies then the rest of us combined. I love my sister, but I would never want to make her mad."

Brooklyn laughed but didn't respond. She followed Declan up the stairs to the concourse where they found Braeden and Andrea waiting for them. Neither looked the worse for wear, although there was something a bit off about Braeden's demeanor when they approached. The fact he was standing around waiting for them instead of flirting with every female that walked by was enough to make Brooklyn worry.

When they got to the car, both Braeden and Andrea had asked to sit in the back seat which was a shock. Since they promised not to fight or even acknowledge each other, Declan said it was okay, but only after asking Brooklyn if she minded. While she had joked earlier about taking a nap on the ride home, she knew there was no way she could sleep, and since it was the sworn duty of the person riding shotgun to keep the driver awake on road trips, she told him she was fine sitting up front.

They chatted about mundane things until they got to the border crossing, then waited with baited breath to see if they'd be one of the lucky few to have to pull over and be searched. Thankfully, they were on their way quickly, settled into a comfortable silence, a local radio station supplying the background noise.

Brooklyn looked over at Declan, enjoying the unfettered ease of his actions. He always seemed so tense and rigid, but the entire evening he'd been relaxed. Knowing he could actually let loose made Declan even hotter. The man always seemed to have the weight of the world on his shoulders, even when he was hanging out with his friends. To see him free of that weight made her happy. She wasn't sure what brought it on, but she hoped it would continue. Brooklyn loved seeing the almost carefree side of Declan.

She turned back to watch the road, her mind wandering toward the realm of what if. When she felt something touch her hand, she fought the urge to jerk it away from her leg. Instead, she looked down to find Declan's hand resting on top of hers. Her heart leaped in her chest, her pulse quickening.

Holy crap, Declan was holding her hand. She had no idea what the hell was happening, but she definitely didn't mind. Without giving it too much thought, she flipped her hand over, so her palm was against his, their fingers laced together.

Brooklyn had no idea when they'd gone from adversaries to holding hands, but she wasn't going to question things. At the moment giving in seemed like the right move. If it turned out to be the wrong decision, she'd deal with the fallout. Until then, she was going to revel in the fact she was holding hands with a gorgeous, wonderful man and enjoy the ride as long as the universe let her.

* * *

There was something magical about birthdays. Even though Brooklyn had been dreading hers, now that she was standing in her sister's living room looking around at her friends and family, she was glad her sister didn't listen to her and threw her a party anyway. The fact Savannah had made sure there were birthday decorations around the room instead of Christmas decorations made the night even more special. The only thing that would have made the night perfect was if Declan had been there.

The minute the thought entered her head, Brooklyn wanted to smack herself. No guy's presence was going to make or break her evening. She might have loved to see him standing across the room talking animatedly to Gabriel, but the party wasn't going to be any less spectacular without him there. The sooner she got that through her head the better. She couldn't allow herself to put the weight of her pleasure on a guy, especially one she wasn't even in a relationship with.

With a barely audible sigh, Brooklyn turned back to her friend Kerrigan who was telling her and Sylvia about her recent trip to California to visit both her and her fiancé's families. Brooklyn loved seeing her best friend so ridiculously happy. After losing her college sweetheart in a car accident their senior year, Brooklyn wondered if Kerrigan was ever going to allow herself to fall in love again. Enter in her childhood neighbor AKA her former crush and Brooklyn had never seen Kerrigan so happy.

Brooklyn couldn't wait until March when she got to watch her best friend walk down the aisle. It was about time the matchmaker had found her match.

"So Brooklyn, your sister's happily married, I'm engaged, and Sylvia is knee deep in dates. When are you going to let me do my thing and find you love?" Kerrigan asked.

"Unless you've got a prince in your arsenal, I'll pass on any blind dates you're thinking about setting me up on. I'm not really in any hurry."

"She doesn't need to be set up because she's got Declan chasing after her. She's gotta work that out first," Sylvia pointed out, which made Brooklyn roll her eyes.

"First, he's not chasing after me and second, there isn't anything going on between us."

"Yeah cause people who aren't into each other usually hold hands for nearly three hours," Braeden yelled from across the room.

How he could hear their conversation from across the room was beyond Brooklyn, but the fact that he'd just announced she and Declan had held hands the night before made her groan. She'd hoped neither he nor Andrea had noticed. They were both supposed to be sleeping in the back seat, but apparently, Braeden had been faking it.

"Wait, when was this?" Savannah asked.

The attention of the entire room shifted to Brooklyn, everyone waiting for her to answer the question. So much for the magical birthday she'd pictured earlier. Now she just wanted to hide in her sister's guest room until everyone went home.

"This was last night on the way home from the hockey game. When we dropped her off, he walked her to the door and kissed her on her forehead. It was sweet in the way that makes me want to throw up in my mouth a little."

"Braeden, come on..." Brooklyn whined.

"What the hell, Brook. Were you ever planning on telling us about this?" Kerrigan asked.

"Not really," Brooklyn admitted. "There isn't anything to talk about. Declan and I are just friends, and even that seems a bit precarious. I'm not sure what Braeden thinks is going on, but really we're just friends."

"Friends who hold hands. Sure. Makes total sense," her sister said the sarcasm in her tone nearly visible.

"Braeden what the hell, you creeper. Why didn't you tell us you were awake? You could have had the front seat."

"And ruin the most action Declan's gotten in a while, no way. Plus, I wasn't awake the whole time, but every time I did wake up your hands were locked, and there'd be looks of longing passed back and forth. It was quite funny actually."

Warmth crept up her neck and over her cheeks as she wished someone would take pity on her and change the subject. Brooklyn could tell by the looks on everyone's faces they were enjoying the show and had no plans on saving her from further embarrassment. Some friends they were. Although, to be fair she probably would have done the same thing if someone else was in the hot seat.

Looking around the room, she realized at least a handful of the people in the room knew about her interlude with Declan at Savannah's wedding. Of course, her parents and a couple of family friends helping her celebrate her birthday were still in the dark. Braeden also had no clue what happened that night. She felt a little bad leaving him in the dark, but figured if Declan wanted him to know, he'd tell him.

"Holding hands is a pretty big step for Declan. Aside from Erin, I wouldn't be surprised if the last person he held hands with was Kara back in high school," Gabriel said.

Brooklyn was shocked he was getting in on the action. She figured he'd at least have some loyalty to her now that he was her brother-in-law, but apparently, that wasn't the case.

"Dude, I think you're right. That chick was hot, but such a bitch. I still can't believe he dated her and it's been eighteen years."

Now this she could get behind. Brooklyn wanted to encourage the guys to spill more of Declan's secrets, but she wasn't sure she could do it casually enough that it wouldn't look like she was digging for dirt. The man was as closed lipped about his past as she was. Maybe they'd both eventually spill their guts, or maybe they'd hold onto their secrets forever. She wasn't really sure what route they'd take, but she knew something would have to give if they were going to explore what was between them.

"So, what's next Brook? Are you guys going to go on a date or something?" Sylvia asked bringing the attention back to Brooklyn.

"Ugh. We're not together. I don't know what the deal is. Maybe you should ask Declan."

"Maybe we should. That's a great idea. Where in the hell is my phone? I'll give him a call," Braeden offered.

Brooklyn pinched the bridge of her nose, wishing that birthday wishes really did come true. If they did, she'd wish for them to change the subject or for her to be transported out of there. At the moment, either one would work for her.

"I'll get it," Brooklyn said when the doorbell interrupted Braeden's mutterings about his missing phone.

She hurried to the front of the house, excited to escape the madness even for just a moment. Pulling open the door, her breath caught when she saw who was standing there.

"Hi," she said tentatively. "What are you doing here?"

"Hey," Declan said back as he handed her the package he held. "I wanted to stop by and give you this. Happy birthday."

Her limbs felt heavy like they were moving in slow motion as she reached out to accept the gift. Butterflies fluttered to life in her belly. She hadn't expected to see him, let alone have him show up to hand her a birthday gift. He seemed to like to keep her on her toes, and while she usually wasn't a fan of surprises, she was beginning to like the ones he sprung on her.

"I wish I could stay, but Erin's in the car, and we've got to get going. I hope you have a happy birthday, Brooklyn," Declan said before leaning forward and kissing her gently on the cheek.

Before she could respond, he ran back to his car. She could see Erin waving frantically from the passenger seat, so she waved back. As they drove off, her hand flew to her cheek, where she could still feel the imprint of his lips. Like a tornado, Declan had come through quickly and left a mess in his wake. Brooklyn felt week in the knees, but also like she was floating in the clouds.

The chill of the December air finally brought her back to reality. She hurried back into the house, closing the door quickly behind her. Standing in the entrance to her sister's house, Brooklyn stared down at the present in her hands. She had no idea what could be in the box, what kind of gift Declan could have possibly gotten her, but she wanted to find out.

Heading up the stairs to Savannah's guest room, Brooklyn was eager for privacy to open the mystery gift. Before she could get halfway up the stairs, she heard her sister calling her name. Stopping, she turned and walked back down a couple of the stairs to answer Savannah.

"Hey, who was at the door?" Savannah asked.

"Ummmm...it was Declan. He wanted to drop off a present."

"Wait. Declan was at the door just now?"

Brooklyn cocked her head and furrowed her eyebrows, unsure why her sister sounded so surprised Declan would stop by. She assumed Savannah knew Declan had plans, but a quick stop really wasn't a big deal.

"Yeah. He told me last night he wasn't going to be able to come to the party, but I guess he decided to make a quick stop anyway. You know he thought you were inviting him over for a Friendsmas party and not a birthday party."

"Friendsmas. Really? What a weirdo. It's really interesting though that he stopped by. I mean it's a bit out of his way."

"Why is it interesting? Do you know what he and Erin were going to do tonight?" Brooklyn asked.

"Yeah, apparently every year they go to Snowflake Lane and watch the show, then get a picture with one of the snow princesses. They do dinner somewhere in Bellevue afterward. They've been doing it since Erin was little."

"Hold on...are you saying Declan drove over here from Issaquah just to drop off this gift then head back over the bridge to go to Bellevue? Shit, yeah this is totally out of his way. What the heck does that mean?"

God, the man was the king of mixed signals. Or maybe she just wasn't very good at picking up exactly what he was trying to tell her. Brooklyn had no idea which it was, but she was confused as hell. Were they just friends? Would a friend drive 28 miles round trip out of their way to drop off a present on a busy Saturday night? Maybe, but probably not. Especially not when that friend had to go to one of the busiest malls in the area a week before Christmas where there was going to be a parade and a crap ton of kids.

"Holy crap," Brooklyn whispered as she looked down at the present and then back up at her sister, then back down at the present.

"Yeah. Do with that information what you will. I don't know what it means Brook. I don't know what you guys are or what you could be, but I do know both of you have baggage. So please take a moment to really think about whether or not you're ready for something more than friendship and if he's the guy to give it to you. I'd hate to see either of you get hurt, but especially you. You've been through so much over the last ten years. I don't want you to have to go through anything else that'll cause you pain."

"Hey," Brooklyn said as she went down the last few steps until she was standing at the bottom next to her big sister. Without a word, she wrapped her arms around Savannah, hoping she could feel just how much she loved her.

"You deserve love and happiness Brooklyn. I want that for you more than anything else in the world. Declan could be the one to give it to you, or he could be a stepping stone on the way to that. I don't know but can you promise me that if you do decide to go down that route, will you please share the details? That man is pretty fucking hot..."

"Savannah," Brooklyn chastised as she pushed her sister away. "I mean you're not wrong, but way to ruin the sentimental moment with your dirty mind. Although really, I should be more surprised you were having a sappy moment than the fact that you sullied it with picturing Declan naked."

"I wasn't picturing him naked."

"Oh, so that was just me then? He looked sexy as hell in the dark suit he was wearing just now," Brooklyn admitted. "Look, I really don't know what's going on or what he wants, but I promise I'll keep you posted regarding anything life-altering...including if we have any more closet rendezvous."

"I mean that's all I ask. Next time something happens, I should be the first to know, not the last."

"I'll keep that in mind. Now I'm going to run upstairs and open this present. I'll be back down soon, but please don't tell anyone what I'm doing. I don't want Kerrigan or Sylvia rushing up here to bother me about this. Or Braeden. Goodness, who knew he was such a gossip."

"Your secret is safe with me...for now. But you better tell me what's in the box."

Brooklyn smiled at her sister then started back up the stairs. "Don't worry; I'll be back down in a little bit."

Of course, when she said a little bit, she meant as soon as she could wrap her head around whatever signs Declan was trying to give her. Which meant she'd probably grow old and die in her sister's guest bedroom. At least she'd die happy. Really confused, but happy.

* * *

Declan

"Dad, I thought we were going to dinner after the show," Erin said as she struggled to keep up while he bobbed and weaved through the crowd of Christmas shoppers. The dress and heels she wore making it even more difficult than usual for her.

The mall was the last place he wanted to be on a Saturday night. Especially a Saturday night a week before Christmas, but he didn't really have a choice.

"The present I dropped off for Brooklyn was supposed to be her Christmas present, so now I have to pick up a new one," he told his daughter before stopping in the middle of the walkway to look around.

He had no idea what he was going to get to replace the autographed Jay Buhner jersey he'd already given her. It had taken him far too long to decide on the jersey in the first place. Finding a balance between showing her he liked her and not overstepping and being creepy had been harder than he realized. Most guys would buy jewelry and call it good, but he felt like jewelry was only an option when you were in a clearly defined relationship. Plus, he'd noticed Brooklyn wasn't much of a fan of jewelry. She couldn't wear much of it when she was working at the bakery and bracelets were out when she was writing.

"I've never seen you this worked up. First, the nerves when we stopped by Uncle Gabriel's house and now this driving need to get Brooklyn a replacement present when I can guarantee she isn't expecting one. Heck, I bet she wasn't expecting the first one. Also, can I just say it's super adorable you rewrapped the present in birthday wrapping paper instead of giving it to her in Christmas paper."

Declan turned to face Erin. He wasn't sure when she'd become so observant, but maybe he could use it to his advantage.

"Okay, since you seem to know so much, help me. The other present was an autographed baseball jersey, so how do I top that without overstepping since we're technically not even dating."

"Oh, silly man...you don't have to top it in the way you seem to think. It's not about the money spent or the size of the present. It's about the sentiment. I'm assuming you didn't get her the jersey of some random player, but one from her favorite player. Doing that shows you listen to her. Think about something else she's mentioned in passing or something you've observed her enjoying or paying close attention to. That is how you woo a woman."

"What do you know about wooing?"

"First of all, I'm a girl, I hang out with girls, we talk...a lot, in case you haven't noticed. Second of all, I watch a lot of romantic comedies, and I read a lot of books. I might be striking out in the boyfriend department, but that doesn't mean I don't know a thing or two about romance."

"I'm perfectly okay with you striking out in the boyfriend department. You can keep that up until your 32."

Erin laughed and patted him on the cheek. "That's cute Dad, but you know that's not going to happen right? Honestly, it's not for the lack of options, but because I feel like it's a waste of my time when I'm going to be leaving for North Carolina in six months."

Declan sighed, not because he was no longer on board with her going away to college, but because he hated she was getting her hopes up. Erin was going to be devastated if she didn't get into North Carolina State, but she kept talking about it like it was a sure thing. Something about putting it out into the universe, so it became real or some nonsense like that. He just didn't want to see her get hurt and he was afraid that was what was going to happen, especially since they hadn't heard from the school yet.

"Well, wherever you end up, I feel like there should be a no boys rule. Distractions won't help you get your degree and trust me boys are nothing but distractions. Hell, girls are too. Look at how easily distracted I am because of a girl. We should be getting dinner right now, not standing in the middle of the mall trying to figure out what to get a woman I'm not even dating for Christmas. Come on, let's get out of here, I'll figure this out later."

Declan put his arm around his daughter's shoulders, pulling her against his side. It didn't matter what he got for Brooklyn if he got her anything. What mattered was that he only had a handful of months left to spend with his daughter. He needed to focus on her. Everything else could wait until she was off to school living life without him. Then he'd be open for all the distractions in the world. Including one gorgeous woman, he couldn't stop thinking about even when he knew he shouldn't be.

CHAPTER 7

Brooklyn

Brooklyn was finding it hard to focus. The freelance assignment she was working on was taking far longer than it should have because her thoughts were all over the place. She hadn't had a chance to talk to Declan since the night of her birthday party. She'd tried to call and got his voicemail. After leaving a quick thank you message, she sent him a text to thank him again for the jersey. Neither of them seemed adequate though. What she wanted to do was thank him in person with a hug and one hell of a kiss.

Instead, she sat on her couch staring at the jersey feeling like he'd changed his mind and now wanted nothing to do with her. Her emotions were already all over the place and then her sister asked her that afternoon if she could stop by after work to talk. She'd sounded so tentative, so unlike herself that it made Brooklyn worry. Of course, her first thought was there was something wrong, some sort of bad news Savannah had to give her.

Since she left work, she'd been a frazzled mess, so it really shouldn't have been a surprise she couldn't get any writing done. She needed to know what the hell was going on. With her sister, with Declan, hell even with herself. She'd been in a weird funk since her birthday party, and it wasn't just because she hadn't heard back from Declan.

All she knew was that she hated the fact she was in a funk a few days before Christmas. This was supposed to be a joyous time of year, but for some reason, she couldn't get it together. Too many things seemed up in the air. On top of that, she hadn't spoken to Meghan in weeks, and she was worried about her friend. Brooklyn didn't want to push her, but she also didn't think Meghan should be alone. Too bad Meghan wouldn't talk to any of them, not even Oliver.

For the hundredth time, Brooklyn checked her phone to see what time it was and was happy to see Savannah would be over sooner than she realized. She was eager to find out what her sister wanted to talk to her about and the wait was driving her crazy. With the time she had left, she contemplated calling Meghan and leaving her another voicemail inviting her to Christmas dinner. She hated that Meghan was going to spend the holiday alone, but she knew there was nothing she could do other than respect her friend's wishes.

A knock at the door startled her out of her thoughts. Setting her phone down, she got up to unlock the door for her sister even though Savannah still had a key. Once upon a time, the house had been Savannah's, back before she met Gabriel and they got a house together. After living with her parents, then her husband, then her parents again, it was nice to finally have a place to call her own, even if her sister did still technically own the place. One day it would be all hers and Brooklyn couldn't wait.

Opening the door, she took in her sister's appearance. Savannah was looking at little more like herself than she had earlier. She was a bit disheveled but smiling like nothing was wrong. Brooklyn stepped out of the way, letting Savannah into the house, then followed her through the living room and into the kitchen. Savannah grabbed a bottle of water out of the refrigerator then took a seat on one of the stools along the island. Brooklyn pulled out the other stool and sat down next to hear, waiting for her sister to finally tell her what was going on.

"I thought this day was never going to end. I need to remember not to give so many people time off during the holidays. Inevitably someone always calls in sick and then we're scrambling to cover shifts during one of the busiest times of the year."

"I told you I could have stayed longer."

Savannah sighed, then took a sip of her water. "I know, and I should have taken you up on the offer, but you looked exhausted and had already worked nearly ten hours."

"Yeah, well staying busy is a hell of a lot better than sitting around here wondering what the hell happened. I could not shut my brain off long enough to get anything done. I have a freelance piece due right after Christmas and it's pretty much a thousand-word essay about how men are jerks, and you can't trust them even when they give you super meaningful gifts."

"Still haven't heard from him, huh?"

"Nope. Not a peep. Has Gabriel heard anything?"

Savannah shook her head. "He even tried calling Andi and couldn't get through to her either. I'm sure it's not what you're thinking. He hasn't just changed his mind about pursuing you. The man got you an autographed Jay Buhner jersey. That's not a throwaway gift, and it's not a gift you get for a buddy."

"I swooned when I opened that gift, Savannah. I fucking swooned. I've never done that before, but then again, I've never had someone buy me such a romantic gift. Frank used to just buy me gifts he'd expect me to like, not something that would actually interest me. I got a lot of jewelry throughout my marriage. I rarely wear jewelry, especially not bracelets, but I swear he must have bought me every bracelet at that stupid jewelry store. Hell, I'm pretty sure a few of them were duplicates, but I just threw them in the jewelry box and only took them out when I was forced to go to fancy events."

"That guy was such a fucking tool. I would love the opportunity to kick him in the junk sometime," Savannah said her hands fisting at her sides.

"Don't worry. I took care of that."

"I know, but I'd like to get one really good kick in myself. It's the least I can do since I didn't protect you from him."

"You know I wouldn't have listened. It literally took me catching him in the act to figure it out. It wasn't that I loved Frank and only wanted to see the best in him, but it was because I was blinded by everything else. If things hadn't gone down the way they did, I probably would have seen him for the cheating asshole he was a lot sooner."

"Still..."

"Now I know you didn't come over here to rehash my awful marriage or the current jerk that has decided I'm not worth it. What's going on Sav?"

"I've got some news, and I wanted to tell you before mom and dad. I'm not sure it's going to be easy to hear, so I wanted you to have some time with it instead of just springing it on you in front of everyone. Especially since we're planning on telling everyone on Christmas."

"Just spit it out already," Brooklyn said even though she had a feeling she already knew what her sister's announcement was going to be.

"I'm pregnant."

The news hit her like a punch to the gut, but Brooklyn shook it off quickly and got up to hug her sister. It was a miracle, one her sister and Gabriel deserved after everything that happened with Gabriel's ex and the accident.

"Oh my gosh, congratulations, Sav. I'm so happy for you guys. This is amazing. What did the doctor say? How far along are you? What do you know so far?"

"Hey, back up a minute. It's okay to not be okay you know. I get that this might be hard for you," Savannah said as she pushed Brooklyn back a little so she could look at her.

"It's not easy, but I'm not going to resent my big sister because she's getting something I've always wanted. That's not how this works. Just because I can't have kids, doesn't mean I'm not fucking elated you're making me an auntie."

Tears filled Savannah's eyes, which in turn made Brooklyn tear up. Savannah's news did hurt, but only in the sense that it reminded Brooklyn of what she couldn't have. Of what her body wouldn't give her. When Savannah had gotten pregnant, but lost the baby in the accident, Brooklyn had been so worried about her sister she never really had a chance to think about the fact that she'd been pregnant and someday she might be pregnant again.

"I appreciate that you told me separately though. Everyone will be focused on you when you make your announcement, but eventually, mom and dad will turn to me to make sure I'm okay. It would have been easy to fake my way through it, but now I won't have to and I appreciate that. Please, do not think for one second I'm not happy for you. I couldn't be happier for you even if I were able to have children of my own."

She pulled Savannah in for another hug; this time tears were streaming from both of their eyes.

"Okay, enough of that. I want details."

"We pretty much started trying right after the wedding. We didn't know how any of this was going to work, whether or not I'd be able to get pregnant or if I'll be able to stay pregnant. We figured we might as well find out sooner rather than later and we're ready for kids now, so there was no point in waiting," Savannah shrugged. "I thought I might have been pregnant before Thanksgiving, but I wasn't quite ready to take a test, so we waited."

"Wait weren't you drinking on Thanksgiving and at my birthday party?"

"No. I was faking it on Thanksgiving, and by your birthday, we obviously knew the truth, so I promise I drank sparkling water all night. I'm almost nine weeks. Because of my history, we've been keeping a close eye on how I feel, and I'm supposed to take it easy just in case. So far, my doctor says everything looks healthy and normal, but with my potentially unstable uterus, we'll have to wait and see…and wait and see… and wait and see some more for thirty one more weeks. It's going to be exhausting."

"Are you scared?" Brooklyn asked.

"Hell yeah. I know what you went through, and I'm fucking terrified this isn't going to work out. But I'm also terrified it's going to, and I'm going to have to take care of a baby. All I know is that what's going to happen is going to happen. I can only take it one day at a time and hope everything works out. There are no guarantees either way, and I can't take a slightly larger possibility of a miscarriage and let it keep me from trying to have a family."

"I've read that there are more than three million miscarriages a year in the US, and most of those women have completely healthy uteruses and have already had a child or will go on to have one. I'm glad you decided not to let fear get in your way. I'm here for you, whatever happens. In the meantime, you need to let me help out with work more, and we should hire more help."

"I'm not an invalid you know."

"I know this, but we don't want to piss off your unstable uterus. Plus, we're going to have to deal without you when you have the baby, so why not start weaning you off of sixty-hour work weeks now."

"I don't work sixty hours a week."

"Bullshit. You might not work in one of the shops for sixty hours a week, but I know you take work home with you. Doing payroll and placing orders counts as work."

"I know you're right. In fact, I'm going to cut back on work and do a lot of stuff from home. Gabriel wants me to stay off my feet, and I agreed with him."

"Holy crap. Did he record the occasion because I feel like that might be more of a miracle than that baby you're growing?"

"Shut up, smartass. We're going to hold off on telling too many people for now. We want to make it past the first trimester and then depending on how I look maybe we'll tell a few more people. We want to hold off as long as we can since there's always going to be a chance things could go wrong."

"Hey, we're going to put positive thoughts out into the universe. This pregnancy is going to be a happy and healthy one. You are going to cook that baby in there until the 40-week mark, and then I'm going to have a beautiful, healthy niece or nephew to spoil rotten."

"I'm due July 20th, give or take. I'm not looking forward to being nearly 40-weeks pregnant in the middle of the summer, but at least it's not August."

"Oh my gosh, I'm so fu...reaking excited for you Savannah. For you and Gabriel. This is really, really great news and I really needed some great news, so thank you for telling me."

"Of course. I wanted to tell you as soon as we found out but I didn't want to put a damper on your birthday."

"Seriously. This is not bad news so quit acting like it. Now tell me, I know it's early but do you think you're having a boy or a girl?"

As Savannah started to talk about the gender of the baby and what their plans were for the nursery, Brooklyn realized it was getting easier and easier to genuinely be happy about her sister's news. Her chest didn't ache anymore. Her heart no longer breaking for what she couldn't have but filling with the love she already had for her unborn niece or nephew.

She hated that even for one second her sister had hesitated to tell her the news, but she couldn't blame her. After years of trying to get pregnant and failing and then getting pregnant only to lose the baby, Brooklyn left her marriage to Frank, a broken woman. Most assumed it was because she'd caught Frank red-handed fucking his mistress in their bed and then later learned he'd gotten his mistress pregnant. Of course, most people thought that because they didn't know about the silent struggle Brooklyn had gone through to make her dream of being a mother a reality.

They didn't know that seeing another woman pregnant with the baby she'd tried so hard to conceive had nearly ruined her. Brooklyn's doctor had almost convinced her that the issue in the baby making department wasn't her. Then she saw the proof that she was indeed the defective one and it crushed her.

It had taken her years to get over it; to move past what she couldn't have and accept what she could. She had options if she really wanted to be a mom. She'd looked into adoption and was saving money whenever she could in case she wanted to go that route. The thought of being the fun aunt, the one that spoiled the kids rotten, then sent them home hopped up on sugar, had a certain appeal.

All Brooklyn knew now was she didn't need to be a mother to feel fulfilled. It had been something she'd become so focused on during her marriage that she lost sight of who she was if she couldn't give Frank the family he kept badgering her for. Now she knew her worth and knew exactly who she was.

Brooklyn would take time to mourn her loss again once her sister left, but she wouldn't dwell on it. And she sure as hell wouldn't dwell on Declan Reese either. She didn't have time to mess around if she was going to be the best damn aunt anyone had ever had. She only had thirty-one weeks to make sure her niece or nephew had anything and everything they could possible need by the time they came into the world, and she didn't plan on messing around.

* * *

Declan

"She's pissed, isn't she?" Declan asked as he deposited a case of wine on the rack inside Arrow's storage room.

"I mean, she wasn't happy with you at all. You gave her a thoughtful gift and then ghosted her. What the hell was she supposed to think?"

"I didn't ghost her. I had a family emergency."

"I know this, but she doesn't. You've been back a few days, and you still haven't called or texted her."

"Because I wanted to tell her what happened in person but we had to get everything squared away at the warehouse first, and I was freaking exhausted from having to deal with my dad for a week. This was not my idea of a Merry Christmas and especially not how I wanted to spend the last Christmas before Erin goes off to college."

"I know, man, I'm sorry, but I wouldn't worry about it too much. I'm pretty sure she's moved on. She's kinda focused on someone else, and I wouldn't be surprised if she forgot all about you."

"What the hell are you talking about? Who is he? Where did she meet him? How could you let this happen, man? I thought you were my best friend."

Gabriel laughed, which pissed Declan off. He might not have told Gabriel how he felt about Brooklyn, but he knew his friend wasn't stupid. How could he let her meet someone else while he was out of town? Whether Declan had disappeared on her or not, Gabriel should have still had his back. He was his best friend after all, but apparently, loyalty changed when you got married.

"Dude, calm down. I'm just messing with you. Well sort of. She is single-mindedly focused on someone else, but we aren't sure if it's a girl or a boy, yet, but we introduced her to him or her before Christmas."

Declan stopped before he picked up another case of wine. Gabriel's words replaying in his head until it struck him.

"Holy shit, is Savannah pregnant? Gabriel, that's fucking awesome news man. Congratulations," Declan said as he hugged his friend, clapping him on the back.

"Hey, keep it down. We aren't telling a lot of people yet, just her family and now you. There's still the potential for something bad to happen, so we don't want to tell too many people until we don't have a choice because she can't hide it anymore. Thankfully we might be able to keep it under wraps longer with winter in full effect. Layers will be our friends for a while."

"I get it. This is great, Gabriel. I'm excited for you. I'm sure everything's going to be fine. You and Savannah will make wonderful parents."

Declan wondered what it would have been like to raise Erin with a mother. To have a partner in all things, to not have to worry about what was going to happen when she went through puberty or started liking boys. Having his sister there was helpful, but an aunt was not the same as a mom, no matter how hard Andi tried.

A strange feeling came over him as he thought about starting over. About doing it all again, this time with someone by his side and not just any someone, but Brooklyn. Could he do it? He'd always said he didn't want more kids, but he couldn't help but picture a child that was the perfect mix of him and Brooklyn.

Just as the picture became clearer in his mind, the panic set in. The worry that he would once again be left behind, a baby in his arms, his heart broken, not just for him but for his child. He couldn't go through that again. He wouldn't.

Shaking off the thoughts, he forced himself to remember the excitement he felt for his friend and his wife. Gabriel and Savannah would be great parents. They deserved all the happiness that came with having a family. Declan hoped everything went well and that there were no complications or issues stemming from Savannah's accident.

"Thanks, Declan. I've been pretty much terrified of everything since the moment we found out. What if something happens? What if I end up being a shitty dad? What if my kid ends up hating me? I didn't really have an excellent role model growing up, so what if I end up screwing my kid up the way my dad nearly screwed me up?"

"Trust me. That shit never goes away. I worry every single day that I'm turning into my dad. You just have to make a conscious effort not to," Declan told his friend. "When Erin told me she wanted to go away for college all I could think of was the millions of horrible things that could happen to her. I couldn't think of a single reason why I should let her go."

"Okay, you're not helping me here."

"Sorry. You kind of get used to it and sometimes you forget all about the horrors of the world, and it's just amazing being a dad. It wasn't how I wanted to go about doing things, but I wouldn't trade having Erin for anything else in the world. Not even for having a long successful career at shortstop for the Mariners. Not even if that career came with a World Series ring. She is absolutely the best thing that ever happened to me, and I'm sure you'll feel the same thing about your child."

"I know you're right. The waiting is going to be the hardest part."

Declan laughed. "That's what you think. Anyway, congrats man. I'll bring something good to your house tonight to celebrate, but we'll tell Braeden it's for New Year's."

"Sounds good. You better get out of here and finish your route. I have it on good authority that someone will be at my house this afternoon setting up for the party tonight. If you happened to stop by to see if I was home and ran into this person...well I mean, it would be just a coincidence, right?"

"Thanks, man. I was hoping to talk to her before tonight. I'll see you later if she doesn't kill me first."

Declan grabbed his hand truck and hurried out of the restaurant. He only had a few more stops on his route before he could drop the delivery truck back off at the warehouse and grab his car. Thankfully, he didn't think Brooklyn would be leaving Gabriel and Savannah's anytime soon, so he didn't have to rush too much. He was just eager to see her, to explain to her what happened. To tell her he'd thought about her every single day they were in Florida.

He just hoped she'd listen to him and not slam the door in his face.

* * *

When he pulled up in front of Gabriel's house, he was happy to see Brooklyn's car was still in the driveway. He put his car in park but hesitated for a moment to get out. He had a damn good reason for being gone and a decent reason for not contacting her while he was away and when he got back. Truth be told, he could have tried harder to call her while they were in Florida, but it seemed like too much.

Dealing with his confusion about her on top of his mom being in the hospital and his dad being an asshole, it was all just too overwhelming. Unfortunately, he could only focus on one thing at a time, and his family had to come first. Seeing his mom and protecting his daughter had to be his priority. He had to hope Brooklyn could understand where he was coming from. And if she didn't...well, then he knew what his decision would be where she was concerned.

He knew he was being a chicken shit. He had to face Brooklyn, tell her what happened and go from there. If everything worked out, then he'd make his new year's plans a reality. If they didn't, then he'd come back later, celebrate the new year and the great news with his best friend and then head home alone just like he had the year before.

He really hoped everything worked out the way he wanted.

"Oh my goodness, he lives. It's a miracle," Brooklyn said as soon as she opened the door.

She stared at him for a moment, then turned to walk back into the house. Since she left the door open, Declan took it as an invitation to follow her. He closed the door behind him, then followed her into the dining room, where the table had been taken over by decorations and various other party necessities.

"Can we talk?" he asked tentatively.

"Only if you can talk and decorate at the same time. Savannah can't help, and Gabriel won't be home until right before the party starts and there's still a lot to do."

"Put me to work then. I'll help however you need me to."

Declan took off his jacket, hanging it on the back of one of the dining room chairs then rolled the sleeves of his shirt up to his elbows. Brooklyn watched him, but he couldn't tell if she looked at him in appreciation or if she was trying to figure out how to kill him and not get caught. As soon as he was done, she handed him a banner and pointed to where it needed to be hung over the mantel. He went to work, quickly knocking a few items off of her to-do list so she wouldn't regret letting him in the house.

"I'm sorry I didn't call you," he said lamely.

It wasn't how he'd practiced his speech or what he'd even intended to say straight out of the gate. Brooklyn made him anxious in a way he'd never experienced before. Even in high school, he'd never felt like he wasn't in control when it came to the opposite sex. He saw someone he wanted and went for it. He'd followed the same rule throughout his adult years whenever he felt the need, but the minute he met Brooklyn everything he knew went out the window. She had him second-guessing his entire life.

"Why didn't you call? Or at the very least text. I don't ask for much, and it's not like I wanted to spend hours talking on the phone about our feelings. I just wanted to thank you for the present."

"I should have, I'm sorry, but things were a bit hectic. The day after your birthday my dad called. Andi and I haven't spoken to him in years. Even though we talk to our mom at least once a month, my dad hasn't bothered to call us to even check on the business since they moved to Florida a decade ago. So when he called, we knew something was wrong."

"Oh god, Declan..."

"Everything's okay now, but my mom was in the hospital. She had a stroke. We flew out to Jacksonville immediately. It was touch and go for a while there, but she's going to be fine. I lost my phone in the airport, Erin forgot hers here in her room. The only one of us that had their phone was Andi, and she doesn't have your number."

"I get it. I'm sorry about your mom. I'm glad she's doing okay."

"That's the thing though; I could have called you if I tried harder. Andi has Gabriel's number; I could have gotten your number from him. It's just...I couldn't deal," Declan admitted. "My dad was always hard on us, but when he found out I got Kara pregnant at seventeen, he turned into something else entirely. You know, until this last week, he'd only seen Erin a handful of times even though we lived in the same house with him for the first six months of her life. Once we moved out, he wanted nothing to do with her or with me. Andi came with us, so he cut her out too."

"Jeezus."

"Everything he has to say to us about the business, he does it through mom or Al, my dad's lawyer. If it weren't for our mom, we wouldn't have anyone other than each other. There was a time where I feared even with mom involved he was never going to leave us the business. Thankfully, Andi proved that her genius was worth more than his pride. When she doubled the company profits her first year working there, dad realized he was going to be set up to get a really nice retirement package. He suddenly became more than eager to sign things over to us and get the hell out of town."

"Wow, I thought Gabriel's dad was a piece of work, but yours definitely wins asshole dad of the century. I don't understand how anyone could be shitty to their kids. Why do people even bother having them if they aren't going to love them unconditionally no matter what they end up doing with their lives?"

"I don't know. I mean I don't want Erin to follow in my footsteps at all, but if she did, I would support her no matter what. I would have never done to her what my dad to me."

"Well, I don't think you have to worry about that happening. Erin's pretty much the most together teenager I've ever met. She knows what she wants, and she's not going to stop until she gets it."

"I hope you're right. I've heard college can be extremely distracting and the boys there are far pushier than the ones in high school."

"Erin can take care of herself. She also knows what to do if someone's giving her a hard time."

"Maybe I should have her take some self-defense classes before she goes."

"It's not a horrible idea. I've taken a few; they're really helpful."

They went back to decorating for a while, neither of them saying much. It was nice not feeling like he had to fill the silence. He loved that Brooklyn didn't feel the need to fill it either. Most women hated silence, it made them feel awkward, and then they tended to overshare or chatter on about nothing important. Like when they'd done the dishes together after Friendsgiving, Declan felt entirely at ease with Brooklyn, and she seemed to feel the same way with him.

Once they finished everything on the list, Declan replayed their earlier conversation in his head. He wasn't quite sure that he felt comfortable with where they left things, so he decided to apologize one last time. He honestly felt bad that he left her wondering why he hadn't called. Now that he was with her again he realized calling her probably would have helped. There was something about her that calmed him that made him feel like everything was going to be okay.

"Brooklyn, I'm really sorry I didn't call you. I should have."

"Hey, I get why you didn't. It's not a big deal. I just wanted to thank you for the jersey. It was a really thoughtful gift."

"You're welcome. I'm glad you liked it. I have a Christmas present for you too."

"Really? You didn't have to do that. The jersey was more than enough."

"I know I didn't have to. I wanted to. It's nothing big, I promise. I saw it, and it made me think of you."

The smile on her face nearly brought him to his knees. Knowing it was all for him, that he was the reason she was beaming from ear to ear thrilled him. This woman made him forget everything he'd been telling himself over the last eighteen years. She made him feel things he'd sworn he'd never let himself feel again.

"I have something for you too. Maybe we can get together in the next couple days to exchange presents?"

He wasn't going to tell her he had her present in his car. That he'd been driving around with it since he got back into town just waiting for the chance to give it to her. Although if he was honest with himself, it wasn't so much giving her the present as it was just being with her. The woman was consuming his thoughts, dictating his actions. Even when he was dealing with stupid family stuff, she was in his head.

"Sure. I don't have a lot going on. Just let me know when you're free."

Brooklyn smiled, running a hand through her hair. "I should get going. Thank you for helping me decorate this place. I've got to head home to get ready, so I can come back over here in a couple of hours to start putting the food together."

"It's nice of you to take all of this on for Savannah, although I'm sure it's killing her not to be able to do things for her own party."

"I take it Gabriel told you the good news."

"Yeah. I'm really happy for them."

"Me too," Brooklyn said quietly.

Declan knew she meant it, but there was something off about the way she said it. Something was lingering beneath the surface. Before he could try to figure it out, Brooklyn was ushering him out the door. They said goodbye on the steps in front of the house before she rushed to her car. She waved at him as she backed out of the driveway leaving him wondering what the hell just happened and how he was going to get her to tell him what he wanted to know.

* * *

With Erin and Andi having plans of their own, Declan didn't have to head back to Issaquah to pick anyone up. Instead of going home for no reason, he decided to go to the gym to blow off steam. The commute back and forth from Issaquah to Seattle wasn't horrible depending on the time of day, but it wasn't one he liked making if he didn't have to.

He would have much rather spent the time with Brooklyn, but something was going on with her. Though he couldn't be sure, he didn't think it was the fact that he'd gone radio silent for a week. There was still so much he didn't know about her, still so much they hadn't talked about. He wanted to know everything though. He wanted to know her darkest secrets and to let her in on his.

The thought of telling someone else about the things he kept hidden usually made him sick to his stomach. Until now, he would have never dwelled on the possibility long, but with Brooklyn, it was all he wanted to do. He had no idea what kind of spell she'd cast on him or how things had gotten to the point where he no longer wanted to wring her neck and instead wanted to get her naked and writhing beneath him.

After the longest, coldest shower he could stand, he was dressed for the evening and headed back to Gabriel's house sooner than necessary. The party wasn't supposed to start until eight, but since he knew Brooklyn was going to be there he wanted to get in as much quality time with her as he could.

She didn't seem surprised to see him when she opened the door and found him standing there. The smile she gave him was the one he couldn't get enough of. Her entire face lit up making it clear she was happy to see him. Within seconds of walking into the house, she had him wearing an apron and chopping up vegetables.

Everything felt so right standing next to her in the kitchen, that he barely even noticed when Gabriel came home from work or when the guests started arriving. He had no idea when doing common household things together had become a part of his norm, but he liked it. In fact, he found himself starting to crave the time they spent together doing the little things like the dishes and putting together a platter of veggies.

By the time the party was in full swing, Declan had found himself standing around with Braeden, Gabriel and surprisingly Oliver. They had to practically beg the man to leave his house and join them. He'd been understandably distant since his wife had gone AWOL. He said it was because he didn't want to get in her way, that she needed the support of their friends more than he did, which was total bullshit. But since Meghan hadn't been around in months, the guys had insisted Oliver at least make it out for New Years. Which had seemed like a good idea at the time, but now that they were all standing around chatting, not so much.

"You know you're not as sly as you think you are," Braeden said suddenly interrupting their conversation about how the Seahawks regular season had ended.

"What are you talking about?" Declan asked even though he had a feeling he'd regret it.

"You. The glances you keep making toward a certain person. The glares you keep sending in the direction of any man who bothers to stop and talk to her. We see them all no matter how hard you try to hide them. You want her, so why don't you go after her? Quit pussy footing around and go for it."

"It's not that simple."

"Why not? What's standing in your way? You can't use Erin as an excuse anymore. She's nearly eighteen. She's going to leave for college soon, and you're going to be sitting around fully aware of how life has passed you by. Get off your ass, Declan. Don't let her be the one that got away. You'll never stop regretting it if you do," Braeden said before draining his drink and walking away.

Declan watched him for a minute before turning to Gabriel and Oliver who seemed just as shocked as he was.

"What the fuck was that?" Declan asked, speaking more to Oliver since he was the one who knew Braeden the best, although it hadn't always been that way.

"I have absolutely no idea. I mean, you all know he's not the goofy fucker he lets everyone believe he is, but that...that was new to me."

"He's not wrong though," Gabriel pointed out, though he didn't need to.

Declan was more than aware Braeden had spoken the truth he'd been trying to ignore. He couldn't use Erin as an excuse anymore. She wasn't a child he had to protect from women he might bring into her life. She was smart enough not to let them hurt her or influence her in any way. Plus, she already liked Brooklyn and would continue to like her whether he dated her or not. Erin had told him more than once he needed to get out there and date and she was entirely in favor of Brooklyn being the one he took the chance with.

"I have no idea what I'm doing," he admitted.

"Do you think I did? Or Oliver? Dude, this shit's confusing, and there's no manual. Yeah, your situation is a bit different than most, but it's time to put yourself out there again. Maybe I'm a bit biased, but I don't think you could have picked a better woman to jump into things with. Just don't hurt her...I really don't want to have to kick your ass, and if you hurt her, I'd be forced to."

"So much for the bro code or whatever."

"Sorry, but my wife gets my loyalty now man. You'll understand someday."

Declan wasn't entirely sure he would, but he didn't say it out loud. He hadn't decided he was ready to date yet let alone talk about marriage. There were so many things he still had to figure out, things that could end up keeping him from ever taking the plunge. So many things still scared him, things he didn't know if he was going to be able to get over. But the thought of not being with Brooklyn was almost too much to bear.

He really needed to figure out which was more important, Brooklyn or his fear. Declan knew he needed to figure it out soon before he lost his chance and he ended up living with his regret instead of her.

CHAPTER 8

Brooklyn

There was a reason she didn't host parties besides the fact she'd gotten her fill of it back when she was married. They were freaking exhausting and difficult to enjoy when you were the one that had to make sure everyone had a drink and that the food was stocked. Gabriel had taken some of the pressure off of her, but Brooklyn still felt like she needed to stay on top of things since her sister couldn't.

Thinking about Savannah reminded her that she needed to make sure she was still sitting on the couch instead of making the rounds. Sitting around doing nothing was difficult for her sister, so Brooklyn had to keep checking on her to make sure she wasn't overdoing it. Occasionally she had to resort to threatening her to ensure she did as she was told.

Looking at the clock, Brooklyn realized they were a mere five minutes away from the new year. She always looked at the new year as a time for new beginnings. A time to leave behind the bad things that'd happened or the stupid things that she'd done and start over fresh. A lot had changed for her in the last year, and thankfully most of it was good. Most of it she didn't want to leave behind.

Brooklyn looked around the room, noticing that those who were a part of a couple were finding their other halves as the countdown to midnight got closer. Her eyes met Declan's, and it felt like her heart skipped a beat. She was tired of fighting what was between them. Tired of pretending that she didn't want him, but she didn't know what was going through his head. She had an idea but couldn't be sure if it was wishful thinking on her part or if she'd been finally reading his signals correctly.

Now here they were, a moment that could change everything and she was hesitating. Did she make the first move? Did she wait for him? What if neither of them moved or if she did and he wasn't interested? Her head swam with uncertainty, but none of it mattered when she saw him start to walk toward her.

It took him less than a minute to cross the room. Neither of them spoke as he grabbed Brooklyn's hand and pulled her down the hallway, so they were out of everyone's line of sight. As the countdown began, he brushed his hand along her cheek, tucking her hair behind her ear. His eyes were locked on hers, the intensity of the moment making her chest feel tight. She had to remember to breathe, but breathing seemed so unimportant at the moment.

Every single part of her was focused on Declan and his hands that she had no idea what was happening around her. She had no idea if the clock had struck midnight, although if it had and he hadn't kissed her, she might have to kick his ass. The world could have been crumbling down around them, and she wouldn't have noticed because all she could see was the way he was looking at her.

He leaned in slowly, almost hesitantly. The minute their lips touched, the tentativeness was gone, and every pent-up feeling they'd been suppressing since her sister's wedding came flooding out. It should have been just a chaste kiss to ring in the new year, instead of their mouths locked in a passionate grapple for dominance. Their need for each other overriding everything that had been holding them back.

They broke apart, gasping for breath. Their eyes locked again, and at that moment she knew they were on the same page.

"Come home with me," she said making sure it came out more like a demand than a question.

She needed him, and she was damn sure he needed her. They couldn't keep circling each other, waiting to see who would break. She had no idea what it would mean or where they would go from there, but tonight they needed to forget everything but what it felt like to be together.

Grabbing her hand, he pulled her through the house. They said quick goodbyes to their friends neither of them caring that every single person there knew where they were headed and why. Most of them would likely say it was a long time coming. Those that knew about the wedding just smiled at them. Brooklyn tried to promise to Savannah that she'd come over in the morning to help clean up, but both she and Declan told her it wasn't happening. She glared at him, but inside she was doing a happy dance that rivaled the Carlton.

She grabbed her purse and both of their jackets from the hallway closet, then let him lead her out of the house and to his car. Although she'd driven to the house earlier, she didn't even bother questioning him or saying she could drive herself. Brooklyn was pretty sure they were both as into the moment as anyone could get, but she didn't want to give him any opportunities to talk himself out of what was about to happen.

If she was honest with herself, she didn't want to give herself the opportunity to talk herself out of anything either. There were so many things that could go wrong, so many reasons why they shouldn't go for it. None of them were as convincing as the feeling she got when he touched her, when he merely held her hand like he was at the moment.

When they got to her house, he parked the car then quickly got out to open the door for her. Chivalry would get him everywhere. More men needed to figure that out. He followed her to her door, waiting impatiently as she unlocked it. Once inside, they kicked off their shoes, then she took his hand and led him up the stairs to her room.

The second they entered her bedroom, clothes started flying. Jackets hit the floor followed by his shirt, then hers. His jeans came next, leaving him in just his delicious boxer briefs that left very little to the imagination. His cock strained against the tight material and her mouth watered at the thought of taking him between her lips. Before she could drop to her knees, he grabbed her chin and lifted her face until her eyes met his.

"While I'm down with what you have in mind, it needs to wait. I don't want to come in your mouth, not yet anyway, and I'm too close to the edge to hold back now."

She looked back down, her tongue darting out to lick her lips. As much as she wanted to give him the best blow job of his life, she didn't have any more patience than he did. With the same speed he'd shown, she opened her belt, undid her black skinny jeans and pushed them over her hips. For a second, she chided herself for not wearing the best of her lingerie, but when she'd dressed earlier, she didn't want to look like she'd assumed this was going to happen. It didn't matter that she knew with every fiber of her being that they were going to end up exactly where they were. Disappointments happened all the time.

"Jeezus, you're gorgeous," Declan said as he took her in from head to toe, then back up again. His eyes lingered on her barely contained breasts a little longer than the rest. He looked like he was going to devour her and she couldn't wait. Like a lamb to the slaughter, she couldn't fight against the pull, and she didn't want to.

They each took a step forward at the same time. Her hands falling against his well-defined pecs, his hands landing on her hips. His chest was something she'd only ever seen on Instagram. She'd never seen something so perfect in real life, certainly not on any man she'd been with. His pecs were covered with a dusting of hair that would usually turn her off but was strangely a huge turn on with Declan. His six-pack made her want to trace each ridge with her tongue down to the delicious V that had been known to make grown women weep.

Brooklyn had always assumed he was one of those perfect specimens that only existed when Photoshop was involved. His broad shoulders and beautifully sculpted forearms had been enough to make her drool. Seeing the man in all his glory was nearly enough to make her head explode. Although his cock was currently covered, she knew from experience that it was just as perfect as the rest of him and he definitely knew how to use it to make her happy.

"You're not so bad yourself," she finally said as her eyes continued to peruse every inch of his naturally tanned skin.

His hands roamed up her sides, leaving goosebumps in their wake. He traced a finger along the bottom edge of her bra, then up along the edge of the cup, across the expanse of skin that her bra couldn't contain. A chill ran down her spine even though she felt like she was on fire. Her hands drifted down over his abs to the waistband of his underwear. She dipped a finger between the elastic and his skin, loving the way he sucked in a breath as her finger brushed the tip of his cock.

"You're killing me."

"But what a way to go right?"

"I'd rather die buried inside you," he said as he backed her up until they were next to the bed.

With deft fingers, he flicked open her bra, then pushed the straps off her shoulders. She let it fall to the ground exposing her overheated flesh to the cool air of her room. Declan paused a moment to take in her breasts, her nipples pebbling as his rapt attention sent a shot of arousal to every part of her that was in need of his touch.

The only other time they'd been together had been a fully clothed, quick fuck in a closet that had ended in tears and resentment. This time, she wanted to savor things, but she was also pretty sure she didn't have the patience to hold out. Carefully, she pushed his boxers over his hips, loving the way his cock sprang free as it was released from the confining material. Once again she fought the urge to drop to her knees in front of him so she could worship his beautiful body.

Slowly, he pushed her panties over her hips and down her legs. Brooklyn was surprised when he followed the last remaining barrier between them. As he dropped to his knees, she was momentarily jealous, but then he nudged her legs apart, his hand skating over her skin until he found her center. She sucked in a breath as he parted her folds, his thumb pressing gently against her clit before being replaced by his tongue.

Her knees nearly gave out as Declan went for an all-out assault on her pussy. His tongue traced a path from her clit to her core and back. Without warning he pushed a finger inside of her, then after a few pumps, he added another, driving her wild with every thrust and retreat. She couldn't be sure if it was because it had been awhile or if Declan was just that good, but it only took a few minutes before she was coming, his name falling from her lips as her head fell back and her eyes closed.

How she was able to stay standing she never quite understood. Declan had wrapped an arm around her waist to hold her against his mouth, but she'd felt like dead weight as she started to come back from one of the best orgasms of her life. The only one that had topped it was the one he'd given her the night of the wedding. Of course, she'd die before she ever admitted that. Now that they were halfway to doing it again, she hoped this time topped that one so she wouldn't be ashamed to shout it from the rooftops.

Declan continued to hold onto her as he stood. He pulled back the covers, pushing them to the end of the mattress so they wouldn't be in the way, then lowered her gently to the bed. The cool fabric was a balm against her overheated skin as she pushed back until she lay in the middle of the king size bed. Once she was in place, Declan settled himself over her; his body notched between her legs. He handed her the condom he'd grabbed from his wallet, and she quickly ripped it open and rolled the latex over his straining cock.

His eyes locked with hers. Her heart was pounding furiously against her ribs. This was it. It would be ten times harder to go back once they took this final step. His eyes seemed to search her face for any sense that she wasn't sure or that she'd changed her mind. To prove to him that she was just as into it as he was, she reached between them and positioned his cock at her entrance. With their eyes locked on each other, she grabbed his ass and pulled him into her, initiating the contact they were both so desperate for.

"Holy shit," Declan muttered at the same time as she moaned an "oh god".

They both stilled, needing a moment to adjust to the immensity of the moment. Her eyes never left his, not even when he started to move and she felt like they would flutter shut. She needed to be connected to him in every way possible as he stretched and filled her. The feel of him inside of her was the most exquisite thing she'd ever experienced. His hands on her skin was almost too much. She nearly lost her mind when he pulled back then filled her again in the slowest most erotic move ever.

He leaned in to kiss her, his tongue slipping into her mouth, as his cock pushed into her over and over. They kissed until neither of them could breathe. They broke apart long enough to catch their breath, before diving back in, their lips and teeth crashing together. His right hand moved up over her hips, brushing against the bottom of her breast. Her nipple tightened with need as she arched her back. He cupped her breast in his hot hand, his thumb brushing over her nipple once, twice and again until her pussy nearly started to clench.

Declan paid equal attention to her left breast, shifting his weight onto his right side so he could lavish her body with attention. Brooklyn was surprised he could multitask as his hips never missed a beat. He continued to fuck her slow, slow, fast, his rhythm only occasionally faltering as he tried to fight against things ending too soon.

She was so close, her body felt like a live wire. Every inch of her ready to go off with just the slightest touch. Her eyes locked with his and it was like he could read her mind. Reaching between them, he pressed his thumb against her clit, and she was off. Her body tensed, her legs squeezing around his waist as her pussy clenched around his dick. Her body arched up off of the bed as she moaned his name.

He continued to pump into her, his timing becoming more frantic as she pulsed around him. Brooklyn could feel his body tensing between her legs, his ass becoming rock hard as he pounded into her harder and harder, his body brushing against her clit with each thrust. She felt herself climbing closer to another orgasm, something that had never happened to her before.

"Fuck...oh shit..." Declan muttered as he thrust hard into her one more time then held her against him as he came.

That final thrust sent her over the edge, spiraling toward orgasmic bliss once again. Her body hummed, her legs shook as her walls milked him for everything he had. When they finally came down, and she could see through the euphoric sex clouds, she realized what'd happened.

Holy shit. It's real.

"What's real?"

"Crap. I said that out loud didn't I?"

"Yeah," Declan said with a laugh as he moved off of her then sat on the end of the bed so he could take care of the condom. Once it was disposed of in the trash can by her bed, he rolled onto his side, propping his head on his arm. Watching him was giving her a kink in her neck, but she didn't quite have the energy to roll onto her side to face him.

"Damn internal dialogue must be on the fritz with the multiple orgasms and all that."

"So, what were you talking about? What's real?"

Finally finding a boost of energy, Brooklyn rolled onto her side so she could face him. Their noses were nearly touching they were so close. "Simultaneous orgasms. I thought they were a thing of myth. Something that only happened in romance novels."

"Seriously?"

"Ummm, yeah. Is it weird that I didn't realize those were real?"

"It just pisses me off. I also do not want to hear that there have been times in your life where you didn't get off first. That will push me into a murderous rage, and I really like this weird euphoric haze I'm in at the moment."

Brooklyn averted her eyes from his not wanting him to see the truth there. Of course, she'd given it away with the fact that she didn't want to make eye contact with him. The last thing she wanted to get into while naked with him in her bed was what happened with her ex-husband. He wasn't worth their attention, let alone Declan's rage.

"How about instead of murdering someone who isn't worth it, you show me what I've been missing all these years. If you're up for it, that is."

Anger flashed over his features for a brief second before her words registered. The smile that graced Declan's face would have melted her panties off had she been wearing any. She knew she was in for it now that she'd given him something to direct his anger into.

"Oh, you're in for it now. It's a good thing we have all night because you just dropped the gauntlet," he said before pushing her onto her back. "Challenge accepted."

* * *

Brooklyn woke with a start, the soreness of her body making her cringe until she remembered why she was so sore. She felt a smile spread across her face as she stretched, a memory of the night before flickering through her head as her hand came in contact with the warm, hard body next to her. She could tell by the sound of his breathing that he was still asleep, so she rolled onto her side to face him. It didn't matter to her if it was creepy to watch him sleep, he looked so peaceful like he didn't have a care in the world. She wished for his sake that he could always be that carefree.

Part of her was freaking out in the way a teenage girl freaked out when her crush finally noticed her. The other part of her wanted to wake him up the best way she knew how. The fact that they'd barely gotten any sleep the night before made her keep her hands to herself, at least for a little while longer.

Even though the evidence was right in front of her, Brooklyn still couldn't believe the night before wasn't a dream. They talked, they laughed, they explored each other's bodies until they nearly lost their minds. It seemed like it was just yesterday they were arguing over something ridiculous, but if she really thought about it, the arguments had been few and far between since their trip to Vegas. Well few and far between if they ignored the whole storage closet incident.

Brooklyn wasn't sure when things had changed; when their relationship had gone from adversarial to something closer to friendship. If she thought about it, she realized it could have been when he saved her from Colin and then stayed with her for hours to make sure she was okay. It was far more than Brooklyn had expected and far more than most guys in his position would have done. Even though it ended with them bickering, as usual, she'd still felt closer to him that evening than ever before.

It also could have been the night of the rehearsal dinner when he'd made her feel better about her wedding. He didn't have all of the details, or really any of them, but he'd made her truly believe that her doomed marriage wasn't her fault. Most people wondered why she couldn't make it work. Not why Frank couldn't make it work or why they couldn't make it work, but why she couldn't. She'd spent too much of her marriage wondering what was wrong with her and then her marriage ended and she again wondered what she'd done wrong.

In all the time she'd known Declan, even when he was pushing her buttons, he'd never assumed she'd been at fault for her marriage imploding. He'd never thrown the failure of her marriage back in her face when it would have been easy fodder for their constant bickering.

"I can feel you staring at me."

His voice was gruff and sexy, like music to her ears. It had been so long since she'd woken up with a man in her bed and even longer since she actually liked the man she woke up next to. He opened his eyes slowly, a smile gracing his beautiful face as soon as their eyes met. God, he was gorgeous. Breathtakingly gorgeous. Even as he was just waking up the man put other men to shame. His jaw was covered with the scruffy start of a beard, which had Brooklyn's mind running wild with possibilities.

"Sorry, not sorry. It's like having a living, breathing painting in my bed. I'd never forgive myself if I didn't try to memorize all that makes up the magnificence that is Declan Reese. I mean truly. Have you seen yourself? It's unreal."

"You're ridiculous."

"No. You're ridiculous. I mean really. I've only seen bodies like this on Instagram. I figured they were as real as those simultaneous orgasms and then here you are blowing both of those myths out of the water for me," she said as she waved her hand from one end of his body to the other.

A blush crept up his neck and over his cheeks, surprising her. Declan had always come across as confident and while not a total douchebag, she always figured he knew how hot he was. For him to start blushing after a few mild compliments made him infinitely more attractive, which did not bode well for her ability to keep him at arm's length.

He recovered from his embarrassment quickly, pulling the sheet from her body before she could grab it. Brooklyn felt her skin heat up as his gaze roamed from one end of her to the other. She was sure she looked like a mess, but he seemed to appreciate what he was seeing. Her nipples tightened as his eyes lingered on her breasts.

Without warning, he rolled her onto her back, his body covering hers. She giggled as their legs tangled with her bedding. Her giggles quickly turned to moans of pleasure with every slide of his hand over her heated skin. Every inch of her body vibrated with anticipation, ready and waiting for his touch.

She nearly levitated off of the bed when he sucked one of her nipples into his mouth, his tongue teasing it into a hardened point. Her body hummed with the need to come as he took the same care with her other nipple. She bucked her hips up against him, hoping he'd get the hint. She tried to reach between them to take hold of his cock, but he moved so it was just out of reach. His fingers lightly brushed over her center then disappeared leaving her wanting.

When his body lifted off of hers, she whimpered at the loss and tried to pull him back against her. The knowing smile on his face made her blood boil. He was getting off on teasing her, and she was playing right into his hands.

"A little eager are we, Princess?" he asked, his tone cocky as hell and more than annoying.

She crossed her arms over her chest and stared up at him giving him her best 'whatever' glare.

"Actually, I'm a bit hungry, so if you could hurry this up, that would be great."

He looked down at her, not saying anything for a moment and then he laughed. A full out, deep roar that proved she hadn't fooled him at all. In fact, she was pretty sure she'd just made things worse.

"Oh, now you've gone and asked for it, you little brat."

His hands coasted slowly up her legs, from her ankles to her thighs. Goosebumps broke out in a trail following his path along her skin. When his thumbs brushed against the juncture of her legs, she bit her lower lip to hold back another whimper. As he continued to move closer to her where she needed him the most she fought the urge to roll her hips knowing it wouldn't help her situation at all.

Move in, then retreat. Over and over he nearly gave her what she wanted then took it back. Brooklyn was so close to cursing his name that by the time he finally thrust a finger into her she almost sobbed in relief. Then when he withdrew from her completely, she was thankfully able to keep her displeasure to herself.

Brooklyn tried to pretend like she wasn't affected, but she knew her acting skills weren't up to par. Declan smiled down at her with a knowing look on his face. His green eyes sparkled with menace and desire. It was then Brooklyn realized that he was just as affected by his teasing as she was. If she could push him to the edge, maybe he'd finally put them both out of their misery.

When he plunged a finger back into her, she clenched around him. As a whispered "Jeezus" fell from his lips, she smirked. He withdrew his finger again and watched her for a reaction. Instead of giving him what he wanted, she gave herself something she was craving. Brooklyn palmed her breasts, kneading the soft mounds of flesh, applying pressure to her hardened nipples.

The shocked look on Declan's face urged her on. Abandoning one breast, she moved her hand down over her abdomen until she reached her sex. As her fingers found her clit, she let out a long, loud moan, her back arching off the bed.

"What the hell are you doing?" Declan asked as he watched her carefully.

"What does it look like I'm doing?" she asked playfully. "I've been responsible for my own orgasms pretty much since I hit puberty."

"First of all the implication there is really fucking sad, second of all, when you're in bed with me, you will never have to be responsible for getting yourself off. That's my job, and I'm really fucking good at my job."

Brooklyn's arousal seemed to skyrocket at Declan's words. Was there anything sexier than a confident man who knew how to please a woman? She didn't think so. And if there was, she certainly couldn't think of anything at the moment. All she could think about was Declan and everything he was capable of.

"Prove it," she dared him knowing he wouldn't back down.

When he moved off of her, Brooklyn worried she might have miscalculated the situation, but then she heard the drawer of her bedside table opening. Throwing a condom onto the bed next to her hip, he maneuvered his body until he was lying between her legs, his head buried between her thighs.

"Fuck, that feels so good," she murmured as he licked and sucked at her like he couldn't get enough.

It didn't take long for her to reach the edge and plunge over. Declan's attention shifted from her clit to her opening and then back up. As she started to come down, he continued his relentless assault on her pussy, thrusting first one finger inside then adding another. Her body clenched around his fingers as he found the spot that drove her wild. She didn't think it was possible to come again so soon, but there she was, her body trembling, her toes curling.

"You're so fucking soaked."

"And ready for you to fuck me."

Declan cocked an eyebrow but didn't say a word. Instead, he sat back on his knees, grabbed the condom from the bed and quickly had it rolled over his cock. Brooklyn watched the entire show, which somehow felt like foreplay. By the time he finished she was even hotter than she'd been before he started.

He settled himself between her legs, his cock barely nudging her pussy. She refused to let him tease her anymore or let him take his time. Grabbing onto his shoulders, she used her weight to roll them over so he was on his back and she hovered over him. Taking his cock in her hand, she moved until she'd taken in just the tip, then before he could take back control, she lowered herself quickly until he was filling her completely.

She stilled for a moment, letting herself adjust to the delicious intrusion. Each time with Declan seemed to get better and better, the way he made her feel, the connection between them. It was about more than the sex, but Brooklyn couldn't let herself go there. Especially not while his hands were gripping her hips and his eyes were urging her to start moving

Taking the hint, she started to move. Slowly at first, but then her need to come took over. It had been a very, very long time since she'd had the opportunity to have morning sex and Brooklyn wasn't going to squander it. Especially not when the person she got to wake up to and then ride until they were both spent, was Declan. It was a dream come true...a very naughty dream, but that didn't matter.

Each time she lowered herself back onto his cock, she circled her hips so she could rub her clit against him. The dual stimulation had seemed like a good idea in the beginning, but the closer to orgasm she got, the harder it was for her to control her body. Using her hands against his chest as leverage, she tried to regulate her movements, but it was no use. Her body shook as her actions became sporadic.

"Just ride me, Brooklyn. I'll take care of you."

Knowing that he would indeed take care of her, she did as she was told. Leaning back, she pushed up until he nearly fell out of her then lowered herself back down. Over and over she repeated the move all while he pressed his thumb against her clit in tiny circles until she couldn't hold back any longer. She cried out as her orgasm blasted through her, nails digging into his thighs as she rode him.

As soon as she started to come down, she couldn't hold herself up anymore. Lowering herself, so she was laying on his chest, she wasn't surprised when Declan took over. His hands grasping onto her ass as he thrust into her in rapid succession. Less than a minute later he was coming, a long moan of her name falling from his lips as he thrust up into her one last time.

They laid like that for what felt like a long time, neither of them able to move after their intense orgasms. Her head rested on his chest, the sound of his heartbeat comforting her. She would never tire of waking up to this man, of waking up and making love to him. Closing her eyes, she mentally chastised herself for jumping the gun again. For all she knew this was a one-time thing. She couldn't get her hopes up.

Though she hated to move, she needed to separate herself from Declan so she could get her head on straight. She slowly moved off of him, rolling onto her back next to him on the bed. Her stomach rumbled, loud and low and embarrassingly long. Brooklyn covered her face with her hands and wished she could melt into the bed.

"You weren't making that up, you really are hungry," Declan said with a laugh.

He tried to pry her hands away from her face, but she wouldn't budge. Her cheeks were no longer just flushed from the fantastic sex, but with humiliation. The only thing that would have been less sexy at that moment was if she'd passed gas.

"It's not that big of a deal Brooklyn. Let me get cleaned up and I'll meet you in the kitchen. I'll cook you one of my famous breakfasts."

Brooklyn peeked out from between her fingers. "Wait. You cook?"

"Don't sound so surprised. I had to feed my daughter somehow, and Andi is what I like to call domestically challenged. It worked out okay though, especially with our schedules. I was always the one home for dinner, so it made sense that I did the cooking."

Before she could say anything else, Declan rolled over and tried to give her a quick kiss but couldn't break through the grip she had on her face. He laughed at her again then rolled out of bed to head for the bathroom. With his back to her, she moved her hands so she could watch him walk away, his perfect ass on display for her to drool over.

Once he disappeared into her bathroom, she searched the floor for something to throw on and found the Henley he'd discarded the night before. She quickly put it on then made the trek downstairs to the kitchen. It felt decadent to be running around in only Declan's shirt. The undeniable scent of him surrounding her, reminding her of what it felt like to be in his arms.

How was it that she'd just been fucked within an inch of her life, yet after smelling his shirt and feeling it against her sensitive skin, she was ready for him to take her again? She was quickly becoming addicted to him, and she couldn't decide if that was a good or bad thing. What she did know was that they needed to figure it out.

It didn't matter to her if they were dating or just friends with benefits. What mattered to her was whether or not they were exclusive. Although she wasn't usually one for casual sex, she wasn't going to pass up what Declan had to offer. But she would if he wanted to have the right to screw other people. There was no way she was going to go through that again. Not even if they agreed upon it ahead of time.

Not knowing what he was going to need for breakfast, she went about making coffee to keep herself busy. She could hear him upstairs, probably looking for his shirt. Brooklyn smiled to herself as she started to shake her ass. She liked the way the shirt felt against her skin, liked that it hit her mid-thigh, so it covered enough, but still felt sexy as hell. Plus, since she was wearing his shirt, he was going to be forced to come downstairs without one on...in all his toned, tanned, delicious glory.

Putting his shirt on was proving to be one of her better ideas all the way around.

"You look damn good in my shirt, Brooklyn."

Spinning around, she squealed in surprise. How the hell had she not heard him come down the stairs? Especially given the fact that a few were a bit creaky. She didn't know why she bothered even wondering. It was the picturing him without a shirt on that had distracted her. Now that she stared at the real thing, the image she had in her head hadn't done him justice.

Brooklyn fought the urge to reach out and touch him as he came closer.

"You look damn good without one on."

A light blush tinted his cheeks under his day-old scruff, once again giving him that carefree look she'd loved the night before. He always seemed so grumpy, but she was loving seeing him enjoy himself more. And she loved feeling like she was the reason why he appeared to be in a better mood as of late.

She handed him a cup of coffee, then made one for herself. While it brewed, she watched him move around her kitchen like it was his, checking drawers and cabinets and the refrigerator for everything he needed. They made small talk while he worked and once her coffee was made, she took a seat on one of the stools at the island so she could watch him.

"Since your kind of a captive audience here, I need to ask you something."

"Okay, go on," Declan said his eyes meeting hers for a moment before he went back to chopping up vegetables.

"I don't want to be that girl that gets pushy and wants everything defined, but what are we doing here? The first time we had sex you pushed me away and said it was a mistake. After we moved past that, you got me ridiculously thoughtful gifts, but still acted like I might be the devil. What is it you want from me, Declan? I want to make sure you aren't going to run out again, regretting what we've done while making me feel like shit in the process. I won't allow that to happen again."

"Look, I don't know what I want. I don't even know what I'm ready for, but I do know that I like spending time with you and I really like having sex with you. I promise I don't think this is a mistake and I'm not going to make you feel like shit. Fuck, I feel horrible that I hurt you. I'll do everything I can to make sure it never happens again. Can we just see what happens from here?"

"I like having sex with you too, and I suppose you're okay to hang out with," Brooklyn said but knew she had to change her tune with the look he was giving her. "Fine...you're more than okay to hang out with. I'm fine with taking things slow and seeing if we can even get along long enough to enjoy this. The only thing I demand in this situation is exclusivity. I will not share the person I'm sleeping with again. To be honest, I'm not ready for much more than sex anyway. I haven't done much...okay, any dating since my divorce and I don't know how to do any of this anymore."

"Well I don't know how to do any of this either, so we'll figure it out together, just us and we'll have a hell of a fun time while doing it. How does that sound?" Declan asked.

She could feel the uncertainty in his voice even though his body gave nothing away. He seemed so sure of what he was proposing, so sure that everything would be fine, but she knew deep down he was just as worried as she was that they were making some kind of mistake. That one of them would end up broken in the end.

She had a feeling it would be her that would end up battered and bruised. Declan was too damn easy to fall for which meant the not wanting a relationship thing wouldn't last for long. At least not for her. It was only a matter of time before her feelings were involved if they weren't already. In the end, she'd only have herself to blame, and at the moment, she couldn't bring herself to care.

If the entire thing came crashing down around her, engulfing her in flames, she would deal with it then. For now, she had to jump; she had to take a chance. She'd told her sister once that even knowing how her relationship with her ex ended she still would have gone through with it. The experience is what mattered, the growth that came from going through something like that. She knew that no matter what happened with Declan, she'd be better for having given in, for having gotten the chance to be with him.

So even though it scared the shit out of her; even though she was destined to walk away with a broken heart, she found herself telling him what he proposed sounded great. She was all in, ready to see where their attraction could take them. One day she'd probably look back on the moment and curse herself, but eventually, she'd get over it. For now, she was going to enjoy every single moment she had with him because she never knew which one would be their last.

CHAPTER 9

Declan

"Dad, hey Dad."

"Declan are you listening to us?"

His cheeks flushed with embarrassment over getting caught not paying attention again. He was supposed to be spending time with Erin and Andi, their last trip as a family before Erin graduated and headed off to North Carolina. Instead of bonding with his family, he couldn't keep his mind off the beautiful brunette he'd left back in Seattle; the one who was knocking his world off its axis.

"I'm sorry, I missed that. What were you guys saying?" he asked as he looked from his daughter over to his sister and back.

When they'd made the impromptu decision to head up to Vancouver for the long holiday weekend, Declan had been gung-ho about getting out of town. He was excited to spend time with Erin, thankful that Martin Luther King Jr's birthday gave her an extra day away from school. Now that they were on their trip, he was struggling with the fact that he missed Brooklyn. He wasn't used to such conflicting emotions.

"You know you could have invited her to come along this weekend," Erin told him.

"Who?"

"Don't play dumb, Dad. We all know what or should I say, who, you keep thinking about."

"I don't know what you're talking about."

He had no idea why he lied. The words just fell from his lips. Probably out of habit, maybe because he wasn't quite ready to talk about Brooklyn with his family. He didn't know how to explain what they were to himself, let alone other people.

"Bullshit," Andi said behind a fake cough.

"Yeah, what she said. We're not dumb. Pretty much everyone knows you and Brooklyn are dating now and we couldn't be happier."

"First of all, we aren't dating really...we're...I don't know. Second of all, who's this everyone, you're referencing?" he asked, turning to face his sister. "Are you guys talking about me behind my back? What the hell?"

"Apparently everyone's been waiting for you and Brooklyn to get together forever. So yes...we talk about you guys quite a bit actually."

Erin laughed a little too hard for Declan's taste. It irritated him a little that his daughter, his sister and apparently his friends all talked about his personal life. He was surrounded by a bunch of damn gossips. He didn't even understand why they thought his life was worth talking about in the first place. He especially didn't understand why Erin was so fascinated by it.

"Dear sister, why are you guys talking about my love life with my daughter?"

"Most of the time she brings it up," Andrea said with a shrug before taking a sip of her wine. She acted as if it was no big deal that his seventeen-year-old daughter was asking questions about his relationship status.

Erin started to laugh again, this time Andrea joined her. He tried to give them both his best disapproving look, but it only added fuel to their laughter. Neither of them seemed to be taking him seriously at the moment. He didn't want his daughter talking about his love life. It wasn't something she needed to worry about or bother herself with. In fact, he needed all of them to stop caring about it.

"Dad, I just want you to be happy, and I like Brooklyn, and I know she likes you. Why else would she have gone through all that trouble to put together those scrapbooks she made for you for Christmas? That was a lot of work. More work than you usually put in for someone who's just a friend," Erin pointed out. "So since you don't talk about what's going on between you two, I have to resort to checking in with everyone else."

"I don't talk about it because it isn't anyone's business."

"But I want to know," Erin said in her whiniest voice.

She looked at him like she used to when she was a little girl, her bottom lip sticking out, her eyes sad and pleading. Damn it. He was always a sucker for that look. Even now that she was nearly a grown woman, he wanted to give her whatever she asked for when she looked at him like that.

"Fine. I honestly don't know what's going on between Brooklyn and me. I like spending time with her, and we've agreed to see each other exclusively, but I'm not sure what that means. I don't know if we're dating or if it's just..." Declan paused remembering that he was talking to his daughter. "Ummm...anyway, we've both got baggage, some we haven't even talked about, so I don't know what that means beyond what's happening right now."

"I'm not a kid anymore. I know you guys are having sex."

Heat flared up Declan's cheeks as he fumbled for words. "We're...what...I mean..."

The girls started laughing at him again, and he felt his cheeks grow even warmer. He had no idea how to turn the conversation around, how to go back to thinking his daughter was innocent and didn't even know what the word sex meant; at least not when it pertained to her dad.

"Jeezus, I'm not talking about that with you, young lady. And now this conversation is over."

"Whatever. I don't care about that part. I care about you moving on from what the Egg Donor did to you."

"Honey..."

"I get it. I do. I know that she isn't the whole reason you haven't been in a relationship since I was born, but I do know her actions scarred you. They scarred all of us, and I think it's about time we all stopped letting her mess with our lives. You both deserve to fall in love with wonderful people and have children and lives that don't revolve around me."

Declan didn't know what to say. Erin's eyes were shiny with unshed tears, which wasn't that surprising given her sensitive nature. Unlike his daughter, his sister hadn't been able to hold her tears back. She turned away from them both, her body shaking as she silently cried. It wasn't like her to show emotion, though she'd been acting a little weird over the last month. He'd assumed it had to do with Erin leaving, but now he wondered if there was something else bothering her.

His heart broke a little as he thought about what Andi had given up when she agreed to help him. She didn't go to college. She didn't get married or have kids of her own. It hadn't bothered him to go without someone to share his life with because he had Erin. He would do anything to give her the life she deserved, even if that meant not bringing strange women into her life.

There was no doubt Andi loved Erin, but he never stopped to think about the fact that she never dated either. She could have. Erin wouldn't have looked at any man she brought around as a parental figure, unlike if he'd brought a woman home. It wouldn't have been as devastating to Erin if Andi's relationship didn't work out. Declan had no idea why Andi had opted not to date throughout the years, but he now worried she'd suffered because she was following his lead. He should have talked to her about it sooner. He should've made sure she knew she was free to be happy even if it meant leaving him to fend for himself.

He didn't understand how he could have missed the fact that she was unhappy. Growing up, he'd always felt like he could read his twin and that she could read him. They had the twin bond that everyone talked about. When she broke her wrist, he felt a pain shoot through his own wrist despite being hours away from her. When he learned about what Erin's mom did, Andrea knew he was in pain even though she was nowhere near the hospital.

Until that moment he'd never really given his connection with Andrea much thought because he was so focused on Erin and doing right by her. She was his sister, no way would that change, but if he really looked, he could see a shift in their relationship. They were still a unit stronger than others, but they'd stopped being honest with each other. Neither of them had spoken up about the fact they were struggling, and he was too blinded by his own issues to pick up on her unhappiness the way he used to.

Anger coursed through him, but he forced himself to tamp it down. This wasn't the time or place to say anything, and he was just as mad at himself as he was at her. He should have paid more attention. She should have spoken up. They were both to blame for letting things go for this long. For eighteen years they just went with the flow, never once questioning what they were doing.

"Oh, Aunt DeeDee, I didn't mean to make you cry. I'm sorry. I just want you both to be happy, whatever that means to you. I don't want to hold you back anymore. So if you want to go back to school or find someone to love or move back to West Seattle...please do it. I'm not going to be sad to come home to visit and not sleep in my childhood room. And I'm not against having siblings or cousins or an uncle or maybe a stepmom. In fact, I'd actually like all of those if you could both work on making those happen, that would be great."

"Sorry, baby, but I don't plan on having any other kids. You're it for me."

"Whatever. You might change your mind. I mean you and Brooklyn are both young, so just never say never, okay."

"Actually, never is the appropriate word here. I also think you're jumping the gun there a bit with Brooklyn. We just started seeing each other. Marriage and kids aren't even in the conversation, let alone the picture."

The minute the words were out of his mouth, flashes of Brooklyn danced through his head. In a wedding dress walking toward him down an aisle. Standing in front of him, showing off her belly swollen with his child. Lying in a hospital bed, a baby in her arms. It was easy picturing her in those situations, sharing those moments with him. Too damn easy. His chest tightened, and for a moment he felt like he was going to start hyperventilating.

He couldn't do it again. Fear clawed at him, reminding him what happened the last time he dated a woman he could picture that with. A woman who he actually experienced two out of three of those moments with. Of course, if he could go back in time, he wouldn't have changed what happened because then he wouldn't have Erin. But he couldn't allow himself to be in that position again, no matter how much he ended up loving someone.

"Okay. Whatever you say."

"Jeezus, can we change the subject already?" Declan asked as he rubbed at a knot in the back of his neck. So much for a relaxing family getaway.

"Only if you both promise me that you'll at least think about it."

"Sure, Bug. I'll think about it. To be honest, I have wanted to move back to West Seattle. I hate the commute to work and back, and the people are just ridiculous in Issaquah."

"Do it. Just not before I graduate because I don't want to deal with that commute either," she said with a wink. "Aunt DeeDee are you okay?"

"Yeah kiddo, I'm fine. I'm sorry I cried...must be getting close to that time of the month."

"Oh come on, Andi."

Once again Declan found himself being laughed at by both his daughter and his sister. It had been that way for as long as he could remember and he really didn't mind. He hated that Erin didn't have a mother in her life, but he would always be grateful that she'd at least had a strong female role model guiding her way.

Declan was pretty sure he'd never be able to show Andi just how much he appreciated what she'd done for him, He knew though that he needed to at least tell her what her sacrifices meant to him. Erin was right. Andi deserved to be happy, and he would help any way he could to make that happen.

In the meantime, his daughter's words had also made him realize that he and Brooklyn needed to talk. They might have decided to wait to see where things went, but if she wanted to have kids someday, then it didn't matter what could develop between them. He didn't want more kids, and he wasn't about to hold Brooklyn back from what she wanted just because he was already halfway in love with her.

He'd been a selfish asshole once already in his lifetime. He wasn't going to do it again...especially not to her. Even if he had to break both of their hearts to make sure of it.

* * *

Brooklyn

She was exhausted. Physically, mentally, emotionally, all of it. Between taking over more of the work at all of the bakeries and dealing with her conflicting feelings about everything around her, she was quickly losing her mind. She'd forgotten how difficult dating could be. The trying to figure out when to see each other and what to do, thinking about what every little thing could mean even though it probably meant nothing at all. Wondering if it was worth the hassle, especially when everything else was up in the air and all over the place.

With Savannah spending more time at home, Brooklyn was working ten to twelve-hour days, almost every day. She'd been able to hire more help to cover some of the labor they were missing with Savannah out, which had been an enormous help, but she was still working far more than she'd ever planned. Thankfully, Savannah was willing to do all of the office stuff from the comfort of her home saving Brooklyn from the tasks she hated the most

Brooklyn would have done it all without complaining, but she was damn glad it hadn't come to that. Payroll sucked and paying bills sucked even harder. She could handle getting up at the crack of dawn to bake cupcakes and the myriad of other goodies they sold. Having to deal with the numbers and other crap like that...she'd rather have someone pry off her fingernails.

Looking over at the clock on the wall above the sink, Brooklyn let out a sigh of relief when she saw it was finally time for her to head home. She still had a freelance project she needed to work on, her last for the foreseeable future, but she wasn't sure she'd have the energy to work on it once she got home. Work wasn't the only thing she had on her to do list, but it was the easiest.

The more she thought about it, the more she realized she'd rather work another ten hours at Delectable Delights then deal with Declan. Things had been different between them since his weekend away with Erin and Andi. In the two weeks since they'd been back, she'd seen him only once when he came to pick up their dog Stitch from her house.

They texted a little, but that was it. They were both busy with work, although the fact that she hadn't seen him during a delivery was a bit suspicious. Of course, he had a reasonable explanation, but it still set off her bullshit meter. Was he running? Had he changed his mind about them while they were gone?

There was a tiny part of her that hoped he had. It would save her the inevitable heartache later. Getting it out of the way now would be a good thing. She could move on, find someone else but just the thought of being with someone else made her nauseous. Which was why most of her hoped his work excuse was legitimate and that their schedules were making it too difficult to get together.

Shaking her head, she chastised herself for being crazy for possibly the millionth time in the last two weeks. She pulled off her apron, dropped it in the hamper by the sink then headed to the office to check the calendar and grab her purse. She already knew she had the opening shift the next day, but she wasn't sure if she was supposed to head out to any of the other locations to check in with them.

When she started working with Savannah, Brooklyn had no idea how much her sister did. Now that she was picking up the slack for her, she realized how little she still knew about what Savannah did on a daily basis.

"Crap," she muttered when she saw she had something else scheduled for the next day.

In all the excitement of the holidays and Savannah's announcement, she'd forgotten all about the wine tasting they'd scheduled to try out new wines for the bakeries. And now with Savannah knocked up, Brooklyn realized she was going to have to go to the tasting alone. She could ask Meghan or Kerrigan to go with her, but they were both wrapped up in their own situations. Although Meghan was making strides, she still hadn't talked to Oliver and Kerrigan was knee deep in work and preparing for her wedding.

As much as the wine tasting would be a nice break for both of them, if she invited either of them, she'd have to explain why Savannah couldn't go and her sister wasn't ready to tell anyone but family about the bun in her oven. Plus, neither of them were at the top of her list of replacements anyway. If she was honest with herself, Declan had been the first person she thought of. It would be the perfect excuse to call him and the perfect reason to get together. She would take whatever she could at this point. She just hoped he was free. Otherwise, she was indeed going to have to go alone.

It took her ten minutes to get to her car and drive home. She didn't live far from the shop, and while she walked to work in the summer, there was no way in hell she'd even think about it in the winter. Especially not at four in the morning.

After taking a quick shower and changing into a pair of lounge pants and a baggy sweatshirt, she sat on the couch staring at the phone in her hand. She'd gone as far as pulling up his phone number, but now that she was faced with the chance to call Declan, she was hesitating, fear pushing her confidence aside. She knew she had to get it out of the way and it wasn't like he'd end things over the phone anyway. That wasn't the type of guy Declan was. If he'd changed his mind about them, he'd at least do her the honor of telling her to her face that it was over. He wasn't that much of a coward or a total dick.

Before she could give it a second thought, she pressed the green call button on her phone. It rang once, twice. She assumed after the third ring the voicemail would pick up. When she heard a faint out of breath "hello" she nearly dropped the phone.

"Hello...Brooklyn? Did you butt dial me? What's going on?"

Realizing that she was still staring at the phone like it was going to talk for her, she put it up to her ear so she could hear him better. He said her name again and then once more before mentioning that he was going to hang up.

"Hey Declan, sorry...I uh dropped the phone. You got a minute?" Brooklyn asked her uncertainty more than evident in her voice despite her attempt to hide it.

"Yeah, of course. I've been meaning to call you. I'm sorry things have been so hectic lately."

"I get it. We're both busy. I'm sure you're trying to soak up every minute you have left with Erin before she leaves."

A weird sense of pride filled her as she thought about Erin getting accepted to North Carolina State. Erin had been so excited when she came to tell Brooklyn the excellent news. When the young girl hugged her and thanked her over and over for helping to change her life, they both started crying. Now that she was working more Brooklyn didn't get to spend as much time with Erin, but she knew she was going to miss the girl a ton when she left for school.

Declan chuckled. "I've been trying, but that girl is busier than I am between school, her volunteer work at the shelter and working at Delectable Delights. She's barely got any free time, and what little she does have she wants to spend with her friends, not with her old man."

"You'll get your time in eventually."

"I know. It's strange. I'm starting to get used to the fact that she's not going to be around every day. It still feels like my hearts being ripped out, but it's getting easier. So how are things on your end?"

"I don't know how Savannah kept up this kind of schedule for as long as she did. It's brutal. But I'll do whatever it takes to make sure that my sister and my niece or nephew stay safe and healthy. If we could just hire one more person, maybe as some kind of roving assistant manager or something, it would be better. The traveling between the four stores is what drives me crazy. Ten hours of baking stuff and chatting with customers, easy. The getting stuck in traffic and dealing with the drama at the other locations...not my idea of a good time. I don't know how you do it. I would lose my mind if I had to do as much driving as you do every day."

"I start early enough that it isn't too bad. I usually crank up the music and focus on that."

"Wait...what kind of music are you listening to? Please tell me that you bop around and sing along to whatever it is. Nevermind too late. I've already pictured it in my head, and the mental image is burned in there. FYI, you were singing along to Never Gonna Give You Up."

"I'm more of a Foo Fighters kind of guy, but Rick Astley is a classic. Who doesn't enjoy a good Rickroll?"

"Oh, I'm really enjoying this information."

"I'm glad I could make your day."

"Thank you...but speaking of making my day. Please tell me you don't have plans tomorrow evening."

"I don't have plans tomorrow evening."

"Would you be interested in attending a wine tasting with me? We're in the market for a few new vendors, and Andrea gave us a list of a few you guys work with. Savannah scheduled a tasting with one of them for tomorrow, but she obviously can't participate, so I need another partner in crime."

"I would love to join you. Maybe we could get dinner after?" Declan's voice wavered with uncertainty.

Brooklyn fought back the urge to do a little dance and instead tried to sound calm and collected. It didn't matter that her insides were doing little dances of their own, her stomach flipping nervously.

"Sure, dinner would be great."

Her words didn't come out as calmly as she'd hoped, but he didn't seem to notice that she was nervous and giddy and quite frankly freaking out a bit. She'd missed him over the last couple of weeks. Sadly, she'd missed him so much she would've gladly gone back to the way they were when they tried to get a rise out of each other. It would've been far more enjoyable than the relative silence. At least with the poking at each other, she knew where she stood.

"Great. What time should I pick you up?"

They made quick plans on when and where to meet the next day before Declan had to get off the phone. He was in the locker room at the gym he frequented, and people were getting annoyed that he was on the phone. She had no idea how he had the energy to go to the gym after working all day. Especially since he got up so dang early and worked a pretty physical job.

Then she started to picture him running on the treadmill, using the bottom of his shirt to wipe at his face, his perfect abs on display. The image then changed to him stripping his shirt off leaving every inch of his gorgeous chest open to her gaze. Pulling her long hair off her neck, she fanned at her face with her other hand, trying to cool down the heat that had taken over her body.

If just talking to him over the phone had elicited the kind of response where she was nearly melting into the couch, she wondered how she'd possibly make it through seeing him the next day without passing out. Or trying to strip him down at the winery or the restaurant. Although the last option sounded like more fun than the first, Brooklyn knew she was going to have to behave herself.

While she worked on that, she'd have to come up with a way to get him to come home with her so she could get her fix. At some point, she'd become addicted to Declan Reese, and without him, she was a horny, distracted mess. A problem she couldn't seem to get rid of without more Declan.

* * *

Declan

Nervous wasn't a word in Declan's vocabulary when it came to the opposite sex. Ladies loved him, even when he was still in school. They chased him around the playground in elementary school, asked to be his girlfriend in middle school, and offered him things they probably shouldn't have when they reached high school.

Even with Kara, he'd never been nervous because he knew she wanted to be with him, even after graduation. At least he'd always thought that was the plan. Even once his relationship with Kara ended, he had no reason to be nervous around women. He only went after ones that were a sure bet, ones that wouldn't get the wrong idea of what he was looking for, ones he'd likely never see again. It made his life easier when it was already filled with complications.

When he met Brooklyn, he knew his easy lifestyle was no longer an option. He was a goner the minute she looked at him then started an argument. Sometimes he felt a sense of peace when he was in her presence. Other times, he felt like he might throw up or pass out or do something so unbelievably stupid she'd never want to speak to him again.

As he sat across from her in the dimly lit restaurant, his palms were sweaty. His stomach flipped each time she looked at him. He'd hoped the bit of wine he'd drank at the tasting would have helped calm his nerves, but he obviously hadn't had enough. The uneasy feeling in the pit of his stomach started the minute he'd gotten in his car to drive to her house to pick her up. Now that they were over halfway through their evening he still felt like he was on the edge of a nervous breakdown.

If he was honest, what he was feeling had started when he was in Vancouver with Erin and Andrea. From the minute they'd had the conversation about what Erin hoped for their future, Declan knew he was going to have to talk to Brooklyn. He knew the bliss and serenity he'd felt over the two weeks prior would potentially turn to heartbreak once they spoke, so he'd avoided her to postpone the inevitable.

It was clear she'd been confused by his actions the day he picked up Stitch from her house on the way home from their vacation. He didn't give her a kiss like he had when he'd dropped the dog off. In fact, he did everything he could not to touch her at all. Instead, he picked up the dog with its pronounced underbite and scraggly fur, said a quick thanks and rushed out of her house.

Then he waited in the car while his daughter gave the woman he was falling for a hug and a huge smile. Two things he should have given her at the very least but couldn't seem to muster up while grappling with fear.

"I'm glad you were able to come with me today. I really appreciate it. I have to admit it felt good to spend some time with you. Hopefully, our schedules will be a bit easier to work around because I missed you."

Brooklyn's admission felt like an ice pick to his chest. He could have easily found time to see her over the last couple of weeks, but he wasn't ready. So instead, he threw himself into work, picking up extra stops, doing some of the paperwork that he detested so that he wouldn't feel guilty.

"I have to be honest with you, Brooklyn. I really have been busy since we got back from Vancouver, but I didn't have to be. I did it on purpose because I was too scared to see you."

Brooklyn looked at him a spark of anger in her eyes, her eyebrows furrowed in confusion, but she didn't say anything. She waited for him to continue with his confession. He rubbed a hand against the back of his neck not liking being under the scrutiny of her gaze. He was really beginning to fucking hate being nervous.

"I felt really good about things after our talk on New Year's. I was happy with seeing where things could go, but then Erin said something on our trip about the things she hoped to see in the future. It got me thinking, and then it had me second guessing everything. I don't know if you know the whole story about Erin and her mother or the Egg Donor as she likes to call her."

"The only thing I know is you have custody of Erin. I always figured if you wanted me to know more, you'd tell me. It's not really any of my business. Although Braeden did say she was a bitch."

Declan chuckled. Braeden was being nice by calling Kara a bitch. She absolutely hated Braeden, Gabriel, and Oliver. She hated that they took attention away from her. None of them ever liked her which should have been his first clue that she wasn't who she pretended to be.

"Well, it's kind of your business now because it plays into what I've been thinking about. Back in high school, I was kind of a big deal when it came to baseball," he admitted although it embarrassed him to do so. "It started when I was little. I just had a natural talent for the game. I played on a bunch of select teams against kids older than me. By the time I reached high school, I had college's already watching me, even though I was only a freshman. I was the first freshman to become a varsity starter while also being invited to practice with local college teams. I lived and breathed baseball."

"I knew you played, but I didn't realize it was that serious."

"I practiced nearly non-stop year-round, running drills and going to the batting cages even during the off-season. My junior year I started dating Kara. She was one of the most popular girls in school and the first girl I dated that didn't feel threatened by my dedication to baseball. She was encouraging and supportive, and it didn't take long before we were in love and planning a future together. She said she would follow me wherever I ended up going to college or if I ended up getting drafted out of high school."

"Wait, you were that good?"

"Yeah, some major league scouts were sniffing around my junior year. It was pretty surreal, but I was pretty firmly on the go to college first track, despite my dad's insistence that I get into the majors as soon as I could. I mean even if I was drafted out of high school, it still would've been years before I was even close to being at that level. He didn't seem to care.

Anyway, everything was set, my future was laid out for me, I just had to get through my senior year and then Kara and I could hopefully head to Tennessee to Vanderbilt, and I'd become a baseball superstar."

"But I'm guessing Erin changed all of that."

"I didn't see much of Kara over the summer because I was playing in a traveling summer league and she was off visiting relatives in Europe. She came back from her trip and broke the news to me that she was two months pregnant. We'd gotten a little careless the night before she left, the first and only time I ever went without a condom. She was on the pill, but neither of us knew that antibiotics made the pill worthless."

Declan stopped for a moment so he could take a sip of the beer he'd ordered when they first got to the restaurant. He didn't want to wait to finish his story because he knew their food had to come soon and he at least needed to get it out before then. He'd wait until after they ate to drop the bomb on her.

"She wanted to get an abortion, but her parents wouldn't let her because they were extremely religious, something I didn't know. Though in hindsight it explained why she never wanted me to meet them. Thankfully since she was underage, she couldn't get it without their approval. So she spent senior year behind closed doors, being homeschooled while my child grew inside her against her wishes. She refused to see me though her mother brought me pictures every once in a while. Kara never once told me what her plans were, so I assumed we would get married as soon as we turned eighteen and we'd raise our child together.

"On March fourteenth, Erin came screaming into the world. I'd never been so happy, even though my home life was in shambles. My dad was furious. Every day he told me I was ruining my future and I should get rid of the baby. When I made it clear that wasn't an option that I wouldn't give the baby up for adoption, he made it clear I wasn't wanted in his house."

"I know I've said it before, but your dad's an asshole."

"I won't argue with you on that. I was at the hospital the second Kara's parents told me she was in labor, but they wouldn't let me in the room. I waited for hours until her father finally came out to tell me I had a little girl, that her name was Erin. I was so excited that Kara had given her the name I'd wanted since it was my grandmother's name. I asked him about

Kara, but he handed me a manila envelope and told me where the baby was then walked away. I didn't open the envelope at first. I was in too much of a hurry to see my daughter. I forgot all about it while I held her for the first time. It was the most surreal amazing moment of my life."

Brooklyn smiled over at him and reached out to place her hand on top of his. She must have noticed that he was starting to get choked up talking about Erin's birth. It had been such a fantastic day that even the bad parts of it couldn't overshadow the miracle that he'd been given.

"I stayed with her until they kicked me out. I was the first to feed her, and I changed her first diaper. Thank god there were nurses there because I had no idea what I was doing. The whole time it never occurred to me that it was odd for me to be doing those things in the nursery. I didn't know any better. I didn't realize that those things should have been happening in Kara's room, that Kara should have been trying to breastfeed her instead of me giving her a bottle."

He watched Brooklyn swipe a finger beneath her eye to catch a tear that managed to escape. She was trying hard not to cry, but he knew it would be difficult for her to hold it in. He should have waited to tell her the story until they weren't in public, but he knew the odds of them talking while in the privacy of either of their homes was slim to none. They'd gravitate first to sex, then maybe they'd talk, but probably not. He'd be too worried of screwing up the post-sex glow that he wouldn't want to say anything.

"I finally opened the envelope when they kicked me out of the nursery. I didn't go far, just to a waiting room down the hall, but it felt like I might as well have been miles away. Inside the envelope were legal documents and a letter from Kara. In the letter, she admitted she never loved me but saw me as a means to an end because I was going to be famous one day and maybe she would be too. She never wanted kids especially not at seventeen. The last thing she said in that letter was that she never wanted me to contact her and I was to never to let Erin contact her either."

"Oh my god. How could she do that? I..." Brooklyn paused choking on the tears that were free-flowing now.

He flipped their hands over so he could squeeze hers. More than that he wanted to go to her side and pull her into his arms. It meant a lot to him that she felt so deeply for him and his child. He wanted to thank her and comfort her at the same time.

"I never got a chance to ask her why. Her family moved right after she got out of the hospital. She'd signed over her rights to Erin and also signed papers saying she'd never come looking for her either. That we wouldn't have to worry about her showing up years later to cause problems. I have to say it has been nice having that peace of mind, but I would have loved for my daughter to grow up with a mother instead."

"It doesn't sound like she would have been a very good mother though. She was selfish and superficial, and I'm sure Erin was probably better off without her."

"I'm sure you're right. In fact, I know you are. When Erin was about ten or so, Andrea went digging online trying to see if she could figure out what happened to Kara. From what little she could find, Kara was on her third marriage but didn't have any other kids. Each of her husbands had been well off and older. It looked like she was living the life she'd always wanted, although none of her husbands had made her famous yet."

"What a piece of work. I can't even imagine how someone could abandon their child like that. I could never imagine doing that."

"I don't know how she could have done it either. I mean, I had my life mapped out for me. Then they placed that squirming bundle into my arms, and I just knew I'd give it all up to take care of her. I loved her the second I saw her. People have asked me if I could go back in time would I change anything and I honestly wouldn't. I mean it was scary as fuck at times, especially when my dad kicked us out, but I love my little girl. I'm thankful that she's a part of my life."

"God, Declan. I didn't realize what you'd gone through and what you'd given up for her. You are a remarkable man."

Before he could respond, their waiter delivered their food, their conversation ending for the moment. They ate in relative silence, a few comments about the food here and there, but nothing as earthshattering as what he still had left to say. Declan watched Brooklyn when she wasn't looking. Even with her cheeks stained with streaks from her tears and her eyes rimmed with red, she was still the most beautiful woman he'd ever met.

For a moment he contemplated not finishing what he'd planned on saying, but then dread filled his stomach, threatening to evict his dinner and he knew he had no choice. Even if what he had to say pushed her away, he had to go through with it no matter how much it hurt. She deserved to know his truth so she could decide if they could continue exploring the connection between them.

Once they were finished eating and their plates had been cleared, Declan took a deep breath, steeling his nerves so he could finish what he started.

"Kara might have done the right thing walking away, but she left a lot of damage in her wake. Trust is hard for me. Letting someone in is even harder. I didn't even think about letting anyone in for the last eighteen years. Not until I met you. I didn't want to ever get Erin's hopes up. I didn't want to introduce her to women only to have them walk out of her life too."

"Oh Declan, I would never...you know I adore Erin."

"I do. I don't worry about that as much now because she's old enough to understand that some relationships don't work. But that's not what this is about. I like you, Brooklyn. I do want to see where this could go, but I feel like you should know that no matter how much I like you there is one thing I won't change my mind about. I'll understand if this is a deal breaker for you. It would be for most people."

"Just spit it out already, Declan. It can't be that big a deal."

"That's what you say now," he said before taking another steadying deep breath. "Fine. I'm sorry, but I don't want any more kids. Not now, not ever."

* * *

Brooklyn

Declan's words repeated in her head and instead of the heartache she'd been expecting to feel, she was elated. The fact she didn't have to be the one to broach the subject was only a small part of her happiness. The rest of it was because when she told him her story, he wouldn't turn away from her. Who better for a man who didn't want to have kids to be with than a woman who couldn't have them.

"Can we get out of here?" she asked.

"Are you okay? Are we okay?"

"Yeah, I just don't want to talk about this here if that's okay. Can we go back to my place? I have something I need to tell you."

A look of panic flashed across Declan's face before he was able to get control of it.

"Don't worry. I'm not about to tell you I'm pregnant. Although, I shouldn't have needed to say that since you've watched me drink a lot of wine in the last few hours," she teased. "It's a story I'd rather not get into in public since there's a chance there's going to be tears and not the silent ones like earlier."

He raised an eyebrow but then turned to find their waiter without saying anything else. He settled their tab quickly and then helped her into her jacket so they could head outside. They didn't talk during the drive back to her house. Thankfully, there wasn't much in the way of traffic, and the lights worked in their favor.

As soon as they got inside, she headed straight for the kitchen. She grabbed a beer out of the fridge for him and poured herself a glass of wine. He'd stopped in her living room, a look of uncertainty on his face. After delivering the drinks to the living room, she shucked off her coat and threw it on the love seat and then flopped down onto the couch. While he followed suit, she took a hefty sip of her wine realizing that she probably should have brought the bottle with her.

She waited until he was settled before she started. "I appreciate the fact that you wanted to be upfront with me. I've been thinking the same thing actually but wasn't sure how to go about it. How do you bring up children with a guy you're only kind of seeing? It's an awkward conversation for sure so thank you for bringing it up first, so I don't look like some kind of clingy chick jumping too many steps forward in a relationship that's not even really a relationship."

"I'm glad I could help...I guess."

Brooklyn laughed then took another sip of her wine. He picked up his untouched beer and downed nearly half of it in one swallow.

"The fact that you don't want any more kids works out for both of us actually."

"What do you mean?"

"Well, you don't want kids and well... I can't have kids, so it seems we make a perfect match."

She tried to play it off, but the look on his face told her that he didn't believe that she was as laissez-faire about the situation as she pretended to be. The fact that he could see that made her chest tighten. She'd hoped she'd be able to make it further into the conversation before she started to cry, but his understanding seemed to be her undoing. Declan put his hand on her knee, and the control over her tears broke.

"Tell me."

It wasn't a command though it wasn't a question either. Brooklyn sucked in a breath, held it for a moment and then let it out in a loud whoosh. She repeated the process a couple more times before she knew she'd be able to speak without a hitch in her breath. She hadn't planned on telling him about the first few years with Frank. They weren't that important to the overall story, but after hearing about Kara, she felt like he deserved to know that he wasn't the only one duped into thinking he was in a loving relationship.

From his pursuit of her after meeting the summer before her senior year to the whirlwind romance where she fell for every line he fed her hook, line, and sinker. The years where he wined and dined her and made her feel like the luckiest woman in the world. He was seven years older than her, gorgeous, sophisticated and rich. He could have had anybody he wanted, but he'd chosen her.

"We got married when I was 24, and he immediately wanted to start trying to have kids. I put him off for another year because I still felt too young even though being a mother was all I'd ever wanted as a kid."

The minute the words were out of her mouth, his face fell. It was apparent he could tell where this was going, although she knew he could only figure out part of her story. The rest was too much like a soap opera for anyone to guess. She still had a hard time believing what happened even though it'd happened to her.

"It only took me eight months to get pregnant once we started trying. I was so excited, I couldn't wait to tell my family, but we decided to hold off until after I was out of the first trimester. I lost the baby the day before we were planning on telling everyone the news."

"Oh, Brooklyn…"

"It took me another two and half years to get pregnant again. It was a long, painful time between pregnancies. Frank was anxious to have a baby. He didn't understand what happened or why it was taking so long. I was still devastated by the loss of the first baby, worried that it was going to happen again. He didn't want me to tell anyone about it, so I suffered alone, not even telling my family because I didn't want to upset him. I had the second miscarriage at ten weeks."

Despite the ache in her chest, she was surprised at how easily the words fell from her lips. The three-year span where she experienced the most significant losses she'd ever faced were the most difficult years of her life. She learned a lot from that time though, and she liked to think that she came out of them stronger than she'd been before. Of course, it wasn't easy, and sometimes she cried herself to sleep at night when she remembered what she lost and what it meant.

"Physically I was told to wait at least three months before we tried again. Mentally and emotionally I was a wreck, and I didn't want to try again at all. Frank was adamant though, so as soon as the doctor gave the okay, we tried again. Two months later I thought I might be pregnant again, so I went to the doctor for a blood test before telling Frank my suspicions. I didn't want to get either of our hopes up plus I wanted to find out what I was doing wrong. So I lied about where I was going."

She paused to take a sip of her wine. "I wasn't pregnant, and the doctor just told me to keep trying. That many things could lead to miscarriages. That I couldn't blame myself and I couldn't give up. So I went home to pretend like I wasn't devastated by the news. When I walked into the house, something didn't feel right. It was eerily quiet even though Frank was home. Then I heard it…a moan followed by another. I forced myself to walk up the stairs, forced myself to walk down the hall to my bedroom even though I knew what I was going to find. The noises had gotten louder, and they were undeniable."

"Jeezus..."

"Yeah, so I walked into my bedroom to find my husband fucking someone else in our bed. He was taking her from behind, so I couldn't get a good look at her, but she was blonde, turns out he had a type, and that wasn't the first time he'd cheated on me. Remember the shitty wedding I told you about, part of that included a good chunk of time where the groom went missing. It turns out he was fucking a friend of his sisters, a beautiful blonde with a tiny waist and big tits. The others I learned about after the divorce all varying shades of blonde, all beautiful. Turns out I wasn't as special as I thought I was."

"I'm gonna kill him."

"He's not worth it. I promise you that," she told him with a thankful smile. "Anyway, so there they were in all their naked, rutting glory in my bed and I just stood there. It took a good couple of minutes for it to really sink in and then I fucking lost it. I threw a shoe at his head, and when it hit its target, I actually let out a whoop of celebration. I picked up a few other things and threw them at him while I yelled at them to get out. It felt good, felt cathartic to take out my anger and pain on him. I tried to be careful not to hit the girl, for all I knew she had no idea he was married so I couldn't blame her. I knew how charming Frank could be. I watched her scramble out from under him and jump off of the bed. She tried to cover her naked body with her hands, but it wasn't enough. She couldn't hide the one thing that could deliver a blow far more devastating than walking in on them together.

"At first, I thought that maybe she was just a little overweight, but then I remembered that Frank was too damn superficial for that. He barely wanted to touch me after I gained a little bit of weight the first time I was pregnant. He'd even gone so far as to say he was glad I lost the weight while I was off limits because he didn't want to have to make me cover up while we had sex."

"You don't have to say anything else, Brooklyn. I always knew the man had to be a grade A idiot to let you go, now I know he's not just an idiot, but a fucking asshole as well. I'm so sorry."

"I realized later that I wasn't as hurt about the cheating as I was about everything else he put me through. He made me sweep my loss under the rug. I couldn't talk about it to anyone, not even him and I had to move past it sooner than I was ready to so I could try to get pregnant again. Then he ends up knocking up someone else, giving her the one thing I wanted more than anything else in the world. If he'd just been cheating on me, I could have left him and moved on a lot quicker. Instead, I've spent the last few years feeling worthless and broken. Like there was something wrong with me because I couldn't give him a baby."

"Brooklyn..." Declan said before reaching over to her and pulling her into his lap. He held her tightly against him, comforting them both as her heart broke again remembering everything she lost. She cried against his shoulder, while he rubbed her back.

"He married her six months after the divorce was final and I'm pretty sure they're still together. I no longer talk to his sister, even though we were friends first. She took his side in the divorce...not sure how that works. I guess family comes first, even if they are lying, cheating assholes. I found out later from Kerrigan that the reason he was so eager to have a kid was because of some clause in the trust that his grandpa set up. To get the final piece of his inheritance, he had to have a wife and kids before he turned forty. Apparently, he was hedging his bet by fucking a bunch of other women at the same time since my ability to make babies was proving to be faulty."

"I don't even know what to say," Declan admitted.

"It's okay. You don't have to say anything. Just know that you're not wanting to have more kids works really well for me. You don't have to worry about any of the rest of it. We can't do anything to change our pasts. What matters now is what we do with the rest of our lives. And I don't know about you, but I plan on enjoying the hell out of my life, and I'd like to start doing that with you right now."

Declan looked down at her as she knew he would. He'd want to check on her, make sure that her body language matched the flirtatious tone of her voice. She smiled up at him, their eyes locking on each other as her hands moved to the top button of his shirt.

"What did you have in mind, Miss St. James?"

"Why don't I show you, Mr. Reese."

And show him she did. On the couch, on the stairs, in her bed and the shower. She didn't question his need to use a condom each time despite her news. It would take a while for both of them to trust the situation, but they'd get there someday. Until then, she'd take every piece of him he was willing to give her and love every minute of it.

CHAPTER 10

Brooklyn

Looking around the room, Brooklyn realized how damn lucky she was to have the group of friends she did. Some, like Meghan and Andrea, were new additions to her inner circle, but fit in like they were meant to be there. Kerrigan had stuck with her throughout her marriage despite the fact Frank liked to try to push them apart. Brooklyn would forever be grateful that Kerrigan had ignored the asshole and continued to come around.

Then there was Savannah. While she hadn't always gotten along with her older sister, Brooklyn couldn't imagine her life without her. Savannah hadn't let Frank run her off either, and despite her ridiculously busy schedule, she checked in with Brooklyn as often as she could. She'd held Brooklyn together even when she didn't realize she was doing it. Their Wednesday night ritual during Survivor season had often been the highlight of her week while she was married and if it had been up to her husband, she would have missed every single one of them.

Girl's night had become a semi-regular occurrence for their group. Thankfully, Meghan was coming around more often now that she'd figured things out. She still hadn't entirely made up with Oliver yet, but Brooklyn had faith that she would. They were made for each other and Oliver was exactly who Meghan needed by her side while she dealt with what life had thrown at her.

Brooklyn was also glad that Declan's sister was starting to join them more often now that she felt comfortable with the group. From the minute she'd met Andrea, she knew they'd be friends, but at the time, she and Declan weren't exactly bosom buddies, so it made things a bit awkward. The closer she and Declan got, the stronger her friendship with Andi got. Brooklyn just hoped that if anything changed between her and Declan, she wouldn't lose Andi's friendship. She'd already gone down that road once before, and it sucked.

The ping of a cell phone grabbed her attention. Checking her phone and not seeing anything, she waited for everyone else to check theirs. The look on Savannah's face gave away the recipient of the text and as her sister started to laugh Brooklyn couldn't wait to find out what it said.

"Hey, stop it," her sister said as Brooklyn tried to grab the phone out of her hand.

Savannah hid the phone behind her back, her growing baby bump giving the hiding place added protection. Every time she saw Savannah, Brooklyn was in awe with the change in her sister. Not just the physical proof that she was pregnant, but the subtle things that most people probably wouldn't notice. Pregnancy brain was a genuine thing it turned out and her sister was knee deep in the phenomenon. Aside from that, she was always smiling, even when she felt sick to her stomach or overly exhausted. She was glowing and happy and ready to hold her baby in her arms.

"Hey, stop using my niece to distract me from whatever was so funny on your phone. Inquiring minds want to know," Brooklyn said as she waved her hand in the direction of the other women in the room.

Savannah smiled but didn't bring her phone out from behind her back. "Trust me, Brook. You don't want to see everything that's on there. The reason I was laughing though is Declan and Braeden. I need to know what the deal is with those two. Gabriel told me that they were best friends until high school and then something happened. Now they barely get along. He's not sure what the deal is, and neither of them will talk about it."

Brooklyn looked over at Andi and noticed that she was picking at the hem of her shirt. She waited for her to speak up, but the other woman continued to pretend like she wasn't paying attention to the conversation. Brooklyn wasn't buying it. If anyone knew what the deal was between her bother and Braeden, it was Andi. She was Declan's twin, after all. She'd been around them since they were kids. She had to know what changed.

"Andi, you have to know the scoop, right?" Brooklyn prodded.

Andi looked up, her bright green eyes wide like she'd been startled out of her thoughts. Her eyes were so much like Declan's Brooklyn often found it distracting. Currently, though she was on a mission to figure out the truth and Andi held the key. The animosity between her and Braeden rivaled that of her brother's, but there was also something lying just under the surface that Brooklyn noticed any time they all got together. Especially when the four of them had gone up to Vancouver for the hockey game.

"I don't know. It all happened around the time that Erin was born, and I was too focused on her and playing referee between my dad and my brother to pay attention to Braeden."

Brooklyn could hear the lie in her tone but would file it away for later. Someday she'd figure out what happened, but she liked hanging out with Andi, so she didn't want to push her too hard. There was something else in Andi's tone that jumped out at her. Something that sounded a lot like regret and a little like longing and she felt the need to test the new theory that sprang to life in her head.

"We need to find Braeden a woman. Maybe that would help the situation. Meghan, didn't you say it's been a while for Braeden?"

"Yeah to my knowledge, he hasn't hooked up with anyone since before our trip to Vegas."

"Wait, didn't he get his own room specifically so he could find someone to bang while we were there?" Savannah asked while Brooklyn watched Andi's face. Andi cringed at Savannah's choice of words, but it was barely perceptible. Brooklyn was fairly certain no one else even noticed since they weren't watching Andi like a hawk.

"That was what he said, but that wasn't really the plan. He's gonna be so mad at me for blabbing, please don't tell the guys. He doesn't want anyone to know. The only reason I do is because he got drunk at our place one night while he was helping me move in and he ended up blabbing about wanting to settle down and that it finally seemed like it was the right time. He told me he hasn't slept with anyone since he realized it was serious between you and Gabriel. Said it was only a matter of time before Declan settled down too and then it would finally be his turn. I didn't know what that meant though…I still don't."

Brooklyn watched Andi's eyes as they lit up, only to fade just as quickly, her shoulders hunched over as she went back to picking at the hem of her shirt. Her hunch had been right. She obviously wasn't 100% sure and she didn't know the whole story, but things had suddenly become a hell of a lot clearer when it came to what happened between Declan and Braeden and Andi. She had a strong feeling she'd find out sooner rather than later what the whole story was and she couldn't wait.

In the meantime, she'd do her friend a solid and change the subject even if it meant putting herself in the spotlight.

"Guys, I think I'm falling in love with Declan."

"I knew it," her sister yelled as she jumped up from the couch doing just the thing Brooklyn had pictured herself doing moments before.

"How could you have possibly known that? I didn't even know it until recently, and it didn't really ring true until I just blurted it out."

"Let's see...you talk about him all the time, you guys spend a ridiculous amount of time together for two people who technically aren't even in an actual relationship, and you are always flipping happy. It's a bit nauseating even for someone who's riding their own happy train at the moment. I'm sure Meghan and Andrea probably want to punch you, and Kerrigan has probably been too busy floating in her own bubble of happiness to notice."

"She's right. It's pretty gross. Especially since the one making you that happy is my brother."

"Well, I don't want to punch you. I think it's great even if it's a constant reminder of what I'm missing out on by not talking to Oliver."

"Oh, Meghan I'm sorry. I didn't..."

"Stop right there. I didn't mean it like that. It's actually helped me pull my head out a bit, Brooklyn, so thank you. In fact, I need a favor for tomorrow, but we can talk about that later. For now, let's hear about Declan. Sorry Andi, but I need details...is he as good as he looks?"

"Oh god..." Andi groaned. "I'm gonna go get a drink so please be quick while you talk about my brother's sexual prowess. Anyone else need anything?"

Andi took drink orders then quickly left the room before Brooklyn could start talking. She didn't blame the woman. If she had a brother, she wouldn't want to hear about how earth-shatteringly good he was in bed either.

"The man is unbelievable, Meghan. I mean...did you know that simultaneous orgasms are real? Like not just in books, but something that truly happens in real life? I never knew that until Declan. Hell, I didn't even know multiple orgasms were real until him."

"Seriously? Oh, Brooklyn, that makes me so sad for past you. What the fuck was wrong with your asshole of an ex-husband?" Meghan asked sympathy and anger warring for dominance over her pretty face.

"He was too busy fucking other women to worry about getting me off. I was just there as a broodmare, someone who would help him get the last part of his inheritance."

"Fucking asshole. I hope his dick rots off," Savannah muttered.

"Hey watch the language around my niece," Brooklyn teased, although she agreed with her sister's statement. "I'm sure the odds are in our favor with that. I will be shocked if he's been able to keep it in his pants with his new wife. That doesn't seem to be his style."

"Enough about that asshat, more about Declan before Andi comes back," Meghan urged a smile gracing her lips. "I know it's of my own doing, but I've been seriously deprived lately…I need, no I deserve, to live vicariously through you."

Brooklyn felt her cheeks warm as she thought about Declan and everything they'd done in the last two months. They'd quickly made up for the lost time from their two-week hiatus and then some. She hated the nights they spent apart even though she knew he was spending those nights with his daughter. Every time she felt a tiny bit neglected, she hated herself for it.

She wasn't a selfish person, but he made her feel like one because she wanted him all to herself. Part of her still felt like the bottom was going to fall out and because of that, she didn't want to waste what time they had left.

"Let's just say there isn't a room or a surface in my house that hasn't been put to the test. I need to pick yoga back up because I'm not nearly as flexible as I used to be. The man knows what to do with his fingers, his tongue, his dick…I mean it's pretty much a foregone conclusion that if we're together, there's an orgasm with my name on it. Unless Erin's with us."

"Are you done talking about him yet?" Andi called from the kitchen.

"It's safe to join us," Savannah told her despite Meghan's protest otherwise.

"It's not just about the sex though. I actually love being around him, even when he's pissing me off. He challenges me, he lets me be myself, he makes me feel like I matter, and he doesn't make me feel like I'm less than because I can't have kids."

Savannah reached over giving her knee a quick squeeze. It'd been trying in the beginning, watching her sister's belly grow bigger with her child, remembering that she'd never have the chance to enjoy the experience. Savannah had been so patient and understanding, knowing how hard it must be for her. The last thing Brooklyn had wanted to do was take away from the happiness of Savannah's pregnancy, so she sucked it up and put her big girl panties on. While it fucking sucked that she'd never have kids of her own, she was ecstatic about being an aunt.

"Are you sure you can't have kids? What if it was just a fluke or maybe your eggs hated Fuckface's sperm," Meghan suggested.

"That can't possibly be a thing, can it?" Andi asked.

"Well, I think it's pretty obvious the problem was with me. Fuckface has since had a child, and I'm still babyless."

"Maybe that's from lack of trying and not because your lady parts don't work. Did you guys ever get tested?" Meghan asked her inquisition grating on Brooklyn's nerves just a little.

"No. He refused. Said it wasn't necessary. Probably cause he was already lining up his backup plans. Look, I get what you're trying to do Meghan, but I've come to accept my lot in life. Plus, if I were able to have kids, it would change things with Declan, and I like the way things are."

"He told you he doesn't want any more kids, didn't he? Damn it, Declan." Andi shook her head as she sighed. "I had a feeling he'd wuss out."

"Declan doesn't want more kids? Why?" Savannah asked.

"Kara fucked him over and broke his daughter's heart. Ultimately, he's just scared. That's the gist of it. When we were in Vancouver, Erin told us that she'd love a stepmom and siblings someday. She also mentioned wanting an uncle and cousins too, so she's a bit delusional, but it freaked Declan out."

"That explains the two-week no-show he pulled. Let me guess. You guys talked after he stopped freaking out," Savannah said knowingly.

Her sister was one smart cookie. Instead of speaking up, she nodded and waited for Andi to say more. She needed more insight into the man she was falling for. She wanted to see more than he was willing to show her.

"Declan is the best man I know, but he struggles to get over what Kara did. What our dad did. We all do. Their decisions changed our lives more than Erin's appearance ever could have. If she'd stayed in the picture and if our dad hadn't turned into a giant asshole, Declan could have probably still gone to college, he could have played baseball. I could have...just our lives would have been different. I know he doesn't regret Erin, but he's also never forgotten how one person...well two people's selfish decisions changed everything."

"I'm sorry, Andi."

"It is what it is. I've come to accept it, and now that Erin's getting ready for North Carolina, I think it's finally time for me to step out of my comfort zone and put myself out there. Kerrigan, I was looking on Finding Love's website a couple of weeks ago and saw you guys were looking into putting together speed dating sessions. Is that true?"

"We're still in the early stages, but yeah. I've been a little pre-occupied with wedding planning, so we pushed them back a bit, but we're hoping to have them up and running by the end of the summer."

"Perfect timing. Erin will be in North Carolina, and Declan will be preoccupied with Brooklyn. I don't think I'm ready for the full blown Finding Love experience, but I think I can handle speed dating. Let me know when it's time to sign up."

The conversation devolved quickly into story after story of some of the worst dates they'd been on and horror stories they'd heard from friends. Brooklyn's stomach ached from laughing so hard by the time it was over. Once again, she thought about how lucky she was to have such a great group of friends. They could talk about anything and everything and still have a good time. No matter what happened with Declan or any man for that matter, she knew she'd always have her friends, and that was more than enough for her.

* * *

Declan

"Thank you for coming to the wedding with me. I know it couldn't have been that fun to sit through the ceremony by yourself."

"I don't know, I was really enjoying the scenery. Right now my patience is proving to be well worth it," Declan said as he moved his hand over the bare skin of her back.

He had no idea who kept picking out Brooklyn's bridesmaids dresses, but he really needed to thank them. The navy-blue gown fit her like a glove. While the halter top didn't give him the nice peek at her cleavage the other one did, it gave him plenty of bare skin to touch and kiss and lick when they finally left for the night. It was all he thought about during the ceremony. He had no idea what Kerrigan or her husband said during their vows because he'd spent the entire time picturing Brooklyn hiking her dress up and riding him until she screamed his name.

It wasn't lost on him that it was a wedding that'd originally gotten him into trouble with Brooklyn. Where he first realized he couldn't deny his attraction to her. Where he realized that he needed her. At least this time he wasn't going to fuck her then say something so monumentally stupid he thought he'd never be able to make up for it.

He pulled her closer until she rested her head on his shoulder. They'd danced nearly every slow song together since the reception started. Declan wanted her in his arms whenever possible. If that meant he had to spend time on the dance floor, he was willing to do it. He never wanted to let her go. Whenever they were apart he felt like a piece of himself was missing. When they were together, he felt like he could do anything, be anyone. She made him finally feel at peace.

He knew without a shadow of a doubt that he was in love with Brooklyn St. James.

The revelation had startled him when he'd realized it the week before. He'd yet to tell her how he felt, but it was only a matter of time. Though they'd never really talked about what they were doing, it was apparent they'd moved past the just seeing where this could go stage and into the full-blown relationship stage. Falling in love with her had been inevitable. He couldn't have fought it even if he'd wanted to, which he didn't. He just hoped she felt the same.

His chances were pretty good, but he'd never underestimate a woman's ability to pull the rug out from under him again. It surprised him how eager he was to tell her how he felt. To look her in the eye and say the three little words. I love you. It would be that simple.

Brooklyn stopped moving her body stiffening in his arms. She pushed back and looked up at him, shock written all over her face.

"What did you just say?" she asked.

"What do you mean? I didn't say anything."

"You said something out loud just now Declan. What was it?"

"Fuck," he murmured as he realized what he'd done. "That wasn't how I wanted that to go down."

"Did you mean it?" she asked the tone of her voice not giving away even hint of the pleading he saw in her eyes.

He smiled down at her, then took her face in his hands. "Brooklyn, I'm so in love with you I can't see straight. You're all I can think about. Every dream I have is about you. You're everything I could ever want and ever need," he admitted. "I had this all planned out, it was going to be a hell of a lot sweeter and a hell of a lot more private, but apparently, my subconscious was tired of waiting for me to tell you that you own my heart. Please be gentle with it, this whole love thing is still new to it, and it's not really sure what it's doing."

Before she could respond, he leaned into her brushing a chaste kiss against her slightly parted lips. Her eyes fluttered closed as he kissed her again. A soft sigh fell from her lips, the sound rushing straight to his dick despite the sentimental tone of the moment. He pulled away, his hands dropping to her waist. She looked a bit dazed when she finally opened her eyes. Then the most beautiful smile spread across her face as she threw her arms around his neck.

Her eyes locked onto his, her feelings written all over her face, her hazel eyes shiny with tears.

"Oh Declan, I love you too. So much it's a bit scary. I've never felt this way before. It's both exhilarating and terrifying, but I wouldn't change it for anything. You have my heart too. You have for a while now. I just didn't know how to tell you."

"Silly girl, all you had to do was say the words. I would have treasured them."

"I was afraid they'd send you running," she admitted.

"Not this time. You aren't getting rid of me that easily. Think we could get away with cutting out early? I need to take you home and make love to you."

"Thank goodness. Let's go. I don't think anyone will notice if we leave and if they do, oh well."

Declan grabbed her hand and led her from the dance floor to their table to grab her purse and their jackets. She said a few quick goodbyes, then waved at Kerrigan who was on the dance floor with Ben. The look on Kerrigan's face told him the redhead knew exactly where they were headed, and she approved. He gave her a small wave of his own then let Brooklyn lead him toward the entrance to the venue.

Once they were in his car, he reached over and took her hand. He needed to touch her, to ground himself by feeling her skin against his. Admitting his feelings out loud made him feel like he was flying high. It was a feeling he wasn't used to, one that made him nervous and a bit uncomfortable.

He'd thought he loved Kara all those years ago, but what he felt for her wasn't anything like what he felt for Brooklyn. Giving her his heart gave her power over him and he wasn't sure how he felt about that. He just knew he wouldn't take any of it back. He wanted to be with Brooklyn more than anything, and he was willing to take on whatever bumps he'd have to face along the way.

* * *

Brooklyn

Being in love was weird. Sometimes she was floating on a cloud of hearts and flowers. Then she'd start to worry about how bad it would be when things came to an end. Brooklyn had spent a lot of time over the last couple of weeks comparing how she felt about Declan to how she felt about Frank, and it wasn't even close. Her feelings for Declan gave him the power to destroy her. Frank only had that power because he lorded her inability to conceive over her for so long, he'd broken her down.

Declan didn't have to break her down. He didn't have to do anything other than be himself. She was a goner no matter what. Every time she started to think about things ending, she reminded herself that it didn't have to end. While there were no guarantees, either way, she couldn't spend her life tied up in knots over what might happen. So instead of focusing on the unknown, she vowed to enjoy every moment they had together.

Starting with their plans for the evening. She looked at herself in the mirror, her make-up nearly finished. A new song started on her phone, one with an upbeat tempo that had her shaking her ass as she combed out her long dark hair. She couldn't wait to give Declan his birthday surprise. It was something she knew he'd love and would have never tried to get for himself. It made her giddy just thinking about how much he was going to enjoy it.

"Now that's what I'm talking about."

Declan startled her from her less than stellar bathroom dancing. He stood leaning against the doorframe watching her. She met his eyes in the bathroom mirror, lust filling them as they roamed over her body, then back up to meet her gaze. He pushed off and stalked toward her like a predator going after his prey.

Her heart rate ramped up, her body aching for him to touch her. But they were on a schedule, and if they did what he had in mind, they'd end up being late. Something that could not happen.

"Declan, we don't have time for that," she told him as she watched him in the mirror.

"I'm not sure how you think I can walk in here, see you dancing around in your tight little tank top and barely-there panties and not bend you over the vanity and fuck you."

"We're gonna be late," she protested weakly.

There was no use arguing, not that she wanted to. Her panties were soaked the second he looked at her like he was going to have her for dinner. He pushed up against her, his big body trapping her against the sink. She pulled her bottom lip between her teeth, the anticipation of the moment driving her crazy.

"I'll make it quick…amazing, but quick. I don't think I'd be able to hold out anyway. Your ass is fucking unbelievable."

She shivered as he ran his hands over her hips under the elastic waistband of her underwear. He pushed them down while spreading her legs at the same time until they caught at her knees. She watched as he moved behind her, positioning her, so her ass was thrust out against him. He swept a finger between her legs, moaning when he met her wetness.

"We don't have all night," she reminded him as she pushed her ass back against his rock-hard erection.

He smirked at her in the mirror, then leaned to his right to open the cabinet drawer and fish out a condom. He quickly freed himself from his pants, pushing them and his boxers down until they were out of the way. Before she realized it he was thrusting into her, his body slapping against hers as he filled her to the hilt.

With his hands gripping her hips, he fucked her relentlessly. He took her fast and hard, and it was magnificent. She watched their bodies, watched his face. He was a sight to behold taking what he needed from her. She pushed back against him with each thrust of his hips, her body gripping at him, trying to pull him deeper.

"Fuck," he moaned as he tensed behind her then started to thrust into her earnestly even though he was barely holding on.

He pulled her back against him, one hand resting against her chest, the other snaking around her waist to the juncture of her thighs. The thrusts of his hips slowed, but the assault of his finger on her clit didn't. She watched in the mirror as he played her like a fiddle, her eyes nearly crossing the second her orgasm hit.

Her walls clenched around him until he could no longer put off his own pleasure. He thrust into her once, twice, then tensed behind her as he let out a long, low growl of satisfaction.

As they came down, he rested his forehead against her shoulder. Brooklyn was fairly certain her grip on the counter in front of her was all that kept them upright, at least it was all that kept her from sinking to the floor.

"Well, that was one way to start my birthday celebration off right," Declan muttered against her shoulder.

"Your birthday has been nothing but sex so far. This morning when we woke up, before and after lunch and now we're going to have to hurry so we don't end up being late all because you needed another quickie."

"Hey, it's my birthday, I should be able to do what I want, and you are exactly what I want. Always," he said.

He lifted his head so he could meet her eyes in the mirror. She might have been teasing him, but she could see he meant what he said. His words filled her with warmth, her body tingling, not from the orgasm but from the love emanating from him.

There was no doubt she was in deep with him. There was no going back to being just friends, no going back to the playful bickering. This was where she wanted to be, in his arms, wrapped up in his love. Always.

*　*　*

"Love looks good on you."

The clang of metal crashing against metal filled the room. "Damn it."

"Too busy daydreaming to realize someone else was in the room? Yeah, love looks really good on you sister dear."

Brooklyn sighed as she leaned down to pick up the cupcake tin she'd dropped when her sister startled her. When Savannah had become as stealthy as a ninja, she wasn't sure. Especially since she'd been facing the direction her sister entered the kitchen from, and she hadn't noticed a thing. Not to mention the fact that Savannah was very, very pregnant, which didn't usually lend itself to stealthy tendencies. The entire situation would have been a bit troublesome if she didn't know exactly why she'd been so distracted.

Declan Reese...the owner of her heart, the man of her dreams and every waking thought. It had been a little over a month since the night they made their mutual declarations. Since then her focus had been all over the place. Thankfully, only a quarter of the time had been spent thinking about when everything was going to go wrong. Brooklyn felt pretty good about the fact that she no longer spent all of her time thinking about the end. The more time they spent together, the more she heard those words from his mouth, the more comfortable she became.

"Sorry. I'm a bit spacey lately," Brooklyn admitted before turning to throw the cupcake tin into the sink to be washed.

"I get it. Love does that to you. It doesn't matter how long you're together. You'll find yourself zoning out, thinking about him, about the two of you and what the future holds."

"I've been waiting for the other shoe to drop."

"Hell, I still do that on occasion. Especially right now. Every time I feel especially fat or especially crazy, I think about Gabriel trading me in for a skinnier, less hormonal model."

"Now that's ridiculous. First of all, you're pregnant, not fat. Second of all, your husband loves you more than anyone else in the world. He's not going to trade you in for anything else, even if you did get fat or your hair fell out, or you officially lost your mind. You've got nothing to worry about."

"Neither do you. I see the way Declan looks at you. He's head over heels in love with you, Brooklyn. I think you can stop worrying about that other shoe and whether or not it's going to drop."

Brooklyn smiled at her sister, more to appease her than to prove that she believed what Savannah was saying. She wanted to, but there was a piece of her that couldn't stop thinking about the end. She feared that piece of her would always be there. It would always be lurking under the surface wondering if this was the day everything went to shit.

"You should sit down. You look uncomfortable."

"I'm not staying long just needed to drop some stuff off in the office. I figured I could bug you a bit before I left. What time are you guys leaving for the auction tonight?"

"Declan's picking me up at five."

"Well thank you for being the Delectable Delights representative and for bringing the auction to my attention. I'm glad we could put together a couple of items for people to bid on. Gabriel said something about the possibility of some celebrities being there?"

"I think there might be a couple of Mariners in attendance and a couple of former Seahawks. I also heard that Chris Pratt might show up since he's from here and all. I'm not sure. I can't believe that Declan and Andi are getting some type of award. I didn't realize they donated so much money to the local shelters, although with Erin's passion for animals, I shouldn't be surprised."

"I didn't know either. Is Declan going to give a speech? If so, can you please record it?"

Brooklyn tucked a stray hair behind her ear as she laughed. The thought of Declan doing any kind of public speaking was ridiculous. He might have been happier since they started dating, but he was still Mr. Grumpy Pants, who hated attention and people nearly equally.

"Yeah, I didn't think so. Well, I hope you guys have a great time tonight, and if Chris Pratt does show up, please get pictures. It seems I'm destined to live vicariously through you and Finley when it comes to being around hot male celebrities."

"Don't forget Meghan and her dalliance with Aquaman."

"Her husband definitely knows how to plan a great date."

"Yes he does," Brooklyn said with a sigh as she thought about the hotness that was Jason Momoa.

It didn't take long for the picture in her mind to shift to Declan, her real-life hottie. She never got tired of looking at him, never got tired of thinking about him. Tonight, she would be proud to be on his arm while people congratulated him and thanked him for his commitment to helping the local shelters. It might've been too soon to admit it to anyone other than herself, but Declan Reese was the man she wanted to spend the rest of her life with. She just hoped he would eventually feel the same about her.

* * *

Brooklyn had never had more fun at a black tie shindig before. She'd been to a ton of them back when she was married. Dull affairs that she despised but had to put on a happy face for because of Frank's family. The charity auction for the Washington State Shelter Foundation was what all charity auctions should aspire to be like, and she held the reason in her hands.

"Are you ready to go?" Declan asked her for the second or maybe the third time.

Looking over at him, she shook her head, then squeezed the furball closer to her chest. She kissed the squirming ball of fluff, then held it up so she could look at it. The kitten was black with one spot of white along its nose. It made Brooklyn sad that black cats were the most common in shelters because of the stigma attached to them. The adorable beauty in her hands didn't seem like bad luck at all.

"Seriously, this is the best party ever. Why doesn't everyone have cats and dogs at their stuffy functions? They'd be far less stuffy if they did and then everyone would enjoy them."

"I think you've held every single animal they brought with them today."

"Of course, I did. They all need some love and who better to give that to them, then me?"

She looked around at the empty pens and kennels and smiled. The animals hadn't just been there to bring joy to those in attendance. They'd been there in the hopes that people would fall in love with them and want to adopt them.

"It's so great that so many of them found new homes. I wish I could take the rest home with me."

"I think one is enough for you at the moment. You can add to your menagerie later once you get the hang of being a pet owner."

"Hey, I've owned a pet before."

"Really?"

"Well, we had a family pet back when I was a kid. And hey, I did a great job watching Stitch for you guys when you were in Vancouver."

"Yeah and I distinctly remember you saying that he was high maintenance."

"He is. Adorable, but super high maintenance. He hated going outside to go to the bathroom when it was raining. He constantly needed attention, even when he was sleeping. And he has cuter sweaters than I do."

"Okay fine. That dog is a bit much, but all pets have their quirks. I think it's smart that you're starting with a cat. They don't need a whole lot, and she probably won't even want to cuddle with you all that much."

"Don't say that. I hope she wants to cuddle with me all the time. I need someone to spoon with when you stay at your house."

"Well, then I hope she does the trick. I don't want you to be lonely. Now, can we go? I want to get you home so I can get some naked cuddling in before heading home. Tomorrow's Mother's Day and we've got a family tradition to uphold."

They gathered their jackets and the care package that came with the kitten she'd adopted. She snuggled the cat into her coat to protect her from the rain as they ran to his car. The drive from the hotel to Brooklyn's place took less than half an hour, which was great for a Saturday night. She quickly got the kitten set up with a litter box and some food before she let Declan lead her upstairs to her bedroom.

Once inside they made quick work of each other's clothes before finding their way to the bed. She knew by the look on his face she was in for a long luxurious lovemaking session and not one of their earth-shattering quickies and she wasn't wrong. He spent more time than necessary bringing her to the brink with his tongue pressed against her clit; his fingers buried deep inside of her. Each time she got close to going over, he'd back off, peppering kisses along her thighs, her pelvis or her stomach before jumping right back into driving her crazy.

By the time he slid on a condom and buried his cock inside of her she was nearly spent. Her limbs were heavy, her heart threatening to pound right out of her chest. Even though he'd proved otherwise more often than she could count, Brooklyn thought for sure there was no way she could come again, no way he could ring more out of her body.

She was never happier to be wrong. His stamina was unrivaled, his ability to hold back his orgasm while he brought her to completion over and over was unbelievable. Another thing she'd only ever read about before Declan. He moved in and out of her slowly, some thrusts were shallow, others as deep as he could get. Lowering his body onto hers, he rocked into her while seeking her mouth with his. His tongue delved into her mouth, teasing her tongue the way his cock currently teased her g-spot.

When he pulled back to catch his breath, she looked up at him, her vision slightly hazy from her current blissful state. She could tell by the look on his face his control was slipping. He pushed her legs back until her knees brushed against her breasts, then pushed them apart allowing him to go deeper.

He circled his thumb around her clit, then pressed it against the sensitive nub, sending sparks flying behind her eyelids. As soon as her body began contracting around him, he started to pound into her. The sound of their moans and their bodies slapping together filled the room. His rhythm faltered quicker than she expected and before she knew it, he was coming hard inside of her, hitting just the right spot to set her body off with another mini orgasm. His jaw dropped open, his head fell back, the muscles in his arms flexed as he pushed into her one last time.

He held her legs back until they were both spent, then he let them fall to the bed. Brooklyn could already tell she was going to be sore from this round, but she didn't care. It was so hot watching Declan come. She'd give up walking for a day, just to see his "O" face.

"Jeezus...that was..."

"Amazing, wonderful, fucking fantastic," she suggested.

"Yeah...all of that and more," Declan said giving her a quick kiss before pushing off of her.

She watched him sit back on his knees so he could pull off the condom. Every move he made was sexy, even one as mundane as disposing of the evidence of their lovemaking. One day she still held out hope he'd feel comfortable enough to do away with condoms. They'd been together for four months, having sex for five. She didn't understand what he was still so afraid of. They were both clean, and there was no chance of her getting pregnant. It bothered her a little that he still insisted on using the thin latex barrier. Like he didn't trust her enough to give himself over to her completely.

"Fuck. Fuck. Fuck."

Brooklyn sat up, her eyes tracing over him to figure out why he was suddenly freaking out.

"What's wrong?"

"The condom fucking broke, that's what's wrong. Fuck. This can't be happening."

"It's not that big of a deal, Declan. I can't get pregnant."

"But you're not on the pill right?"

"No, but I spent half a decade trying to have kids and couldn't make it happen. We're fine."

"You can't be sure," he said as he jumped off the bed. Her agitation level skyrocketed as he started pacing back and forth from one side of her room to the other.

"I'm pretty fucking sure, Declan. Stop freaking out."

The more he talked, the more he paced, the angrier she got. Her hands clenched into fists in her lap, her teeth ground together, her jaw tensed as she waited to see what he said next. She had a feeling she wasn't going to like it any more than she liked the bullshit that had already come out of his mouth.

"You could get the morning after pill so we can be one hundred percent positive."

Her vision went black for a second, her nails digging into her legs as she took a deep breath. She held that breath until her lungs screamed and then some. When she finally let it out, she repeated a new mantra in her head.

I will not murder him. I will not murder him.

"Seriously?" she asked. "A...those aren't 100% effective, and the side effects are shitty, and you know what...FUCK YOU."

He stopped, his eyes locking with hers. She could see the panic written all over his face. The fear that gripped him but she didn't care. He was throwing her pain, her failure, back at her and she hated him for it.

"I can't go through this again, Brooklyn."

Anger propelled her out of her bed. She wrapped the sheet around her body as she marched toward him.

"Wow...I....you need to go," she said as she gathered up the clothes that he'd discarded earlier.

"No. We need to talk about this. I need you to understand."

"No," she said as she shoved his clothes into his arms, tears starting to stream down her face. "I need you to get the fuck out of my house."

"Brook..."

"If you loved me, Declan, you would have never asked me to take that pill. If you loved me, you'd know that I could never, would never abandon any child I was blessed with. I am not Kara, and I could never be like Kara," she said her words catching on her sobs. "The fact that you're even a little worried about that tells me everything I need to know. Get the fuck out of my house, Declan. I never want to see you again."

She pushed him backwards through the open door of her bedroom, then slammed it in his face. Leaning against the door, she tried to hold it together. He said her name a few more times, but then finally gave up. She could hear his footsteps on the stairs and the opening and closing of her front door. A sob tore from her throat, her shoulders shaking with each ragged breath she took. She could no longer control the pain, no longer control the anger.

Throwing herself down on her bed, she let herself cry until she had nothing left to give. Even through her stuffed-up nose, she could smell him on her sheets. She could feel him on her body. With her tears all cried out, she went about eradicating his existence from her sanctuary. She took a long, scalding hot shower, then pulled the sheets and blankets from her bed.

Once the sheets were loaded into the washer, she laid down on the couch, a cheesy movie on the tv and her new best friend perched on her chest. She absently ran a hand over the kitten, loving the way her purr seemed to comfort her. It was exactly what she needed to help her through the rough night.

Come the morning she would suck it up and move on. She always thought what they had would end, that it was inevitable. She was prepared for it in a way. Her brain was on board to forget all about him. Now she just had to talk her heart into getting with the program something that she knew was going to be easier said than done.

CHAPTER 11

Brooklyn

Sometime during the three weeks since she threw Declan out of her house, Brooklyn had found herself becoming a philosopher of sorts. She spent most of her time thinking about time and how it seemed unfair that when she was enjoying life, time seemed to fly by. In the blink of an eye, a month had passed, and memories started to fade away. Then when life was miserable, time seemed to come to a standstill, memories of horrible moments sticking out like beacons in her brain to keep her from forgetting all about her pain.

In the three weeks since the breakup, Brooklyn had found herself flashing back to the moment where Declan ripped her heart out and threw it onto the floor. She couldn't seem to remember the moments before it when they were happily making love or the weeks before that when they were going to baseball games together and holding hands while out walking his dog.

In the blink of an eye, her entire life changed, and she couldn't even entirely blame him for everything that happened. Maybe they could have talked it out; maybe she could have gotten him to see reason. She knew in the moment that he was too wrapped up in his fear to see what he was saying or doing. At least that's what she wanted to believe. The fact that he hadn't spoken to her since that night, sort of proved her wrong...if she bothered to think about it too long.

With Declan out of her life, she threw herself back into work. She didn't have anything else to do so she baked and cleaned and ran around to each of the shops. While they were dating, Brooklyn had started working more regular hours, eight maybe nine hours every day. Now ten, sometimes twelve-hour days were her new norm, and it didn't even bother her. She was pretty sure she needed them more than anything else. When she wasn't working, she was thinking, and thinking was terrible for her health.

"Are you sure you don't want me to help out more?" Savannah asked from the chair she'd dragged behind the counter of the shop.

Thanks to the holiday, they were too busy to allow Brooklyn to hide out in the kitchen like she'd prefer. Instead she was stuck managing the register, putting on a happy face for the customers that came in. Savannah was too swollen to stand for very long and too pregnant to hop up on a stool, so Brooklyn had made a space for her next to the register.

"You're over seven months pregnant, and while I know you're fully capable of kicking butt here, I need something to distract me. So I'm going to use your pregnancy as an excuse to work more. Spend your free time with your husband or taking or a nap or heck plan world domination, whatever, just let me have this. I can't sit at home and think about what happened."

"I still can't believe..."

"I know, I know. That's not the Declan you know. Well, it's the Declan I know. I don't want to talk about it anymore."

"Fine. Just please let me know if there's anything you need. I hate the idea of you hurting and holding it all in."

"I'm fine sis...or I will be. I promise."

"I know. I just worry about you. I'm sorry you have to...what is he doing here?" Savannah asked drawing Brooklyn's attention away from her sister and to who her sister was looking at.

Standing across the room talking to his daughter was Declan. Her chest tightened as she took him in. She hadn't seen him since the night at her house when everything ended. His eyes were shielded by a Mariners baseball hat, his jaw covered by a beard that was a few days from being unruly. He'd never let his facial hair get that out of control when they were together or before that even. That knowledge made her feel a bit better about not knowing how he was taking things. It was clear by his appearance that he was feeling as shitty as she was.

"I need to go check on something in the back."

"The hell you do. You're not running away from him. You've got customers to see to," Savannah pointed out. "Well fuck...nevermind, maybe you should run to the back."

"What are you ta..."

"Hi, Brooklyn."

Her stomach rolled as she turned toward the person who spoke to her. She didn't need to look at him to know who it was. She'd never forget the voice of the man who'd broken her. Apparently, she hadn't gotten the memo that it was everyone who'd hurt Brooklyn day at Delectable Delights. Part of her wanted to turn and run, but she was stronger than that. She could face her past head-on and not let it affect her.

It didn't matter that the two men who'd broken her heart were in the same room. One definitely didn't matter. The other mattered too much. But she couldn't let either of them see her break down. She'd save that for the minute they were both gone. Until then she'd show them both she didn't need either of them.

Plastering on her best customer service smile, she took in the people standing in front of her.

"Welcome to Delectable Delights, Frank. How can I help you today?"

* * *

Declan

"Do you think it's fair for you to be here?" Erin asked the minute he walked into the bakery.

The answer was most definitely no, but he couldn't help himself. It'd been three weeks since she'd kicked him out of her house and he was losing his mind. He missed her like crazy, but he couldn't forget what had happened and the overwhelming panic that enveloped him the minute he discovered the broken condom. She didn't understand, and there wasn't anything he could do to make her see where he was coming from.

"I had to bring you your wallet. I'm not staying."

"I could have met you outside. You didn't have to come in."

"You're working."

"And you knew she'd be here, and you wanted to see her. It's okay, you can admit it."

He didn't know what to do with the fact that his daughter was so damn good at reading him. It was a bit scary but surprisingly helpful. If only he knew himself as well as she seemed to.

"Look, Dad, you're both miserable. Do something about it."

"I can't."

His chest ached as he said the words out loud. They felt final, and he hated it, hated himself for not being able to do something about the fact that both of their hearts were breaking. He'd barely looked at her since he walked into the bakery knowing that it would only add to his pain. Part of him feared she would be handling things a hell of a lot better than he was, that she didn't miss him as much as he missed her.

He tried to catch a glimpse of her now, to see if she looked even remotely as miserable as he felt. She spoke quietly to Savannah who was sitting behind the counter a scowl marring her beautiful face. Savannah spoke animatedly until she stopped suddenly her eyes trained on someone standing behind Brooklyn. Her demeanor quickly changed, her eyes narrowed, her jaw clenched.

Declan tried to see who Savannah was staring daggers at, but couldn't quite make him out through the child on his hip and the woman standing next to him. It was apparent Savannah wasn't happy to see him. When Brooklyn finally turned to face the man, she plastered a smile on her face that he could tell was more fake than genuine.

When she said the name Frank with the sunshiney voice she reserved for asshole customers, he felt himself take a step forward and then another. Thankfully Erin grabbed onto his arm, her presence reminding him that it wasn't his place to rush to Brooklyn's side anymore. That wasn't going to stop him from watching the interaction to make sure the asshole didn't hurt her again.

Declan could tell her ex's presence was doing enough damage without him even saying a word. He was pretty sure his presence wasn't helping matters much, but he couldn't cut out now. There was no doubt in his mind that she could hold her own against anyone, but he also wanted her to know that she didn't have to. Even if they were no longer a couple, he was still going to have her back, especially when it came to her asshole ex.

"Dad..." Erin warned as Declan took a step closer.

"I won't do anything, I promise."

He wanted to be able to see both Frank and Brooklyn, so he slowly adjusted his viewing spot. Erin followed him closely, probably to make sure he behaved, which he couldn't blame her for doing.

He glanced over at Brooklyn and smiled. To anyone who didn't know her, Brooklyn looked as if she was helping any other customer. There was no tension in her body, no anger in her voice. The smile on her face seemed completely normal, but he knew better, and he had a feeling Frank did as well. Declan knew he wouldn't have been able to remain as calm if he came face to face with Kara after all these years.

"Brooklyn it's so good to see you. I'm sorry the writing thing didn't seem to work out, but it's nice of your sister to give you a job. You remember my wife Courtney, don't you? Although I guess she wasn't my wife back then, you were. And this is our daughter Samantha. She's the most precious child and everything I ever hoped for, but you couldn't give me."

Despite every fiber of his being screaming at him to stand up for the woman he loved, Declan stayed where he was, his hands fisted at his sides. The man hadn't said much, but every word out of his mouth packed a vicious punch. He'd insulted Brooklyn left and right, yet she stood there, her demeanor not changing at all. He was so fucking proud of her. He wanted to rush in and swoop her up in his arms like some kind of scene out of a movie.

"Why you..." Savannah started but paused when Brooklyn held her hand out.

"It's great to see you again, Courtney. With your clothes on that is. Samantha is adorable. Thank goodness she looks nothing like her father. Now how can I help you guys? We've got a great deal we're running this weekend on cupcakes. Buy three get one free for Memorial Day only."

Frank's face reddened, his mouth falling open then shutting quickly. Declan held back a laugh knowing it would disrupt the scene in front of him. It was only a matter of time before Frank tried to strike again since Brooklyn hadn't taken the bait the first time.

"Oh Courtney, maybe we should take them up on that deal. You are eating for two again, we could get one for each of us and then an extra for the baby," Frank said, his eyes never leaving Brooklyn. "Isn't it great, Brooklyn? Two happy, healthy babies. This one's another girl, we're naming her Macy, after my grandma. Maybe next time we'll get the boy we've been hoping for."

Jeezus, the man was even more of a piece of work than he'd ever realized. To rub his wife's pregnancies in the face of the woman who wanted to be a mother more than anything. A woman he had at one time pledged his love to. Declan couldn't understand how someone could be so terrible to another human being. Not even Kara had been as hurtful as this asshole was.

Brooklyn remained stoic, a barely perceptible twitch of her mouth was the only thing that gave away that she was anything other than happy. He wanted to rush to her side and tell the asshat, that Brooklyn was a partner in her sister's business not just an employee, that she was in love and that she was pregnant with his child. His heart pounded in his chest as he replayed the last part in his head. Why would he even think something like that after everything that'd happened? It wasn't something he wanted, so why would he want to pretend? Why would he want to shove it in her ex's face?

"Congratulations Courtney. That's amazing news, although I'm sorry that it means you had to have sex with this one again. I mean the man is pretty horrible in bed. Did you know that you can have more than one orgasm during sex? No, I didn't either until recently. How about simultaneous orgasms...did you know they're a thing? Yeah, me neither. I missed out on a lot of orgasms while I was with Frank. I hope you're at least giving them to yourself every once in a while to make up for it. Now, what kind of cupcakes did you guys want?"

Declan nearly started to applaud while Frank fumed, his face getting redder by the second. The entire bakery was silent, everyone in the store waiting to hear what Frank had to say next. Instead, he turned his back to the counter and told his wife to take care of it. She picked out cupcakes and paid quickly, never saying anything more than please, thank you and the flavors she wanted. She looked remorseful and like she had more to say, but kept looking over her shoulder at her husband.

Frank was out of the store as soon as his wife gave the word. He didn't even hold the door for her as she waddled behind him. By the time she reached the door, her shoulders were hunched over, her head hanging low. Declan almost felt sorry for her, but then remembered she'd been the mistress of another woman's husband and later married him knowing the kind of man he was.

The minute the door closed behind her a collective sigh sounded around the room. Customers went back to having their own conversations, while Brooklyn looked like she was about to pass out. She looked around the room, their eyes meeting for a brief moment before the bell above the door grabbed her attention. He followed her gaze, surprised to see Frank's wife standing there.

"Sorry, pregnancy brain, I forgot my wallet," she said as she walked toward the counter.

For a moment, he thought she was being malicious, but then realized she was speaking far louder than necessary. Declan looked behind her and saw the reason standing on the sidewalk behind her looking angrier than he had when they walked out. She waddled slowly to the counter, the door shutting behind her.

"I'm sorry for all of that. He's an asshole," she said once the door closed.

"Yeah. Sorry, you have to deal with it."

"It's my own fault, so don't feel bad for me. I did it to myself. This is the life that greed and desperation will buy you. But you should know..." she paused to look over her shoulder. "The baby isn't his. Neither of them are."

Brooklyn's mouth dropped open, but before she could respond Frank pushed the door open.

"Hurry up, I don't have all day," he yelled before backing away and letting the door shut again.

Courtney cringed, but turned away and waddled slowly back to the door. She looked over her shoulder at Brooklyn once, then joined her husband outside. Declan watched the door, waiting to see if either of them would come back. When the door didn't open after a full minute, he turned to check on Brooklyn, shocked to see tears streaming down her cheeks.

Her eyes met his, neither of them looking away until a sob left her throat and she turned and ran through the doors that led to the kitchen. He took a step to follow her and then remembered that it wasn't his place. All he wanted to do was wrap her in his arms and hold her while she cried. He wanted it so badly his body ached with it.

He glanced away from the door and found Savannah staring at him. She seemed to be waiting for him to make a move, but he had no idea what that move was supposed to be. He was probably the last person, aside from Frank, that Brooklyn wanted to see. Going to her wouldn't change their situation, it might make things worse. As much as he hated walking away, that was the only thing he could do.

"I'll see you at home, sweetie," he said to Erin before kissing the top of her head.

She looked like she wanted to say something to him but kept quiet. He had a feeling he knew what she would've said. She'd been very vocal thus far that he should fix things with Brooklyn. Of course, she didn't know the whole story and she never would. The fact that she looked at him like he'd messed things up reminded him why he'd never brought someone into her life when she was growing up.

He never wanted to disappoint her. Unfortunately, it seemed like he'd done just that.

* * *

Brooklyn

Watching Erin and her classmates throw their caps into the air celebrating their graduation sent a shot of pride through Brooklyn's veins. She jumped up and cheered for them with the rest of the audience, a huge smile on her face. She couldn't help it, even though it made no sense. Erin wasn't related to her, yet Brooklyn couldn't help but feel like she had a hand in the girl's success. She'd known her for a year and a half, barely a blip on the timeline of Erin's life, but she still felt it all the same.

Following the crowd out of the auditorium, she looked around for Erin. It still felt a little weird to be there, the only person other than her aunt and dad to watch her graduate, but she couldn't have declined the invitation even if she wanted to. She had no idea when she would see Erin again since she was leaving the next day to head to North Carolina with her dad.

Two months of bonding before school started, she'd said of the adventure they were going to take. Brooklyn wasn't sure she could handle that much time in a car with Declan, but Erin assured her they wouldn't spend the entire time on the road, just the first few weeks. After that Declan would hang out with her near campus, helping her to get the lay of the land before school and her new job started.

Two months of not seeing him at all. Two months of not hoping to run into him around town accidentally. Two months of not having to avoid group get-togethers because he was going to be there. He'd miss the birth of Savannah and Gabriel's baby. He'd miss...not her obviously. The thought made her feel like she couldn't breathe.

It'd been over a month since the night of the great condom incident and yet it wasn't any easier remembering that they were over. She still thought about him all the time, dreamed about him all the time. She worked herself until she was sick and tired so that she wouldn't spend every minute of every day going over what happened and how much she missed him.

Tears pricked behind her eyes, but she wouldn't cry, not in front of hundreds of strangers. She closed her eyes, took a deep breath then let it out. She repeated the process a few times before finally feeling close to normal again. Her emotions had been all over the place since the break-up, she'd found herself on the verge of tears too many times while working the counter at Delectable Delights, she had to come up with a trick to keep the tears at bay.

Opening her eyes again, she scanned the scattered groups of families looking for Erin. She spotted them several yards away, Declan giving Erin a hug, Andrea standing next to them a bright smile on her face, tears in her eyes. Brooklyn stayed where she was, not wanting to interrupt the family moment. When Declan's eyes met hers, she offered him a small smile, but still didn't move toward them. He stepped back from Erin, said something to his daughter and then looked up at Brooklyn before turning to walk away.

Her heart ached, but she knew it was for the best that they didn't interact. She wasn't sure she could handle it, and he didn't look like he wanted to. The beard from a few weeks earlier was gone, whether it was because he was over things or because he wanted to look presentable for Erin's graduation, she didn't know. But he looked good, better than she felt. Surprisingly, she hoped he felt good too. She knew that sending Erin off to college was going to be hard for him. He didn't need to be suffering from their break-up on top of that.

Once Declan was clear, she made her way over to Erin. The minute she was close enough, she opened her arms, not surprised when Erin ran into them. They hugged for a long while, both of them letting the tears flow. This time Brooklyn cried happy tears for Erin and what she'd accomplished. There were a few tears of sadness mixed in because she was going to miss the young girl...now woman. They'd become close over the last year between working together at the bakery and the time they spent working on the essays Erin had needed. It wouldn't be the same without her around.

"I'm so proud of you," Brooklyn said the minute they disengaged.

"Thanks. That means so much to me. You...I owe you, Brooklyn. I really do."

Brooklyn shook her head. "You don't owe me anything, Erin. I didn't do much. This is all your doing, and I know you're going to give them hell at NCSU."

"Heck yeah, I am," Erin responded with a smile. "I'm gonna miss you, Brooklyn."

"The beauty of technology, I'm only a phone call or text away, but I'm gonna miss you too, kiddo."

"He's miserable you know."

Brooklyn sighed. "It doesn't matter."

Although it did, a little bit, at least it felt like it mattered. Brooklyn sighed again trying to remind herself that it was over. There was no way they would ever agree about one simple thing, something that shouldn't even be a conversation, but ended up being the mountain that they'd both die on.

"I know. I just had to put it out there," she admitted with a shrug. "I obviously don't know what happened, but I know neither of you is happy with how things turned out. I hate seeing two people I love hurting themselves and each other the way you guys are right now."

"Erin...."

"No, I'll stop. I'm sorry, it's none of my business."

"I get it, but it is what it is," Brooklyn said with a shrug of her own. The motion was supposed to express to the teenager that what was happening wasn't a big deal. Instead, it made her feel like a fool. It was a big deal, the biggest deal, but there wasn't anything that could be done.

She talked with Erin and Andrea for a little longer, then said her goodbyes. She gave Erin another hug, this one lasting longer than the first. It felt like a goodbye instead of see you later, the realization adding another crack to Brooklyn's already fragile heart. The Reese family had wormed their way into her world, and now they were leaving her behind.

Tears sprang to her eyes, so she walked faster, the dam breaking before she could reach her car. She swiped at them with the back of her hands so she could see what she was doing, but then let them fall freely once she was inside the privacy of her car. It didn't matter that anyone walking by could see her crying.

She was long past caring and only wanted to get the crying jag over with so she could drive to her sister's house and drown her sorrows in pizza and chocolate fudge sundaes. Although she wanted to drown her sorrows in wine, drinking wasn't currently allowed in the Archer household because it made Savannah jealous. Not that it mattered since Brooklyn had barely touched alcohol since the break-up. With her emotions all over the place, it just made her feel even more depressed.

It took her fifteen minutes to calm down and another forty-five before she reached the safety of her sister's house. The tears started again the second she walked in the door. Savannah rushed to her side immediately to comfort her. Gabriel stood off to the side, watching them closely, but not saying a word. Brooklyn wondered for a second what it was like for him being caught in the middle of something so frustrating and heartbreaking.

She tried running through her calming ritual again, but her nose was stuffed up from crying, and her body still felt like it needed to release some of her pain. She choked back a sob before trying again. The last thing she wanted to do was spend the evening crying. It should have all been over and done with. She should have been all cried out by now.

"Let's go into the kitchen and get some water. The pizza just got here. We can eat and watch a movie or something."

Brooklyn didn't try to speak, unsure of what might happen if she did. She nodded then followed Savannah into the kitchen. The scent of freshly baked dough, marinara sauce and spices filled the space. Her mouth started to water, but not in the way it usually did when she was faced with devouring a delicious piece of her favorite food.

Her hands flew up to cover her mouth, her eyes going wide as her throat constricted. She turned and ran toward the downstairs bathroom, her stomach lurching. She barely made it to the toilet before she lost her lunch. Over and over she heaved until there was nothing left. Tears streamed down her face as she rested her head on her arm.

"I thought you said you were feeling better," Savannah said as she placed a cold washcloth on the back of her neck.

"I was," Brooklyn croaked out before the need to throw up overtook her again.

She dry heaved a few more times before slowly sitting back. The room spun a little, but overall she felt mostly better. Reaching out blindly, she lowered the top of the toilet, then pulled down the handle to flush it. Her stomach was still on shaky ground, but Brooklyn felt safe enough to back away from the toilet until she was leaning against the bathroom wall.

"Obviously I was wrong," she murmured. "I'm sorry. I should go. The last thing you need right now is to get sick."

Her sister looked down at her, brows furrowed like she was contemplating something she couldn't quite figure out. Without a word, Savannah walked out of the room. Brooklyn could hear her talking to Gabriel but couldn't make out what she was saying. A couple of minutes later she returned with a glass of water and something Brooklyn never thought she'd see again.

CHAPTER 12

Brooklyn

Looking up at her sister, Brooklyn was fairly certain she'd lost her mind. Pregnancy was eating her brain cells or something.

"Not sure what you plan on doing with that, but we already know you're pregnant and we know I can't be."

Savannah sighed, propping the hand holding the pregnancy test on her hip. Even eight months pregnant, she was sassier than most. Her exasperation would be evident even to a blind person.

"Do we?" Savannah asked, the tone of her voice making Brooklyn feel like she was in trouble. "I'm not sure we do know that, Brook. You've been tired as hell lately, and you've thrown up more in the last few weeks than you have in the last few years."

"It's because I've been working so much. I just let myself get worn down. It's not a big deal."

"You've been an emotional wreck…"

"I just had an emotional breakup," she countered.

"When was the last time you had your period?"

It was Brooklyn's turn to sigh. She didn't like the road her sister was going down. What she was suggesting couldn't be right. It just wasn't possible.

"I don't know. It's always been spotty and erratic."

"Okay fine you can explain away those things, but can you tell me why your boobs look bigger and you're looking a little fuller around the waist?"

"Is that your nice way of telling me that I've gained weight?" Brooklyn asked sarcasm dripping from her lips.

She didn't want to admit she'd noticed everything Savannah had pointed out. She didn't want to admit she'd noticed the change in her body, the fullness of her curves, the soreness of her breasts, even the difference in the size of her nipples. She'd explained it all away in her head because there was no way it could mean what Savannah thought it meant. There was absolutely no way she could be pregnant.

"Take the damn test, Brooklyn. You heard what Courtney said that day just as clearly as I did. Those kids aren't Frank's. What was the point of her coming back to tell you that if it wasn't for you to see that you weren't the problem in that equation? Frank is shooting blanks."

"Except that doesn't work since I did get pregnant twice."

"That means the asshole's shooting blanks and duds. It doesn't mean you're infertile. Neither of you was tested back then because he wouldn't let you. I would bet that's because he knew the truth and refused to face it because of the money. Just take the test, Brooklyn. What's the worst that can happen? Either the test comes back negative and you can go back to believing you can't have kids or it comes back positive like I think it will, and you finally get to live out your dream of being a mom."

Brooklyn closed her eyes. "I'm scared."

"I know."

"Do you? Either way, this is a mess. It's all I've ever wanted, but it's going to make things even worse with Declan. He's going to hate me. And if I take that test and I'm not pregnant, I'm going to be devastated all over again. I'm trying hard right now not to get my hopes up, but it's impossible."

Brooklyn's shoulders started to shake as she fought back her emotions. Savannah placed a hand on her shoulder and squeezed it. Knowing that her sister was by her side gave her confidence that everything was going to be okay no matter what happened. She didn't have support the first few times she'd gone through the highs and lows of pregnancy, but she did now, and she knew it would make a difference.

"No matter what, you don't have to go through this alone. I'd sit down there on the floor with you, but I'm pretty sure I'd hurt myself getting down there, and I'd need a hell of a lot of help getting back up. But other than that, I'm here to hold your hand, to watch the clock while we wait for the timer to go off. If it's positive, I'll go to the doctor with you. If Declan can't get over himself and see what a miracle this is, I'll kick his ass myself."

Her sister's strength helped to bolster her confidence. She could take the test and deal with the outcome no matter what it was. She could take things day by day, minute by minute. A plan of action wasn't needed at the moment. All she had to focus on was taking the test. Then she could figure out the rest. Figure out what she'd tell Declan if the test came out positive.

Holding out her hand, she looked up at her sister, her best friend. "Okay, how does this work? It's been a while since I've taken one of these."

Savannah handed her the glass of water. "Chug this first. Then you get to pee on this bad boy; a couple of minutes after that we'll know if you need to make a doctor's appointment."

She gulped the water down, then sat in silence for a few minutes while she worked up the courage to take the next step. Once it was time to pee on the stick, she sent Savannah out of the room so she could have a little privacy. It took longer than usual to get things started which only added to her anxiety. Her hands shook, but she held on tight to the stick, afraid she might accidentally drop it in the toilet.

Savannah reentered the bathroom once Brooklyn was finished with her business. The stick that would dictate her future sat on a wad of toilet paper on the sink, her phone with the timer running sitting next to it. Instead of staring at either of them, she hugged her sister tight. In a mere three minutes, her life could change forever. The thought nearly had her doubled over in front of the toilet again.

When the timer went off, neither of them moved. Tears sprang to Brooklyn's eyes. Her heart felt like it would break free from her chest at any second. Her lungs didn't seem to want to work, and for a moment she thought she might start hyperventilating.

"Maybe you should sit down. If you faint, I can't catch you, and I sent Gabriel to the store to pick up ice cream."

"You're the best big sister a girl could ever have. You know that right?"

"Yes, I do. Now sit down so we can take a look at that stick."

Brooklyn smiled as she wiped away her tears. Savannah was definitely right; sitting down was the best option. No matter what the stick showed, she wasn't sure her legs were going to be able to hold her much longer. The entire situation was too much. It took Savannah leading her to the toilet for her to sit down. She took a few deep breaths then let them out slowly, trying to calm her shaking hands. It wouldn't do her any good if she dropped the stupid stick on the floor, which sounded about how things usually went for her.

"Just do it already," her sister urged.

With shaking hands, she picked up the stick and looked at the tiny screen that would tell her whether she was pregnant or not. The sheen of tears in her eyes blurred her vision slightly, making her thankful that the test in her hand was one with actual words and not the stupid plus signs that were hard to make out. Blinking a couple of times, she focused on what she was seeing. Her eyes widened, her breath caught in her chest as the word registered in her brain.

"Holy shit."

* * *

"How is this even possible?" Brooklyn muttered for at least the tenth time since the doctor gave her the news.

Savannah sat next to her holding her hand. Neither of them had done a very good job holding back their tears when the doctor came in and announced that the blood test confirmed what the home pregnancy test had already told them. She was pregnant. Fucking pregnant.

Everything she thought she knew had been a lie. Everything she believed, the heartache that she'd gone through, the future she believed to be hers...none of it was real. She could have children. She was having a child.

And she was freaking the fuck out about it.

"How...I just..."

"Why don't you put the gown on so you're ready when the doctor comes in. We can ask her when she comes back."

Brooklyn wasn't sure how she managed to take off her clothes and put on the gown without falling. She felt like she was having an out of body experience. Like she was floating above everyone watching a dream version of herself getting the one thing she'd always wanted. The one thing she never expected to have. And the one thing Declan was clear he never wanted to happen. She was torn between being elated and being heartbroken.

Any hope she had of working things out with Declan went out the window the minute she saw that one word on the test. He would never forgive her for getting pregnant, even if she would never even think of abandoning him and their child.

"So let's see what we've got going on in here," her doctor said as she came back into the room, a technician pushing an ultrasound machine following behind her.

"I still can't believe this is happening."

"Normally we don't do ultrasounds this early on, but since you indicated when you called that you didn't think you could get pregnant and you had no idea when your last period was, we decided to check things out," Dr. Ross explained as she took a seat next to the exam table. "Do you mind me asking why you thought you couldn't get pregnant? Did you have tests done? I didn't see anything mentioned in your file."

"Well no...my ex-husband wouldn't allow it, but we tried for almost five years. During that time, I was only able to conceive twice and both times resulted in a miscarriage."

"There are plenty of things that can contribute to a miscarriage. Most likely there was a chromosomal abnormality which is the most common reason. Other than that, the health of the parents can be a factor, their age and lifestyle choices. The fact that you're currently pregnant and you said ex-husband leads me to believe he's not the father of the child you're carrying now, so the fact that you tried for years and only had two pregnancies, could mean that his sperm and your body were incompatible."

"Wait, that's actually a thing?" Brooklyn asked surprised that Meghan had been right.

"Yes. Of course, it's a bit more clinical than that, but just because you weren't successful before doesn't mean you were the one at fault."

"I always thought I was at fault because he got another woman pregnant."

"We recently learned though that they aren't his kids and I'm betting he's shooting blanks," Savannah interjected.

"Thanks for making my life sound like a soap opera, Savannah."

Dr. Ross laughed and shook her head. "This isn't even close to the craziest thing I've heard in this room. Go ahead and lie back, since you aren't sure about the date of your last period, do you have an idea of when you might have conceived?"

"Ummm, well we had an incident with a broken condom before Mother's Day. We were always very careful about using condoms, so that has to be it."

Brooklyn almost pointed out how compulsive Declan had been about using condoms, even after she told him about her past, but she kept it to herself. The doctor may have heard crazier things in her office, but Brooklyn didn't have to contribute to them.

"Well condoms are only ninety-nine percent effective plus you aren't on any other kind of birth control correct?"

"I stopped taking them when I was married, and after my divorce, I never felt the need to get back on them. My periods were always light, and I didn't think I could get pregnant. I didn't see the point."

"I'm not judging you, just verifying information to see how far along you might be. It's probably a good idea that you didn't put those chemicals and extra hormones in your body if you didn't need them. Alright, let's take a look. The gel is going to be cold, sorry."

Brooklyn stared up at the ceiling, one hand clutching her sister's the other holding the bunched up gown over her breasts. She shivered as the doctor squirted freezing cold gel against her stomach. Dr. Ross hummed quietly while she moved the wand over her body, pressing down lightly at first and then a little bit harder.

It felt like forever before anyone said anything. Brooklyn wanted to see what was going on, but for some reason, she couldn't pull her eyes away from the boring ceiling tiles. Savannah squeezed her hand, pulling her attention over to her sister's smiling face. She hadn't stopped crying since the doctor had given them the news and now she looked like she was shedding even more tears than before.

"Oh Brooklyn..." her sister said through a hiccup.

"Ms. St. James, I'm not sure how to tell you this."

"Oh god...is it..." Brooklyn's breath caught, her heart ready to break into a million pieces with the doctor's next words.

"No, no...its good news, I promise. Sorry, that was probably a horrible way to start this given your history. What I was trying to say is that your timeline is a bit off."

"What do you mean?" she asked confused about how her timeline could be wrong.

"Well, I'd say you're measuring closer to twelve weeks than eight so the incident you spoke of before was not the night of conception."

"How could I be that far along and not know?" Brooklyn asked as she turned to look at the doctor. "I knew the first two times."

"It's easy to explain away the symptoms, Brook," her sister said. "You were heartbroken and worked too much which wore you down. A lot of women gain weight after a break-up. On top of that, you just thought you had the flu. You would never have guessed you were pregnant."

"It's not all that uncommon, especially for women like yourself who've had issues with previous pregnancies," Dr. Ross added, but her words did nothing to comfort her and instead reminded her of something else entirely.

"Do I have to worry about another miscarriage?" Brooklyn asked fear suddenly clawing at her chest.

"I won't lie to you and say you're completely out of the woods. You're still within the first trimester when miscarriages are a bit more common. Late trimester miscarriages are less likely to occur and are usually due to medical issues like thyroid conditions or diabetes, neither of which you have."

"So there's still a chance?"

"Yes, but you shouldn't go into this situation filled with fear about the unknown, there's too many of them to count. If you give in to that fear, you'll end up drowning in it, and you won't be able to enjoy your pregnancy or the child you bring into the world," Dr. Ross said matter-of-factly. "Now, there's one other thing you should know."

"Of course there is. Why not throw one more thing into the mix...it's not like my mind hasn't already been blown twice today. Let's go for the hat trick."

"I love a good hockey reference," Dr. Ross said before moving the monitor so Brooklyn could see the two spots she was pointing at. "Congratulations, you're having twins."

"Holy shit."

* * *

Declan

Leaving Seattle in his rearview mirror had been surprisingly easy the day after Erin's graduation. At first, he'd been solely focused on enjoying the time he had left with his daughter. They'd spent months planning out the route of their epic road trip, deciding where they wanted to stop and what they wanted to see. Things had gone well as they drove to Montana for their first night. They'd even stopped briefly in Idaho so they could cross it off their list of states to visit.

Things started to change the minute they reached Yellowstone. As they hiked around checking out the sights, Declan remembered a conversation he'd had with Brooklyn about wanting to go there. After that, she was all he could think about. Every stop they made reminded him of her; especially when they made their way from one Major League ballpark to the next, which was another item on Brooklyn's bucket list.

Whoever said "out of sight, out of mind" had never met Brooklyn St. James. If they had, they'd realize what Declan had quickly realized during their road trip across the country. She was unforgettable no matter how much he tried to push her out of his mind so he could focus on Erin.

He knew it was apparent to his daughter that he was suffering, but she never said a word. At least not about what he should have been doing. When they stopped in Baltimore for a couple of games at Camden Yards, she mentioned how much Brooklyn would have loved to have been there.

She'd named her cat Ripken after one of her favorite baseball players Cal Ripken Jr. He hadn't known that since the last time they spoke was the night she adopted the cat.

Not thinking about Brooklyn got even more difficult once they reached Raleigh. Although Erin still had a few weeks before school started, she'd found a job at a local veterinarian office that began as soon as they arrived leaving him on his own for longer than he would have preferred. Without Erin to distract him, he thought about Brooklyn, wondering what she was doing and if she was thinking about him too.

Since the day they met, they had never gone long without talking. Even though they didn't like each other that much and fought constantly, they still saw each other at least once a week. He hadn't seen her in almost two months and hadn't spoken to her in even longer. It felt wrong, but he had no idea what to do about it. They still had fundamentally polarizing opinions on a topic they both considered a deal breaker.

How did anyone move past that? Declan wished he knew. He wanted to move past the fear that kept him from moving on, the fear that was ultimately keeping him from Brooklyn. He didn't know how.

Declan spent his last night in North Carolina watching ESPN in his hotel room alone. He could have gone out to explore while Erin went to an orientation for her program and then a meet and greet with the faculty. She'd offered to hang out with him after everything was over, but he didn't want to get in the way.

The next morning she picked him up from his hotel so they could go out to breakfast before she took him to the airport. He woke up in a shitty mood which he tried desperately to hide from Erin. Thankfully she spent most of their meal talking about her night and how excited she was to start classes later that day. Her excitement was infectious and at least for a little while he was able to put on a happy face.

The drive to the airport was a completely different story. He wasn't looking forward to leaving his only child alone in a strange city on the other side of the country, and he had no idea what to expect when he got home. So many pieces of his life had changed and not necessarily for the better. Once he got on the plane, he'd have to face the fact that he'd no longer get to see two of the most important people in his life every day.

He looked over at Erin as she carefully maneuvered around the weaving airport traffic. Tears pricked at the back of his eyes, but he refused to cry in front of her. The last thing he wanted was for her to feel bad or regret her decision. He'd deal with his feelings once he was sure she was happy and secure.

"I'm sorry I wasn't the best company. This isn't really how I wanted to spend our last two months together."

"You haven't been that bad...most of the time. I could tell you were a little sad though. I wish I could do something to fix things."

"I know you do. I wish I could have given you everything you wanted while you were growing up. Like a mom and a pony."

"I was definitely more upset about the lack of a pony then I was the lack of a mom. I didn't need one of those. Would I have liked to have one, sure, but mostly because I would have loved for you to have someone to spend your life with."

"I did...I had you."

"I don't count, and you know it," she said before sticking her tongue out at him as she pulled the car over to park against the curb. "You wasted a lot of time being alone. I never wanted that for you, and I certainly don't want it now. Don't let the best thing that ever happened to you get away."

"You're the best thing that ever happened to me."

"Okay then, the second best thing that ever happened to you."

Declan sighed as he looked out the windshield at the cars that were pulling in and out in front of them. He didn't know how much to say or even what to say. She was right. He was letting the second best thing that ever happened to him get away, but he wasn't sure how to stop it. He could feel Erin staring at him, so he turned to face her.

"You don't know what happened."

"Did she cheat on you?"

"No."

"Do you love her?"

"Yes."

"Then nothing else matters. Can you honestly say that whatever's holding you back is more important than Brooklyn is? Means more to you than Brooklyn does?"

"I'm afraid of history repeating itself," he admitted, surprising them both. "I'm afraid that I'm going to plan a future with her only for her to turn around and decide she doesn't want me or the life we've built."

"She's not the Egg Donor, you know. Brooklyn is ten times the woman the Egg Donor could ever hope to be. In a million years I don't think Brooklyn could ever walk out on her family the way the other one did. But here's the thing, Dad. There are no guarantees in life. The divorce rate in this country is ridiculous. I'm pretty sure none of those people went into their marriages assuming they'd be divorced one day. You can't let fear keep you from what you want the most. Isn't striking out better than never getting a chance to play the game?"

Declan loved the fact that his kid had just used a sports reference during a rather serious conversation. He gave her a small smile as he reached out and brushed a lock of hair from her forehead. He couldn't believe that he was sitting in a car getting relationship advice from his 18-year-old daughter. Times had definitely changed.

"How did you get so smart about this kind of stuff?"

"I read a lot of books. Aunt DeeDee got me hooked on romance novels when I was 13," she told him. "You should read them. You'd get some great ideas on how to treat a woman and how to get her back after messing up big time."

"Maybe I'll pick one up in one of the airport shops."

"Look for Kristen Proby or Samantha Young or Colleen Hoover. They're my favorites."

He mentally shelved her recommendations, serious about looking into picking up a book while he waited for his flight. There was no doubt he was going to need a hell of a lot of help to win Brooklyn back. The things he said, the way he treated her...he didn't deserve her forgiveness, but he was going to try like hell to get it. He loved her more than he ever thought possible. There was no way he could let her walk out of his life without a fight.

"I love you, Bug."

"I love you too, Dad. Now go home and win back your woman. I feel like it's about time I get that mom I've always wanted."

CHAPTER 13

Declan

Six hours had never felt so long. Six hours of sitting in a cramped seat on a crowded plane playing his daughters words over and over in his head. At least when he'd been waiting for his flight he could get up and walk around. The movement helped keep his mind off of things. Unfortunately, they frowned upon pacing on planes, so he was stuck with his thoughts and the romance novel he bought because his daughter recommended it.

He'd actually given the book a chance at the beginning of the flight. The writing was pretty good, and the characters were believable. Declan found himself enjoying the book until things got a little hot and heavy. His face flushed as he slammed the book shut and looked around to see if anyone noticed.

As he waited for his luggage, his face grew warm thinking about that scene. He couldn't believe a book had gotten him hot and bothered and then he remembered his daughter had read the same book and he knew he wouldn't be able to finish it. Thankfully he'd already gotten some helpful tips that he hoped would help him win Brooklyn back.

Knowing he needed to see her as soon as possible, he took an Uber home so he could take a quick shower and pick up his car. He was in and out in less than half an hour. Back on the road, he tried to work out what he was going to say. A simple sorry wasn't going to cut it. He would need to prove to her that he wasn't scared anymore, that he was ready for her and whatever the future held for them.

The parking Gods were looking out for him as he reached West Seattle he found a spot right in front of Delectable Delights. He hadn't checked to make sure she was working, but since Savannah had given birth a month earlier, he was fairly certain the bakery was where she was going to be. If she wasn't there, he'd go to her house and then Savannah's. At the risk of sounding like a stalker, he'd drive all over town until he found her. He'd do whatever it took to see her.

He just hoped wherever she was she was alone. His heart sank as he realized he probably should have asked someone if Brooklyn was still single. It hadn't been that long since they broke up, at least not in his eyes. But it had. Especially since he hadn't given her any indication that there was a chance they'd be able to work things out. She would have been well within her rights finding someone who could love her and trust her the way she deserved.

"Fuck," he muttered as nausea overwhelmed him.

It would be his own fault if she moved on while he was gone. He'd be devastated, but he would be to blame. Fear tried to suck him back in, but he wouldn't let it. He couldn't stop now. The not knowing would eat him alive. Taking a deep breath, he held it and glanced at himself in the rearview mirror. A second passed, then another before he let out the breath and closed his eyes. This was it.

If he let himself think about it too much, he'd chicken out, so he quickly climbed out of the car. Once on the sidewalk, he could see her standing at one of the tables talking to customers. Her back was to the window, but he'd know that ass and those legs anywhere. Her long hair was hanging loose down her back in a cascade of waves.

Shaking his head, he tried to snap out of the trance she'd put him in. If he was this affected by her hair and her backside, how the hell was he going to survive seeing her beautiful face and her stunning hazel eyes? Taking another calming breath, in through his nose, out through his mouth, he moved toward the door and pulled it open.

The bell above the door announced his arrival, and he watched a few people turn to see who'd walked through the door.

"Welcome to Delectable Delights," she said as she turned.

Her eyes widened, her mouth falling open the minute she realized he was there. Neither of them moved or said anything. She closed her mouth and stared at him, her brows furrowing like they did when she was confused. He stared back, taking her in like a man starved. He'd missed her so much it took a moment to register what he was seeing and when it did he had to grab onto the doorframe to keep from falling over.

"Declan..." she said as she hesitantly took a step toward him.

Without thinking he took a step back. He shook his head like it would erase what he was seeing. He closed his eyes, then opened them yet everything was still the same. He pinched himself and reveled in the sting of it, even if it didn't prove what he was seeing was a dream.

She took another step toward him, and he shook his head again. Their eyes met. He felt her pain, but it barely made a dent in the hold the fear suddenly had on him. He'd thought he'd mastered it or at least figured it out on the six-hour flight home, but he hadn't. He was still its bitch, still a coward.

The tears in her eyes felt like a punch to the gut. He couldn't breathe, his arms and legs tingled. He had to get out of there. Running was the only answer. Going there had been a mistake. He should have left her alone, left everything alone. He shook his head at her one more time then turned and hurried back to his car.

"Fuck, fuck, fuck," he yelled as he slammed his hands against the steering wheel one he was locked inside.

How the fuck had she ended up pregnant? How the fuck had he not known? How come nobody told him? He knew baby bumps well enough to know that she was close to the midway mark. He'd only been gone two months, but there was no way Gabriel didn't know she was pregnant and he'd bet money Andi knew about the pregnancy too. Why the fuck didn't anyone tell him?

Why hadn't Brooklyn?

Anger coursed through him, hot and sharp, stealing his breath. Betrayal. It felt like he'd been betrayed by the people he loved the most. His trust in them fractured because they kept a monumental secret from him. A life-changing secret that he'd deserved to know about.

The drive home felt like it took forever. When he realized that Andi wouldn't be home from work for another hour, he took his anger out on plastic cup she'd left on the counter. A satisfying cracking sound filled the room as it bounced off the wall. Picking it up, he threw it a few more times until it was in pieces.

Knowing it would drive him crazy to sit around and wait for his sister, he killed time unpacking then throwing his dirty clothes in the washer. His phone buzzed in his pocket, but he refused to even check it. Eventually, he turned it off completely, never even looking to see who had called and texted before.

Finally, he heard Andi's car pull into the driveway. He barely let her walk through the door before he pounced.

"Why didn't you tell me?"

"That's not something you tell someone over the phone," she said knowing exactly what he was talking about. He wondered if someone had called her to warn her that he'd found out or if the twin bond had told her all she needed to know.

"Why didn't she tell me?"

"Again, see answer number one."

"I deserved to know."

"Yeah, you did. We all agreed about that, but we also agreed over the phone was not the way to drop that bomb. Did you expect her to fly to North Carolina to give you the news?"

"Of course. If it was so important she had to tell me to my face, then yeah I expect that she should come to tell me."

"She almost did. I told her not to."

"Jeezus Andi, why would you do that?"

"Because you needed time to figure shit out. Plus, she was afraid of what you'd say, how you'd react and I didn't think she should have to deal with that by herself in a state all the way across the country far away from the people who'd have her back. Not to mention the fact that she's not the one who fucked up in the first place."

Declan bristled at the accusation. "How can you say that?"

"Why didn't you get a vasectomy?"

"What?"

"It's simple. If you were so hell-bent on not having any more kids, why didn't you get a vasectomy? Other birth control methods aren't one hundred percent effective every single time. So why didn't you do more?"

"I..."

"And if you weren't willing to go under the knife, how could you expect a woman to take a pill that would essentially kill her chance of a child? Especially, when that woman believed with her whole heart that she couldn't get pregnant anyway. That's like punching her in the face even though her nose is already broken. It's overkill."

Words escaped him. Andi was right. He didn't have a good reason for never getting fixed. Maybe deep down he knew that someday he'd meet the woman that completed him and he'd want a family with her. Maybe deep down he knew he'd eventually defeat the fear that was holding him back. The fear that he was allowing to keep him from living the life he wanted.

He thought about the situation he was in, thought about what it all meant and realized that he was more upset that no one had told him about the baby, then he was about having another kid. Fear wasn't clawing at him, wasn't trying to hold him back. He felt lighter than he'd felt in a long time.

As the shock lifted so did the anger. They were replaced by happiness and the memory of seeing Brooklyn standing in front of him, her body swollen with his child. It filled him with a longing he'd never felt before. He needed her by his side. He needed their child in his arms. He needed to make it right.

"How far along is she?" he asked tentatively.

"You should ask her."

"I'm pretty sure she's never going to speak to me again after the way I reacted."

"Oh no, what did you do?"

"Took one look at her and ran away."

"You're a fucking idiot."

"I know," he said earnestly. "What do I do, Andi? I went there to beg her for forgiveness and tell her that I love her. I'm not sure that's going to work anymore."

"You won't know until you try."

"I don't deserve for it to be that easy."

"No, you don't. But you deserve to be happy, you both do. So suck it up and figure out how to win her back."

He closed the gap between them and pulled her into his arms. "Thank you for everything."

"I'll always be here for you Declan. It's what sisters are for. Although, you should know I want to sell the house. I found a condo in West Seattle that I'm going to rent. I've already signed the lease.

"You're not moving because of all of this are you?"

She stepped back, shaking her head. "Of course not, but the fact that you're going to have your hands full was the catalyst I needed to me get my ass in gear. Erin was right. We need to move on and live our lives, and we can't do that if we're always in each other's pockets. We need our own space. Maybe not too much space though…the condo isn't far from Brooklyn's place, FYI."

He smiled and pulled her back in for another hug. "I'm happy for you sis. I hope you find whatever it is you're looking for. Just promise me that you'll let me know if you need anything."

"I promise," she said before stepping back again. "By the way big brother, I need your helping moving in two weeks."

Declan laughed, a full-bellied, guffaw that would have been embarrassing in front of anyone else. It felt good to enjoy a moment with his sister. To enjoy the uncomplicated nature of their relationship before he started wracking his brain trying to figure out how to get Brooklyn to forgive him and take him back.

He had a lot of work to do to convince her he wanted everything she had to offer. He had a feeling he'd also have to prove to her that he wasn't just in it because of the baby. He loved her more than he ever thought possible, baby or not.

This time he wasn't going to let anything stand in his way. Not even himself.

* * *

Brooklyn

"He just turned and ran away. He took one look at me and ran the fork away. Who does that?" she asked incredulously before shoveling another spoonful of ice cream in her mouth.

Savannah laughed which made Brooklyn scowl at her in response. "Hey I wasn't laughing at what he did I was laughing at the fact that you censored yourself. While I appreciate you being sensitive to Ryan's delicate ears, she's still a long way away from picking up your bad habits. Fork? Really?"

"Hey, it's not only my bad habit. Plus, I'm gonna need to get the practice in now since I'll have my delicate ears to protect in a few months. Holy fork..."

"Again with the fork."

"Sorry, I got it off this show with Kristen Bell in it. I have a lot of free time since I'm not working as much and I don't have a social life anymore. So when I'm not over here with you ladies, I'm at home binge-watching things on Netflix. I wish they'd stop asking me if I'm still watching. Makes me question my life choices a little."

Savannah laughed again, but this time Brooklyn joined her. She had to admit that her life was a bit laughable. Once again her life seemed like a soap opera. And Declan Reese was her very own leading man rushing in to shake up her world and then disappear without a trace.

Except there was a trace of him now. He knew the secret she'd been keeping from him almost since the minute he left town. She shouldn't have listened to Andi. She should have flown to North Carolina and told him the truth. Hell, she should have met them along their route and told him in whatever city she could find them in.

Finding out the way he did was not how she'd planned it out. It would have been hard to hide her bump, but she wanted to at least sit him down and talk to him about it. Instead, she had the privilege of watching him freak out then hightail it out of Delectable Delights as fast as his legs would carry him.

"Has he called or texted or anything? I get that he got the shock of his life, but once that wore off, I would have thought he'd contact you. He was at DD for a reason. Even if that reason no longer stands, I would hope he'd still have the decency to talk to you about it."

"Between me and Gabriel, I'm pretty sure we blew up his phone earlier. He probably turned it off. But no, I haven't heard a peep from him since he caught a glimpse of me and then took off like he was trying to steal a base."

"That doesn't..."

"I know, I know, that doesn't sound like the Declan you know. Well, apparently we know two different Declan Reese's. I'm not giving up on him though. Even if it doesn't work out between us, I know he'll be there for the babies. He might not be able to face his fears, but he definitely won't let those fears keep him from his kids."

"He'll be there for the three of you no matter what. I believe that much," Savannah agreed before shifting her infant daughter from one breast to the other.

Brooklyn watched her sister smile down at her daughter, and everything else seemed to fade away. In no time, she'd have her own little bundles of joy to fuss over and love. A zip of anxious energy coursed through her as she thought about doing it without a partner in crime. One baby was a ton of work; two would be overwhelming. While she'd have her family around to help, she wanted what Savannah had with Gabriel.

Like she conjured him with her thoughts, Gabriel walked into their living room beelining it straight for his wife and daughter. He barely even acknowledged her presence as he sat down next to Savannah and gave both of his girls a kiss on their heads, his arm going around Savannah's shoulders. The moment was almost too intimate for Brooklyn to watch. It was too painful, jealousy flaring in her chest.

Excusing herself, she went into the kitchen to rinse her spoon and bowl, the ice cream she'd devoured no longer comforting her. She took a few minutes to herself, while she fought back the overload of emotions that had taken over. When she returned to the living room, Gabriel was holding Ryan against his chest while he kissed Savannah like he was a starving man and her lips were the sustenance he needed.

"Hi Brooklyn, bye Brooklyn," he said quickly after pulling back from his wife. He walked out of the room just as quickly, but his presence had done exactly what she'd hoped it wouldn't.

"Your husband is hot...and with a baby in his arms...jeezus."

"I know, right?" Savannah said with a laugh.

"Ugh, now I'm picturing Declan with a baby in his arms, and it's fucking hot."

"What happened to the censoring thing?"

"Forking hot doesn't have the same intensity. God, when I saw him standing in the doorway today, I was so happy. Not only because he was there and I missed him, but because I'm so damn horny I can't stand it. I don't understand how that's even possible given the fact that I feel like a damn blimp."

"Ah, the beauty of hormones. I went through the same thing. He'll come around, and when he does, you can use all those hormones to make up for lost time."

Brooklyn sighed, she'd give up slaking her need for something much more important. "I don't even care about that...although it would be so nice. I would give it up in a heartbeat if it meant he'd be with me tomorrow at the appointment. I pushed back finding out the gender of the babies because I wanted him to be there for that. Now he's home, and I can't get ahold of him to ask him to come."

"I'm sorry, Brook," Savannah said as she got up from the couch and joined Brooklyn on the loveseat. She wrapped her arm around her sister and pulled her in for a hug. No matter what happened Brooklyn knew she'd always have Savannah and that made the uncertainty of her life at the moment more bearable.

"It is what it is. Hopefully, with time everything will work itself out."

"It will and in the meantime, I'll be at the appointment tomorrow holding your hand while we try to see if those babies have tiny little penises or not."

Savannah squeezed her shoulder as they laughed together. For the first time since she found out about her miracle, she was genuinely feeling like everything was going to be alright. Declan knew she was pregnant, she'd made it into her second trimester a milestone she'd never hit before, and everyone was healthy and thriving. She knew deep down that Declan would come around. It might be just for the babies and not for her, but she'd deal with that heartbreak if it happened.

For now, she'd revel in the love that she felt for the two beings growing inside her. The rest could wait if it had to.

* * *

"Alright Brooklyn let's get you back to the exam room so we can see if those babies of yours are cooperating today," the nurse said before guiding her through the door and then down a long hallway. "You're in room eight. I'll send your sister back as soon as she gets here."

Brooklyn thanked the nurse before walking into the room at the end of the hall. Once inside she turned to close the door behind her, then turned to climb onto the exam table. She let out a squeak of surprise when she realized she wasn't alone in the room.

"What are you doing here?" she asked her hand flying to her chest to cover her rapidly beating heart.

"We need to talk, and I thought surprising you was my best option. Sort of rethinking that decision right now though," Declan said as he rubbed at the back of his neck a sheepish grin on his face. "Are you okay?"

"You should never surprise a pregnant woman. It's a bad idea on so many levels. I almost peed just now. That would have been mortifying."

"I'm sorry. I just wasn't sure you'd talk to me if I showed up at your house. When your sister told me about your appointment, I had her help me set this up with the clinic. I wanted to be here for you. I should have been here for you the entire time."

"I should have told you sooner."

"I get why you didn't. And honestly, now that I've had time to think about it, I'm glad you didn't. I needed to get over my shit. I don't know if I would have been able to do that knowing you were pregnant. I would have jumped right into dad mode because of obligation and not because I faced my fear."

"Did you get your shit together? Did you face your fear?"

Declan took a step toward her. When she didn't flinch or take a step back, he took another one and another until he closed the gap between them.

"I came to see you yesterday to tell you that I love you. That I would rather take a risk with you, then sit back and watch life pass me by. When I thought about you falling in love with someone else and making a life with them, it felt like I'd been stabbed in the heart. It was the most painful thing I'd ever felt. Far more painful than anything I felt because of what Kara did."

Brooklyn sniffled, trying to hold back the tears, but it was no use.

"You and our children..."

"Children?" she asked interrupting him before he could go on. If someone told him about the twins, she was going to be pissed. She wanted to be the one to tell him especially since she didn't get to tell him that she was pregnant.

"Erin and the baby. She's going to be pretty ecstatic about this entire thing. She's always wanted a sibling, and she told me that I need to come home and get you back so I could give her the mom she's always wanted."

The tears flowed harder over her cheeks as she thought about the girl that she loved like she was her daughter. The fact Erin would want her to be her stepmom meant the world to her and made her happier than she'd ever thought possible. They could be a family; the five of them. The family she'd always dreamed of but never thought she'd get.

"I love that girl."

"She loves you too. We both do. Brooklyn, I'm so sorry about the way I acted the night the condom broke. I'm sorry that I left without making things right. I'm sorry that I couldn't see through past hurts long enough to realize what I was losing."

"You did. It just took you a while. I get it. I had to deal with my past too. Then to learn that I was pregnant when I thought that was an impossibility. It didn't feel real. Sometimes it still doesn't. Can we forget about all of that and move on from here?"

"Are you sure? I feel like you're letting me off too easy. I don't deserve it. Especially after the way I reacted when I saw you yesterday."

"Declan, I know all about fear. It can be crippling and unforgiving, but you can't let it win. We have to promise each other that we'll talk things out from now on instead of letting something stupid pull us apart. I want to fight for us, fight for our family and I can tell you do too. It won't be easy. There will be a lot of hard work ahead of us, but if we have each other, we can conquer it all."

"God, I love you so fucking much."

"I love you, too."

Without another word, he pulled her into the kiss of all kisses. His lips were hesitant at first like he wasn't sure if the kiss was the right move, but when she wrapped her arms around him and pulled him against her, he let go of his control. Passion, lost time and love fueled the kiss, their lips parting, tongues teasing each other. She felt like she was going to combust, the pent-up sexual need that had filled her over the last few weeks threatened to burst free.

A knock on the door kept their reunion kiss from being a reunion fuck in the office of her ob/gyn. He jumped back before the door swung open behind her.

"Well, hello there. Who's this Brooklyn? I thought your sister was coming with you today," Tina the clinic sonographer said as she walked into the room.

"This is Declan. He's the father. I wasn't sure he'd be back in time for the appointment. He's been in North Carolina getting his daughter set up at college."

"Ahh, so you've been through this part before."

"Actually, no I never got to go to any of the appointments the first time around, so I'm pretty excited to be here."

Brooklyn looked over at Declan a pang of guilt hiting her in the chest. She'd been so close to keeping him out of the process again, and she hated herself a little for it. Shaking her head, she reminded herself that they were past that. That they were good now. Everything was going to be okay.

"Well that's a shame, but we're glad to have you here today. Brooklyn, go ahead and get up on the table. Since you're wearing a dress, we won't need you to put on one of those ridiculous gowns."

With the help of Declan, Brooklyn got situated on the table, her dress bunched up over her breasts, her baby bump on display. She shivered when the cold gel hit her skin, fairly certain that she was never going to get used to the feeling of it. With her head propped up on her arm, she watched Tina's face for signs of what she was seeing. It felt like she took forever to look at the scan before turning the monitor for her to see it.

"Both babies are measuring at twenty-one weeks, so we're still looking at a January fourth due date. Of course, twins are usually early, so you'll probably end up delivering around mid-December or so. They both look good. I don't see anything concerning so how about we see if they've got their legs open."

Brooklyn felt Declan squeeze her hand the second Tina said both babies. She'd meant to tell him before the ultrasound started, but between the declarations of love and the panty-melting kiss, she'd forgotten.

"Twins? Seriously?"

"Oops. Was that..."

Brooklyn shook her head. "No, it wasn't a secret or anything, I just hadn't had a chance to tell him. We've, well...he's been gone and well..."

"I'm an idiot. Let's just leave it at that," he said before looking down at her. "Holy shit. We're having twins."

"That's exactly what I said when I found out. We're finding out the gender today...if they cooperate that is. I was hoping you'd be here for this part. We get to find out together."

He squeezed her hand again, then looked up at Tina who was watching them with a smile on her face.

"Alright let's see...baby A here, come on...there," she said as she turned the monitor again so it faced them. "See that right there? This one here is all boy."

Brooklyn's eyes teared up as she looked from their baby to Declan and then back to their baby. They were having a boy, a son, a mini Declan.

"Okay now baby B," Tina said before moving the wand around on Brooklyn's stomach. "Ah, there we are. We got another one. There it is right there."

"Two boys?" Declan asked his eyes widening.

"Yep. It looks like we've got two healthy little boys in there. Even though they each have their own sacs and placentas, there's still a chance they could be identical since they're the same gender. Odds are more likely they're fraternal, but it's still a possibility."

"Holy crap…"

"I'll let you two have some time. Here's a picture for you and we'll send you a copy of the video like last time."

Tina quickly excused herself from the room after handing Declan the picture. He stared down at it like it was the most wondrous thing he'd ever seen. The man next to her never ceased to amaze her. She'd expected him to freak out a bit more when he heard the news, but he didn't. Instead, he filled the room with his happiness and love. Her heart felt so full, like it might burst from her chest. The feeling left her breathless.

This was her life. A man who loved her. Babies that she thought weren't possible growing inside of her and a beautiful young woman she hoped to someday call her daughter. She felt like her life couldn't get any better, yet she'd barely gotten started. The best chapter of her life was just beginning, and she couldn't wait to see how it played out.

EPILOGUE

Declan

"Why the fuck did I want this so damn bad?" Brooklyn growled as her sister wiped at her forehead with a cloth.

It was killing him to see the woman he loved in so much pain. Gabriel had warned him about what to expect, but nothing his friend said could have prepared him for the reality of the situation. The contractions had started the evening before, but they were far enough apart that her doctor had told them to wait before coming to the hospital. Of course, the instructions sounded ridiculous to Declan, but Savannah and Brooklyn both insisted that the doctor was right.

When her water broke at home, he nearly panicked, thinking that his sons were going to be born right there in the living room. Somehow he'd been able to keep it together enough to gather up Brooklyn and the bag they'd packed for the hospital. By the time they were checked in the contractions still weren't very close together and she wasn't as dilated as they expected her to be, whatever that meant.

At the time he thought the waiting had been brutal. Watching Brooklyn deal with the sharp pain every ten minutes, every five minutes while nothing else seemed to happen, was horrible for them both. He felt useless and in the way. When he could, he rubbed her back and pressed a cold rag to her forehead. He did whatever he could to just be there for her.

He barely spoke while they waited, having heard from Gabriel that his voice was the last thing she wanted to hear. His platitudes and assurances that she was doing great would only make matters worse which he didn't want.

As time passed, he began to realize how thankful he was that he hadn't sat through any of this the first time around. At 17, it wouldn't have meant as much. He would have been too young to understand the meaning of it all. He would have messed things up for sure and traumatized everyone involved.

"Okay Brooklyn, you're doing great. We're ready for you to start pushing now. Baby A seems a bit eager to make his way into the world," Dr. Ross said as she positioned herself between Brooklyn's legs. "Here we go, push...."

Brooklyn took a deep breath as she bared down and leaned forward. He helped to support her with his right hand, while she squeezed the life out of his left. She groaned, a long, painful sound that he thought might haunt him for the rest of his life. He'd done this to her. He'd been the one to bring this pain upon her. It didn't matter that she wanted to have a baby more than almost anything else. While she was suffering, he felt responsible.

"Ugh...Declan, I'm never letting you touch me again."

He fought back a grin knowing that what she was saying was just a side effect of the pain. So far, he'd gotten off easily. She hadn't threatened his manhood or his life yet. There was still plenty of time and a whole other baby to go. Declan was fairly confident he wouldn't leave the room unscathed.

"You're doing great, Brooklyn. A couple more pushes, and you'll get to meet your son. Let's get those shoulders out of there."

Brooklyn started to push again after very little rest. The bones in his hand ground against each other as she squeezed it again. It didn't matter to him at all. The pain was nothing compared to what she was going through. Brooklyn flopped back against the bed, her chest heaving with her rapid breaths. Savannah mopped the sweat off of her sister's forehead while she whispered words of encouragement.

"I can't do this..."

"Yes, you can Brook. You're doing an amazing job. Just one more push. I promise that you can do this," Savannah said as she helped Brooklyn sit up one more time.

Within seconds, Dr. Ross was holding his son in her hands, and he felt an unfamiliar wetness roll down his cheeks. His chest felt like it was going to burst from the love that filled him. Love for the woman of his dreams that had just gone through so much to give birth to his son. Love for the son that he never in a million years thought he would have, but had fallen in love with the minute he saw his tiny body on the ultrasound screen.

He cut the cord quickly while the nurses worked to take care of him. It took no time before he was letting the world know that he was there. His cries filled the room as they weighed and measured him and checked him out to make sure he was healthy.

Declan looked over at Brooklyn amazed at her strength and resilience. She was the most amazing woman he'd ever met. He'd never be able to repay her for all that she'd given him, for all that she brought into his life, but he'd try. She gritted her way through another contraction, but followed Dr. Ross's instructions and didn't push. Baby B was still breech and needed to turn around before he moved down. Either that or they'd have to do a c-section, which they all hoped wasn't necessary.

While Dr. Ross worked to move the baby into a better position, one of the nurses placed their son on Brooklyn's chest. She looked down at him, love shining through the tears in her eyes. Declan wrapped his arm around her shoulder and traced a finger down the soft skin of the baby's cheek. He kissed Brooklyn on the top of her head as tears rolled down his cheeks again. The moment almost too much for him.

Their son looked like an impossibly perfect mix of him and Brooklyn. Her nose, his chin, the shape of her eyes, his mouth. They continued to stare at him until the nurse came to take him away because it was time for Brooklyn to push out Baby B. Declan resumed his position supporting her shoulders and holding her hand.

"Okay Brooklyn, after much maneuvering we've got Baby B headed the right direction. Let's see if we can't get him out here to join his brother."

With the next contraction, Brooklyn gritted her teeth together and pushed, her face turning a fierce shade of red, sweat beading up along her forehead. Like the first time around, they went through the motions until their other son came screaming into the world, twenty minutes after his brother. Brooklyn only managing to threaten bodily harm once, nothing compared to Savannah threatening to rip Gabriel's arms off and beat him with them.

When they placed him onto Brooklyn's chest, Declan marveled at the resemblance and how much he too looked like a perfect blend of them. They wouldn't know until they performed blood tests if the babies were identical or fraternal, but they looked pretty identical to him. Especially when the nurse placed the other baby in his arms and he looked at them side by side.

As he stared at his sons, he was aware that things were happening around him. Other parts of the birthing process that involved stuff he didn't want to know about but made him appreciate and love Brooklyn even more. Savannah excused herself so she could update the crowd of people in the waiting room, but neither of them registered her absence as the reveled in the existence of their sons.

When it was time to take his sons away to give them a bath and exams, he almost protested. Now that they were here, he didn't want them out of his sight. After assuring him they wouldn't be gone long, he let them go and turned his attention to Brooklyn. He knew she'd say she looked like a mess, sweaty and splotchy, her hair ratty like she walked out of an 80's hair band music video. But to him, she'd never looked more beautiful. The mother of his children, the love of his life. The strongest, most amazing person he'd ever met.

"I love you," he whispered before placing a kiss on her forehead.

She smiled at him lazily, spent from the hours of labor and the demands of delivery. He moved back so he could look into her eyes and in that moment, he knew. This was what he'd been waiting for.

"Thank you for giving me everything I thought I never wanted. You've lit up my life Brooklyn St. James. You've filled it with love and laughter and beauty. I don't think I deserve you, but I'm too selfish to ever let you go. I know this is probably the worst time and place to do this, but I don't want to wait any longer. This damn ring is burning a hole in my pocket and has been for months."

Brooklyn blinked up at him, her hand flying to her mouth. "Declan..."

"Marry me. Marry me and make me the luckiest man in the world. I can't see my life without you in it. Will you marry me, Brooklyn?"

Her head moved, nodding as tears slipped down her cheeks. "Yes...oh, yes...I'll marry you. Tomorrow. Can we do it tomorrow?"

Declan smiled, a laugh bubbling out of him as he took her hand in his and slipped the ring onto her finger. She stared down at it for a minute, then looked up at him, her eyes sparkling like the diamond on her finger.

"Darling, I'd marry you right now if we could, but we'll probably want to wait while we get the babies situated. I was thinking June after school gets out for Erin so she can be there."

"You've thought about a date?" she asked, her words catching on a hiccup.

"It's all I've thought about since I bought the ring in October."

"October?" her voice tinged with disbelief.

"Well, I started looking in September."

"What? We'd barely gotten back together by September, and we weren't even living together in October. You've been planning this the entire time?"

"Brooklyn, there's a part of me that has always known you were the woman I was going to marry. Long before we ever got together, you had a piece of me, even if I wasn't willing to acknowledge it. Once I moved past the fear that was holding me back, I wanted to make you my wife. I wanted to make a home together, one that our children could grow up in and come back to. I only waited to propose until now because I didn't want you to think I was rushing into things because of the babies."

"I wouldn't have thought that."

"Well I also had this cool plan about using the babies to propose, but that was shot to shit cause after everything you just went through, I couldn't hold out any longer. I love you, Brooklyn. More than I ever thought possible."

"I love you too, Declan. So much."

Their moment was interrupted by the nurses returning with their sons, turning the moment into one he couldn't describe. For the next hour, Brooklyn breastfed their sons while he changed their diapers. They each got a chance to bond with the babies, getting skin to skin contact with the little miracles. But they both knew that they couldn't keep their family and friends waiting for too long, so they sent a nurse out to send them back a few at a time.

Erin came first. She'd been able to fly home two days earlier as soon as her finals were over. Declan had been more than thankful that her brothers had decided to stay inside their mother long enough for their sister to come home. Everyone had thought they'd come a little before the 37-week mark but instead had waited until 37 weeks and five days like they knew they had to wait for her.

Tears filled her eyes as she took in her brothers, holding each of them one at a time. She was followed by Brooklyn's parents and Savannah and Andrea; each taking turns to hold the newborns who slept through the whole thing.

"So who's who and how are you going to tell them apart?" Brooklyn's dad Michael asked as he looked down at his grandson.

Each baby had been given a different colored cap to wear to make telling them apart easier. The baby he held was wearing a blue cap while the one his wife held wore a green one.

"Daddy you're holding Cayden James Reese, formally known as Baby A. Momma you're holding his stubborn little brother Wyatt Andrew Reese. Both of them are healthy and whole and totally perfect. We don't know yet if they're identical or not, though if they aren't, they're pretty damn close. For now, we're going with different colored hats to tell them apart. We'll probably end up using the painting the fingernail trick until they start showing their little personalities."

They spent time passing the babies around, telling everyone what their measurements were and where their names came from. Andrea started to cry when they told her that Wyatt's middle name Andrew was in honor of her. Brooklyn's parents got misty-eyed when they explained that Cayden's middle name was in recognition of their family name. Declan had never been a part of something so filled with emotions that it brought happy tears to everyone's eyes.

He hated that Erin's birth wasn't as happy a moment for everyone involved. His daughter deserved better than what she got, and he was thankful that she was getting that now from Brooklyn's family. They each hugged Erin and congratulated her on the new members of her family. Everyone made sure to include her so she didn't feel like she was being pushed aside for the new additions and it made him love the people in his life even more.

His heart was so full it felt like it might burst. His world turned into something he never thought he'd want, not in a million years. As he watched his family and friends, he couldn't have been more grateful for the woman lying in the bed next to him for showing him what he was missing.

Love. Pure unadulterated love.

* * *

6 months later

Brooklyn

"Attractive men carrying babies around is just unfair. I mean I'm pretty sure ovaries all over this place are exploding right now. Even mine, and I don't even like kids much but that over there is doing it for me," Finley said as she stared at the men across the room from them. "Of course, your kids don't count. I love those ones, so maybe that's why that scene is turning me on so much, I don't know."

Brooklyn couldn't help but laugh at the nonsense coming out of her friend's mouth. Well, almost nonsense. It was true that there was nothing hotter than a man carrying around a baby. Of course, it helped when the man in question was her brand new husband, and the baby in his arms was her six-month-old son Cayden. She looked at the other two men in question and realized that they too were hot as hell and that Finley was actually making a lot of sense. Gabriel held his 11-month-old daughter Ryan in his arms, while Liam, Finley's fiancé held her other son Wyatt in his arms.

"She's right. The three of them standing there are like sex on a stick. They're hotter than anyone has a right to be," Brooklyn admitted.

"You better be careful Finley. Before you know it, you'll want to look at that all day long. It's even better when he's shirtless, holding your baby against his bare skin..."

"Woah, hold on. Isn't it enough that I finally said yes to getting married? I don't think this baby nonsense is ever going to be my bag. How about you two keep having them and let my man hold them. Then I can reap the benefits without actually having to deal with the poop and the throw-up and the crying and the snot."

"Sure Fin, you say that now, but someday you're going to give in and want one of your very own."

Savannah's comment was met with a death glare from her best friend causing her and Brooklyn to laugh. They both knew that Finley was most likely always going to just be the cool aunt. Some people really didn't want to have kids and Finley was one of those people. She was great with kids that she liked, but had no patience for children in general. No matter how great a mom Brooklyn thought Finley would be, she knew it would never happen.

"I guess you guys will have to come back up in about seven months or so to hold this one," Savannah said as she placed a hand on her flat stomach.

"What? Are you serious?" Brooklyn asked, nearly shouting the question so everyone in the reception hall could hear.

"Keep it down," Savannah scolded before nodding. "Yes. We're about eight weeks along, so please don't tell anyone. I haven't even told mom and dad yet. I just couldn't help it. Especially since the night we conceived this little peanut, I jumped Gabriel's bones because of how hot he looked taking care of our daughter. It just fit the conversation to blurt out that I'm pregnant."

"Oh my gosh, Savannah, that's amazing news. I'm so excited for you guys."

"Me too," Finley said as she finally stopped staring at the men long enough to hug her friend.

As the three of them hugged, they garnered strange looks from their men. Brooklyn waved Declan off but wasn't surprised when the three of them joined them anyway. Liam tried to hand Wyatt to her but was intercepted by Finley. Brooklyn tried not to laugh, but couldn't hold it back when Savannah started to giggle.

"I hate you guys," Finley muttered. "But I love you, little man. Yes, I do."

"Hello, sorry, can I get everyone's attention real quick? Sorry to interrupt, but before we move on with the festivities, I've got something I need to say."

Brooklyn looked over to where the DJ was set up to find Erin with the microphone in one hand a gift in the other. She looked stunning in her strapless silver dress, like the amazing grown woman she was becoming. It brought tears to Brooklyn's eyes as she realized the girl she'd met was growing up before her eyes. They'd celebrated her nineteenth birthday three months earlier by flying her home for a quick family getaway. They would have gone to her, but the babies were still too little to fly. It hadn't really hit her then just how grown up Erin was, but now standing in front of their friends and family, it was more than obvious.

"I know usually only the best man and maid of honor give speeches, and you usually don't have the bride and groom open gifts at the reception, but I couldn't think of a better time and place to do this than now, here in front of the people we love. Brooklyn, Dad, could you guys come up here please?"

Brooklyn looked over at Declan who shrugged as he handed Cayden off to her sister. He reached for her hand as they walked across the dance floor and she took it, squeezing it softly as they approached Erin. Every eye in the building was on them, watching something that Brooklyn had a feeling was going to be monumental.

"The moment I met Brooklyn, I felt a connection to her. I knew that I could talk to her about anything and everything, that she would be there for me anytime I needed someone. This was long before she and my dad ever started dating. In fact, they could barely stand being in the room with each other, but Brooklyn never turned that animosity around on me. She helped me even though my dad hurt her. She kept my secrets even though she knew it would make things worse between them if he found out. For the first time in my life, I realized what it must feel like to have a mom."

Brooklyn choked back a sob at the revelation. She had no idea Erin had felt that way, that they'd both felt the connection. Declan placed his hand on the small of her back, his touch soothing her. Erin watched them for a moment, then handed her the box she held. With Declan's help she pulled the lid off of the box and peeled back the tissue paper. The second her eyes fell on the documents contained within the box she started to cry.

"Now that they're married, I can call her my stepmom, but that doesn't feel like enough. It's not what I want, and I'm hoping it's not what you want either. Uncle Braeden helped me draw up the papers in that box, and I'm hoping that the two of you will sign them. I want you to adopt me, Brooklyn. I don't want to introduce you to people as my stepmom. I'd much rather tell everyone that you're my mom, biology be damned."

"Oh Bug," Declan said as he reached out for his daughter. He pulled her into a hug. Their sobs carried out into the room by the microphone still clutched in Erin's hand.

Brooklyn stood next to them, the box on the floor at her feet, the paperwork clutched in her hand. Since the moment Declan Reese walked into her life, her world had been turned upside down. It ceased being just about her and now revolved around so much more. She was blessed with a man that loved her beyond reason. She was given a miracle she didn't think possible with two sons she loved with her entire being. And she was given a daughter, a beautiful, amazing daughter who wanted to call her Mom and make it legal.

She gathered them both into her arms, tears streaming down her face for what seemed like the millionth time in the last year. Once again, they were happy tears; ones brought about because of the love that overwhelmed her at times. She could hear sniffling around them, murmurs from the crowd that watched them. Pushing back from Erin and Declan, she looked out at the faces of their family and friends and said the one thing that seemed the most pressing.

"Does anyone have a pen?"

Acknowledgements

To my readers (man I love being able to say that), thank you, thank you, thank you. Your encouragement and kind words mean the world to me. Your desire for the next book has kept me going and allowed me to prove to myself that I could do more and be more. Thank you

To Tarryn Fisher, thank you for creating the Write or Die Writer's Conference. I learned so much in those two days, not only about writing but about myself. Without it, I don't know if I would have had the courage to accomplish what I have over the last year.

To Rachel Hollis, thank you for being such an inspirational badass. My ten minutes with you at Write or Die changed my life. You'll probably never read this, but for anyone that does, you need to listen to this woman's words. She speaks the truth.

To the best team a girl could have, Christina, Taracina, and Sami, I owe you guys so much. You make me better; you make my books better. Thank you for being my rocks during this crazy process. I wouldn't be able to do it without you.

To my family, Lori, Randy, Desmond, Melissa, and Izaiah, thank you for your support while I try to figure out how to navigate this adventure. I still have no idea what I'm doing, but it's getting a bit easier every day. Thank you for helping me make my dreams come true.

About the Author

Paris Hansen was born and raised in Seattle, Washington. She started telling stories at a young age, garnering invitations to writing conferences while in elementary school. Aside from a writer, she also aspired to be a lawyer and an actress as a child, but as a teenager realized she was far better behind the scenes than in front of a crowd.

When not writing, Paris devours as many books as she can get her hands on. After a long day at work, unwinding with a good book, a glass of wine and a decent TV show is her idea of a great evening.

She also loves cupcakes, sexy heroes and popcorn, but not always in that order.

Connect with Paris

E-Mail: paris@parishansen.com
Facebook: https://www.facebook.com/AuthorParisHansen/
Website/Newsletter: http://www.ParisHansen.com
Twitter: https://twitter.com/ParisAja13
Instagram: https://www.instagram.com/parisaja13/

Made in the USA
Columbia, SC
12 November 2018